Stuck in the Middle

Stuck in the Middle

A Novel

Virginia Smith

Revell
Grand Rapids, Michigan

Published by Revell
a division of Baker Publishing Group
P.O. Box 6287, Grand Rapids, MI 49516-6287
www.revellbooks.com

Second printing, February 2008

Printed in the United States of America

          Library of Congress Cataloging-in-Publication Data
Smith, Virginia, 1960–
     Stuck in the middle / Virginia Smith.
        p.   cm. — (Sister-to-sister ; bk. 1)
     ISBN 978-0-8007-3232-5 (pbk. ; alk. paper)
     I. Title.
  PS3619.M5956S78 2008
  813′.6—dc22   2007037179

Published in association with Books & Such Literary Agency, 52 Mission Circle, Suite 122, PMB 170, Santa Rosa, CA 95409-5370

For Susie and Beth.
God blessed me when he made you my sisters.

~ *1* ~

Brrring. Brrring.

From the desk behind the sales counter in the rear of the showroom, Joan Sanderson scanned the empty store. Fluorescent ceiling lights cast a harsh glow that reflected off the polished wooden surfaces of the furniture artfully arranged for display. Where was . . . oh yes. Rosa would be a couple of hours late this morning, after her daughter's doctor appointment. She reached for the phone and punched the button for the first line. "Good morning, Abernathy Sales and Rental."

"I'm going to kill her."

Joan closed her eyes. *Patience. I need patience.* "Hi, Mom. What has Gram done?"

"She alphabetized my underwear drawer."

"She *what*?" A snort of unladylike laughter blasted through Joan's nose.

"It's not funny, Joan. My bras are all in the first row, color-coded alphabetically from left to right, and then a row of panties, all folded in little squares, and then slips.

And socks along the back row. Everything's so neat it makes me want to throw up."

Joan picked up a pile of invoices on the edge of the desk and shuffled them into a tidy stack. "C'mon, Mom, your underwear drawer is a disaster. What's wrong with a little order?"

"That is not the point, and you know it. She went into my room! She touched my underwear. She invaded my privacy! I've been sitting here for the past twenty minutes afraid to look in the closet. What if she got in there too?"

A hint of panic colored the anger in Mom's voice. Gram was harmless, but she did have an obsessive-compulsive tendency to alphabetize everything she touched. Lately everything she did grated on her only daughter's nerves like a snowplow on icy roads. Joan feared one day Gram would do something to push Mom over the edge. The front page of tomorrow's *Advocate-Messenger* flashed into her mind:

CRAZED WOMAN SLAUGHTERS
ALPHABETICALLY CORRECT MOTHER

"I'm sure your closet is fine." Through the glass doors Joan watched a red pickup zoom into a parking space near the store. "She was only trying to be helpful, you know."

Mom huffed. "She can organize the cans in the pantry and the jars in the spice rack all she wants. But three women living under one roof have got to have boundaries. Bedrooms should be off-limits."

"So tell her that. Gram understands the need for boundaries."

A couple emerged from the truck and made their way toward the store. The door alarm bleeped a stuttering double tone as the pair stepped from the clammy Kentucky heat into the air-conditioned store. They were college freshmen if Joan was any judge, much too young to be shopping for furniture.

"Be with you folks in a minute," she called, then spoke in a lower voice into the phone. "I've got customers. I need to go."

Mom ignored her. "Do you think I haven't told her that a dozen times? She pays no attention to me and does as she pleases. I don't think I can take this much longer."

Joan clutched the receiver, a cold lump settling in the pit of her stomach. "What do you mean?"

After a pause, Mom sighed. "I don't know. I wish I did. But really, we've got to do something before—"

Joan's mouth went dry. Something in her mother's tone hinted that she was about to launch into a subject that left Joan sick with dread. She couldn't get into this right now, not on the phone, and not when she was the only one in the store. She turned her back toward the watching couple and spoke quietly into the receiver. "I've got to go, Mom. We'll talk about this later. Goodbye."

The phone clicked down into its cradle harder than she intended as she sucked in a slow, deep breath. Time to calm down. She could think about Mom and Gram later.

A professional smile plastered on her face, she weaved her way through the furniture displays. Her young customers stood just inside the door as though they had happened across a patch of superglue. The guy looked a little shell-shocked as his gaze slid around the store, taking in the clusters of living room furniture to the right, the bedroom suites to the left, the appliances lining the rear wall, and finally settling on the dinette sets in the center. The girl, on the other hand, watched Joan like a cat in front of a fishbowl.

Oh, puh-lease. Joan stifled a chuckle. *I'm twenty-five years old! Your college boy is safe with me.*

Stale cigarette smoke assaulted her nostrils as she approached them, strong enough that she struggled not to take a step backward to escape the stench. Both wore jeans and flip-flops. The girl sported a belly shirt revealing a glimpse of silver in the center of an incredibly tiny waist; the guy, a loose, rust-colored T-shirt. Still eyeing Joan warily, she had a grip on his arm like a monkey with a banana in a cageful of hungry primates.

"Hi, I'm Joan."

Miss Belly Button gave her the once-over, no doubt comparing Joan's straight brown hair to her own shiny blonde curls. Through narrowed eyelids, the girl's gaze swept downward. Joan kept her face impassive, denying the grin that threatened to break free in the face of such fierce teenage possessiveness. She knew she would pass muster. What were comfortable polyester slacks and sturdy shoes compared to Levi's so tight the numbers on a credit card could be read through the back pocket?

He's all yours, honey. Besides, I'm not looking for a babysitting job.

The youngster relaxed and released the guy's arm long enough to allow him to engulf Joan's hand in a calloused grip. The girl didn't offer her hand, but dimpled. "I'm Stacy, and this is Josh."

"Nice to meet you. What can I help you with today?"

Josh cleared his throat and spoke directly to the sofa behind her. "Yeah, we need a table. You know, like, to eat on."

"With chairs," Stacy added.

Interesting. Maybe one of them had gotten lucky enough to find an off-campus apartment. More likely a group decided to go in together and rent a house for the school year. "Okay, and are you looking to purchase or rent?"

"Rent." Stacy gave a short giggle. "We don't have the money to buy anything. We just got married."

She turned an adoring gaze toward her husband, who was now staring at a table lamp and fidgeting with a set of car keys in his free hand. Shocked, Joan struggled to keep her smile from slipping. They couldn't be out of their teens. And they were *married*? She tried not to be obvious as she stared at Stacy's tiny waist again. The girl didn't look pregnant.

"Congratulations." She hoped she sounded sincere. "Here at Abernathy's our monthly payments are pretty low. I'm sure we can find something to fit your budget." She watched Josh's expression relax a fraction, and he actually made eye contact. "And we have a great rent-to-own plan too. As long as you make your payments, anything you rent under the purchase contract becomes yours at the end of the contract period."

"How much is the down payment?"

11

Joan shook her head. "There isn't one. The payment is a few dollars more than the regular rental fee, but not that much."

A couple of creases on his forehead cleared. "Sounds like a good deal."

"It is." She made sure to include Stacy as she spoke. "We help lots of people furnish their first homes."

The telephone rang from the back of the store. For a moment, she was tempted to let it go to voice mail. But that was bad business. Where was Rosa, anyway? Shouldn't she be here by now? Joan smiled at the newlyweds and took a backward step toward the sales counter.

"Feel free to look around." She edged toward the desk. "The dinette sets are here, with formal dining room furniture over there. You'll find the payment amounts and contract periods on the yellow labels."

As she reached the telephone, her customers' feet came unstuck, and they wandered toward the dinette displays. "Good morning, Abernathy's."

"Did you just hang up on your mother?"

Joan winced at her sister's scolding tone. Word traveled at roughly the speed of light in the Sanderson family. "Hi, Allie. I guess she called you?"

"Of course she called me. She's upset. I would be too if you slammed the phone down in my ear."

"I did not hang up on Mom." Joan picked up a pencil and rolled it between her fingers. "Not technically, anyway. I said goodbye first. But all she wanted to do was complain about Gram, and I had customers. They're still here, by the way."

A disgusted grunt sounded in Joan's ear. "Okay, okay, I'll let you go. But you call her and apologize, you hear?"

"When I get a chance."

Joan replaced the receiver with extreme care. Having Mom upset with her was bad enough. Best not alienate her big sister too.

Half an hour later she waved goodbye to Josh and Stacy, promising that their new dinette set and washer-dryer combo would be delivered before noon tomorrow. A glance over their credit application went a long way toward soothing her stinging ego. They were nothing but kids, too inexperienced to even know how poor they were. Whereas Joan drove a nice car with a free-and-clear title, paid no rent, and banked almost every cent she earned. True, she didn't have a husband or even the prospect of one, thanks to Roger the Rat. But at least she was financially solid. She had no reason to be jealous, and she refused to waste another minute comparing herself to a couple of kids.

Her thoughts turned to her mother's phone call as she keyed their order into the computer. Sometimes Gram's behavior did get a little weird, but that was nothing new. She had always been a stickler for organization. And who cared if she alphabetized the laundry? She was still the same sweet woman they moved in with thirteen years ago, after Mom divorced Daddy. The way Joan figured it, at eighty-three, Gram could be forgiven the occasional kooky impulse.

She pressed Print on the computer and waited for the laser printer to spit out the delivery order.

Mom, on the other hand, lost her temper forty times a day. She was deep in the throes of menopause, and Joan sometimes wondered if all those herbal supplements she gulped down every morning were doing the job on her wacky hormones. Everybody got on her nerves. Well, except Allie, who would give birth to the first Sanderson grandchild soon. All Allie had to do was whimper into the telephone, and Mom rushed across town to rub her back and bring her a half gallon of Moose Tracks.

As a sheet of paper slid into the printer's tray, she picked up the folder containing the orders scheduled for delivery tomorrow. Glancing through the contents, she organized them by street address and distance from the warehouse, her thoughts still hovering around that disturbing phone call. Mom had dropped several hints lately, all centering around "doing something about Gram." It didn't take a genius to figure out the comments had something to do with the town's new assisted living center. Her stomach churned at the thought of Gram in an old folks home. Well, Mom could just forget it. There was no way Joan would allow her grandmother to be shut away in a home. No way.

Bleep-bleep. Another customer. This place was as busy as shift change at a factory today. Rosa had better get here before lunchtime. Assuming her practiced smile, Joan pushed thoughts of Mom and Gram from her mind and went to the front of the store, ready to sell more furniture.

The drive-through line at Wendy's wrapped all the way around the building. Joan whipped her car into an empty parking space and shoved the shifter forward. The line inside the restaurant was long too. Joan suppressed a sigh as she walked through the door. This quick run to make the daily bank deposit was taking longer than expected. But when Rosa finally showed up at the store, she had forgotten her lunch, so Joan volunteered to pick something up on her way back from the bank.

As she stepped into the queue, a little girl in a pink sundress skipped across her path. Joan stopped just short of trampling the child. A man, presumably her father, followed behind carrying a laden tray from the pick-up counter.

"I'm so sorry." He gave her an apologetic smile. "She's excited, and isn't watching where she's going."

An unmistakable look of pride as he watched his daughter brought an answering tightening somewhere in the region of Joan's heart. She swallowed, her throat dry. Fathers and daughters always got to her. She dipped her head to acknowledge the man's apology, then stepped around him to take her place in line. She tried not to watch as he got his little darling settled with a cheeseburger and fries.

"Well, look who's here."

At the sound of a disturbingly familiar voice behind her, all thoughts of the father and daughter fled. There went her mood for the rest of the day, right into the toilet.

She arranged her smile before turning. "Hello, Roger. What are you doing here?"

He gave her the crooked smile she remembered so well. Once upon a time that smile would have made her stomach flutter. Now that obnoxious grin set her teeth together.

"I had some stuff to take care of in town this morning. We're actually on our way to work now."

We? Ah, the office bimbo must be waiting for him in the car. Of course. He never made a move without her. Joan awarded him a stiff nod before stepping forward as the line progressed toward the cash register. Just her luck they decided to stop here.

"I guess you heard my good news?"

Good news? Was his little wifey pregnant? Lovely. Let's rub salt in the wound, shall we? Steeling herself against the coming blow, she turned a polite smile his way. "No, I can't say I have."

"I got a promotion, a big one. We're moving to St. Louis next week."

A knife twisted in Joan's gut while she struggled to keep her mouth from gaping. He'd had his eye on a job at his company's headquarters a year ago, back when they were still together, but Joan talked him out of applying. Who wanted to live in a big city and deal with all the crime and the traffic?

Apparently Roger the Rat. And his wife.

"Congratulations." She followed the woman in front of her forward another step, keeping her back turned. Maybe he would take the hint and shut up.

No such luck.

"You know, Joan, I was thinking the other day. When I leave, you're going to be about the only one from our graduating class left in Danville."

Joan kept her gaze fixed on the menu behind the cashier's head. "There are a few of us still here. I saw Mary Beth Kurtz just the other day."

"Then she must have been visiting her folks. She got a job as a Web designer at some big company down in Orlando and moved a few months ago."

Joan hadn't heard that. She always wondered why someone as good with computers as Mary Beth didn't go someplace where she could make a lot of money instead of working in an administrative job for the mayor's office. Apparently she had decided to do just that. "Well, Frankie Belcher's still here."

As if that spoke volumes for the city. Frankie worked at the factory out on the bypass. He'd made the newspaper a couple of times when he got busted for possession of marijuana—which meant he hadn't changed a bit since high school.

"That's true." Roger's bland tone tried unsuccessfully to hide a touch of sarcasm.

"And Sherry Dorring's still here too." Sherry Dorring would never leave Danville. She went to college in town at Centre, married a local attorney, joined the country club, and proceeded to have the requisite two kids, a boy and a girl. Joan ran into her at the grocery store every so often. Her kids were adorable.

Was it true? Had everyone else gotten terrific jobs and moved away from their hometown? Out of 287 DHS grads, was she really the only one left besides a stoner and a society wife?

The woman in front of Joan took her change and stepped away from the register. Joan approached the counter, thankful that Roger seemed to have decided he'd tormented her enough. She stared at the menu on the wall. She wasn't hungry anymore.

Yep. Her mood was definitely in the toilet. Flush.

⚜

The fragrant steam rising from a plate of crispy fried pork chops in the center of the table stirred up a rumble in Joan's empty stomach.

Gram fixed her with a bewildered blue stare beneath a crown of white finger curls. "I just can't imagine Carla being upset over a little laundry."

"She's not upset about laundry, Gram. She feels like her bedroom is private, and that you and I shouldn't go in there without her permission."

They sat opposite one another at the dining room table, a southern feast spread out between them. The tangy odor of fried apples, mixed with the savory smell of pork and the heavenly aroma of freshly baked biscuits, sent Joan's nose into ecstatic twitches as she filled her plate. Trying to get Gram to cook healthy was an effort in futility. Joan gave it up years ago. She'd just have to run an extra mile or two tomorrow to make up for all the delicious food tonight.

While Joan had changed into a pair of gym shorts and a light T-shirt, Gram wore a floral print blouse, long-sleeved despite the summer humidity that their window air conditioners couldn't manage to dispel. The white curtains at the kitchen window above the sink had been pulled closed, but the sun still radiated heat through them. Joan dabbed at her damp forehead with a napkin before spooning buttered red potatoes onto her plate.

For as long as Joan could remember, Gram insisted on sitting down at the table for supper. Even now, with only three of them left at home and Mom working second shift at the hospital, she still cooked a big meal every night. Allie and Eric doubled their number a couple of times a week, but since last year when Tori graduated from U.K. and moved into her own apartment in Lexington, the table usually had only two seats occupied—Joan's and Gram's.

As they traded bowls, Gram shook her head. "But what am I supposed to do with the folded laundry? Put it on the floor outside her door? I can't put clean laundry on the floor."

"You don't have to do our laundry at all." Joan halved a potato with her fork. "Mom and I are both perfectly capable of washing our own clothes. You're not the maid here."

Gram dismissed the suggestion with a wave before picking up her knife to cut into a chop. "Three of us doing separate laundry? That's nothing but wasteful. There's a water shortage, you know."

Actually, there had been no water shortage in central Kentucky for several years, but Joan didn't correct her. Instead, she watched Gram's laborious attempt to slice her meat. Her knuckles looked swollen again. Though her face remained passive, the sawing motion must have hurt.

"You want me to cut that for you?"

"See? We help each other. That's what families are for." She pushed her plate across the table. "With you and Carla both working, I don't mind doing the housework. Gives me something useful to do."

"Okay, but maybe from now on you could just leave Mom's clean clothes on the folding table in the laundry room instead of putting them away for her."

The pork chop cut into bite-sized pieces, Joan slid the plate back across the table. Gram speared a small chunk with her fork and, smiling her thanks, held it before her lips. Their eyes met, and Gram's twinkled with a secret grin.

"Her drawers were such a mess." She lowered her voice and confided, "Even as a little girl she kept her drawers a mess. I don't know how she finds a thing in there. Yours aren't, though. Your clothes are nice and neat, like mine."

A mouthful of potato kept Joan from responding. Gram had been rummaging through her dresser as well. Her drawers were full of clean clothes. And the various perfume and lotion bottles on her dressing table had been arranged in size order, left-to-right, small-to-large. Joan had experienced a flash of irritation when she noticed that this evening. For a moment she knew how her mother felt.

"There was a car in the Marlowes' driveway today."

Distracted from her momentary battle with ire, Joan looked up from her plate. "Really? Did you see anyone?"

Gram nodded. "Two young men. They stayed inside for close to a half hour. I thought the one with the key must be the realtor, but I didn't recognize him."

"They probably hired a new one."

About time too. That house had been empty for over

a year and hadn't been shown more than a handful of times. They chewed for a moment, Gram's gaze fixed on something faraway.

"He was a nice-looking young man. I can't imagine why any woman would let her husband look at a house without her, though."

"Maybe she couldn't get off work. Or maybe he's single."

"Oh, surely not. Why would a single man want to live in a house instead of an apartment?"

Joan shrugged and scooped a forkful of apples into her mouth. Gram was far more interested than she cared to be in the goings-on of the neighborhood. That was understandable, since Gram had lived in this house for most of her adult life. When she and Grandpa built it, the road wasn't even paved yet. She had watched families come and go over the years and made sure she knew every one of their names. Not a person moved onto the street without receiving a pie or a plate of cookies from Grace Hancock, the self-appointed welcome wagon lady of Elmtree Drive.

"I hope he's not a drug dealer," Gram said suddenly.

She looked so alarmed Joan couldn't help laughing. "What makes you think he could be a drug dealer?"

"If he's single, there's only one reason he wouldn't want to live in an apartment. He wants to avoid nosy neighbors. Those people live right on top of each other in apartments, and they can hear right through the walls. No privacy at all. A drug dealer wants his privacy, you know. And besides, it takes money to buy a house, and drug dealers make good money."

Her blue eyes were round as glazed Krispy Kremes, and Joan laughed again. "You've been watching too much television. And besides, not all apartments are like that. Look at Tori's."

That silenced her. Joan fell silent as well, and stabbed at a piece of pork chop while battling a flash of envy at her baby sister's incredible good luck. Tori lived in a beautiful two-bedroom apartment in a gated community. No roommate. She could afford to pay the outrageous rent because her salary was nearly twice what Joan made. She landed a job as a marketing analyst with a ritzy advertising firm straight out of college.

Joan, on the other hand, still lived at home. That had not been her plan. She stayed home during college to save money, as did all three sisters, and planned to move out when she got a job after graduation. But when Grandpa died during her senior year, she couldn't make herself leave. Gram had been devastated, and Mom had her hands full with her nursing job at the hospital and with Tori, who had just started at the university. Allie had graduated two years before and moved into her own place, and the house seemed to echo with the silence Grandpa's absence created. So, instead of leaving her small hometown, Joan became the manager of Abernathy Sales and Rental, figuring in a year or so she'd look for a job that made use of her English degree.

That was three years ago.

"Well, anyway," Gram said, setting down her fork and dabbing at her mouth with a napkin, "if he *is* a drug dealer, he'd just better watch out. I'll call the police. We have a school right around the corner, and I won't put up with a drug dealer when all those children walk down this street every day."

She pressed her lips tight and raised her chin high. Joan didn't doubt her for a minute. Drug dealers didn't stand a chance on Elmtree Drive.

~ 2 ~

"Would you please explain why I'm sitting on a hard chair, breathing someone's armpit smell and sweating like a basketball player?"

Joan bore the brunt of her sister's glare, watching her work feverishly to generate a breeze with her program. Allie did look miserable. Sweat beaded on her red forehead, and though Joan thought her older sister a beautiful woman, her damp hair had formed a blonde skullcap around her face that wasn't all that flattering.

"Shhh." Joan glanced around to see if anyone had overheard. Folding chairs crowded the gymnasium so closely together that a private conversation was nearly impossible. She couldn't be sure about the source of the odor, but someone sitting in the vicinity could certainly benefit from a prolonged encounter with a bar of soap and a stick of deodorant. She leaned toward Allie and whispered, "You're here because Tiffany's mom had to work at the restaurant tonight, and no six-year-old should play in her first piano recital without a cheering section. And Gram didn't want to miss *CSI* on television."

"Rosa is *your* employee." Allie's eyebrows drew together as she pouted. "Why do I get stuck watching her kid while she works at her second job? I work all day long too, you know."

"You didn't mind the free nachos she gave us last week. And don't forget, we're going for ice cream when this is over. My treat." Joan grinned at her sister's scowl, and managed not to make a comment about Allie's cushy job as a state employee for social services. Allie's brusque manner didn't fool her. She was a softie when it came to kids. And bribing her with ice cream didn't hurt any, either.

"I'm having a double dip too. With sprinkles." Allie sat back in her chair and sucked in a loud breath, rubbing the gigantic bump of her belly. "Ooh, she doesn't like the heat, either. She's kicking me."

"Where? Let me feel!"

Allie took Joan's hand and placed it on her side. Joan sat breathless for a moment, waiting for her niece-to-be to perform the only trick she had managed to master yet—kicking the eager adults counting the days until her arrival. Finally, Joan felt a firm poke beneath her fingers.

"Wow. That kid's getting strong!"

Allie arched and placed a fist in the small of her back for support. "Tell me about it. Her favorite playtime is right after I go to bed. Try sleeping with a kangaroo on your bladder."

Joan pushed against Allie's belly, thrilled when the baby pushed back. They were still playing their aunt-and-niece game when a woman in a beige blouse and straight skirt walked onto the stage. The audience of about fifty or so grew quiet to hear her voice echo in the gymnasium without benefit of a microphone.

"Hello, and welcome to our summer recital. We've got a full program for you tonight, so I want to get started. But first let's get a few housekeeping rules out of the way."

"Full is right," Allie grumbled. "Have you seen the number of kids on this program? We're going to be here all night."

"Shhhhh." Joan gave her a disapproving stare, and then pointedly turned her attention toward the stage.

The piano teacher told them how to find the bathrooms, which the sisters already knew because the location of the nearest bathroom was at the top of Allie's priority list. Then the teacher explained that the performers would play in order of the number of years they had been taking lessons.

Joan leaned over to whisper in Allie's ear. "That's good. Tiffany only started playing a couple of months ago."

"God must love me after all." Allie answered loudly enough that a woman two rows ahead twisted in her seat to stare.

From the stage, the teacher's volume rose a notch. "Please give our performers the courtesy of your attention *and silence* as they play."

She cast a stern look their way, over the heads of all the parents sitting in front of them. The sisters locked gazes and giggled. As a kid, Joan often got in trouble because of Allie's incessant chatter and a voice that tended to carry to the front of any room. Funny how some things never changed.

When Tiffany stepped out onto the stage and took her place at the piano after only two other performers, Joan cast a wide smile toward Allie, who rolled her eyes and blew her bangs off her moist forehead. But then they both sat up straight in their chairs, giving little Tiffany their full attention. She only messed up a couple of times, and started over once. When she finished, she stood and bowed like a miniature Liberace, and Joan clapped so hard the palms of her hands stung. Beside her, Allie shouted "woo-hoo" like she used to do at football games, which made several people turn around to get a look at the rowdy pregnant woman on the back row. The sound drew another glare from the piano teacher. Joan avoided the woman's gaze. She wouldn't dream of shouting in public and had never completely outgrown being embarrassed by her lively sisters.

Joan and Allie sat through a few more performances before catching Tiffany's eye to wave goodbye. She would ride home with another kid's mom, and the sisters had an appointment with a couple of ice cream cones for which they didn't want to be late.

True to her word, Allie ordered a giant waffle cone with two dips of butter pecan praline ice cream.

"More sprinkles," she barked when the high school kid behind the counter tried to hand her an insufficiently covered cone. Then she softened her bark with a grin. "I deserve it. After all, I'm eating for two."

"You're going to deserve all that time on the treadmill after this baby is born too." Joan leveled a pointed glance toward Allie's rear end.

Allie winced. "Sisters can be so cruel."

Her jibe earned Joan a punch on the arm before Allie took the cone being offered to her over the counter. If there was actual ice cream under all those sprinkles, Joan couldn't see it. Her nose filled with the heavenly sweet scent of freshly made waffle cones, tempting her to follow Allie's example. She ran a finger inside the waistline of her jeans. They'd been a little tight the past week or so. Ice cream by itself was enough of a splurge—no sense adding more calories. She ordered a single scoop of chocolate in a cup and joined Allie at a table by the window.

They ate in blissful silence for a moment. When Allie had licked off every last sprinkle, she caught Joan in a direct stare across the table.

"So, Mom says Gram is losing it."

Joan didn't bother hiding a grimace. "Mom needs to let up a little. Gram is eighty-three years old. If she wants to alphabetize the laundry, let her."

Allie shook her head. "That's not what Mom's worried about, Joan. Gram is getting forgetful too. I've seen that myself. And she's alone in that house for a good chunk of the day. What if she decides to do something worse than alphabetizing? Something dangerous?"

"That's ridiculous. What would she do?"

"I don't know. Maybe she'll forget she put something on the stove and burn the house down."

"She's been cooking for more years than any of us have been alive. She's not going to do that." Joan shoved the plastic spoon into her ice cream, avoiding her sister's eyes. No one knew that she came home a couple of weeks ago to find a pan of green beans burned dry on the stove and Gram in the bathroom cleaning the medicine cabinet. "Besides, Mom is there until almost four o'clock when she leaves for work, and I get home by 7:15. Gram is only alone in the house for a few hours."

"Mom sleeps most of the morning. You know that. And a few minutes is all it would take for a disaster to happen."

Joan thrust her chin into the air. "Nothing is going to happen. Mom is menopausal, that's all. She finds fault with everything Gram and I do."

Allie concentrated for a moment on licking the melting rivers of ice cream that ran down the side of her cone onto her fingers.

"I'm going to say something you don't want to hear. I've noticed a change since you and Roger broke up. You've gotten defensive."

"Defensive?" Joan sat straight up and glared at her sister. "What are you talking about?"

"You're doing it right now."

A tiny flame of anger flickered as Joan forced herself to relax against the plastic seat back. If defending her grandmother from unjustified insinuations that she was losing her mind set Joan against her mother, so be it. She could handle Mom. But to have her older sister throw her failed romantic relationship in her face was not fair. "I don't see what Roger has to do with any of this."

"I'm not talking about Roger. I'm talking about you." Allie examined her ice cream cone for a moment before continuing, her voice gentle. "I know you expected to marry Roger. Feeling a little desperate is normal."

"First I'm defensive, and then I'm desperate?" Joan sucked in a quick breath. "I'm not exactly over the hill, you know."

Allie's eyebrows rose. "I didn't say anything about being over the hill."

"Well, whatever you're trying to say isn't coming through." With a degree in social work and a few psych courses under her belt, Allie loved to analyze everyone. Usually Joan tolerated the armchair psychology with good grace, but this came close to crossing a line.

Allie leaned forward, and Joan had no choice but to lock eyes with her. "You and Roger dated for nine years. His absence leaves a hole in your life. It's almost like a death or a divorce. Maybe you're feeling a little desperate to think you might lose someone else important to you."

The flicker of anger disappeared. Joan swallowed, her throat tight. Truth rang faintly in Allie's words. She and Roger started dating their sophomore year in high school and losing him *had* felt like a divorce. Not one of her choosing, either. To have him marry someone from his office a few months later left her humiliated and aching. And lonely.

She raised her chin. She was not prepared to discuss Roger the Rat with Allie or anyone else. Instead, she focused on a message Allie had not actually said but insinuated.

"What do you mean I might lose Gram? Does Mom want to send her away somewhere?"

Allie heaved a sigh. "Mom wants what's best for her mother. She doesn't know what that is. I don't think she's ready to lock Gram away in a home against her will, if that's what you're worried about."

"That's good, because I won't let that happen. I'll hire someone to come in and stay with her during the day before I let her go into a home."

"Tell that to Mom." Allie reached across the table with her free hand and grabbed Joan's. "She loves Gram as much as you do. She's worried about her, and she feels like she's facing this alone because you get defensive whenever she tries to talk to you about it."

Allie squeezed before pulling away, leaving Joan's hand sticky with butter pecan praline. They returned to their ice cream, letting the sounds of the restaurant fill the silence between them: fifties music playing faintly from speakers recessed in the ceiling; the giggling of two teenage girls flirting with the kid who had served them; a woman at a table in the corner talking into her cell phone. As the woman's voice droned on, Joan realized with a flash of guilt that she had not talked to her mother in the three days since hanging up on her in the furniture store. They rarely saw one another since Mom didn't get home from work until after 4:00 in the morning and was asleep when Joan got out of bed for her morning run at 6:30. Most of their conversations took place over the phone, and Mom had not called again. Joan knew she had been too abrupt. No wonder Mom felt like they couldn't have a civil conversation about Gram. Joan scooped the last bite of chocolate from her cup, sucked the spoon dry, and put it on the table.

"Maybe you're right." Meeting her sister's blue gaze across the table, Joan gave a twisted smile. "I've been pretty hard on Mom. I probably need to sit down and talk with her."

A smile lit Allie's face. Even with limp hair and the

makeup sweated off her face and about twenty extra pounds she carried as a result of her overindulgence with ice cream since the beginning of her pregnancy, Joan thought Allie was one pretty woman when she smiled.

"Good. Now go interrupt the flirt fest up at the counter and get me a pint of chocolate ripple."

Joan stood. "You're taking it home for Eric?"

"Eric can get his own ice cream." Allie settled against the back of her chair and took a bite of waffle cone. "That's for my bedtime snack. And don't forget the sprinkles."

"He's not a drug dealer," Gram announced a few days later at breakfast.

Joan looked up from the newspaper she always read over her morning oatmeal, a flash of alarm tickling her mind. Drug dealer? What in the world was Gram talking about?

Gram munched a mouthful of Cheerios, obviously waiting for Joan to react to her news. Pink plastic curlers peeked from beneath her pale blue nightcap, a few wisps of white hair flying free to wave above her forehead.

"Who's not a drug dealer?"

"You know. The man renting the house next door."

Memory restored, a flush of relief washed over Joan, followed immediately by guilt. She had started watching Gram, apprehensive of every word, wondering if her grandmother really was becoming too forgetful for her own safety. But this time, Joan's memory was the faulty one.

"How do you know he's renting, and how do you know he's not a drug dealer?"

"Because I met him yesterday when he came to bring some boxes to the house and try out his keys. He works nights at the hospital." Gram grinned. "Actually, he *is* a drug dealer of sorts. He's a doctor."

"Really?"

A doctor moving to Elmtree Drive? And renting? Now that was an interesting bit of neighborhood gossip. The homes on their street were nice but not up to typical physician standards. They were old enough to be a bit dingy but new enough to be uninteresting to anyone who liked old homes. Most of the houses were single-level brick crackerboxes, though some, like Gram's, had a few more rooms and a split-level floor plan. The yards were all clean and kept free of junk but were more likely to have plastic garden gnomes than fancy statues or fountains as decorations. Why would a doctor want to move here?

"And he's single." Gram's eyebrows waggled a few times. "I told him about my beautiful granddaughter who runs the furniture store on the other side of town."

Joan slumped in her chair, groaning. "Oh, Gram, you didn't!"

Well, there went any desire to get a glimpse of the new neighbor. If there was a single dating humiliation worse than being fixed up by your grandmother, Joan couldn't imagine it.

Gram spread her hands wide. "He asked! He needs furniture."

"Why would a doctor rent furniture? Or a house, for that

matter? Why not buy one of those fancy designer homes in a neighborhood like Heartland or Argyle, where all the other doctors live?"

"He can't afford to buy a house or furniture, because he's a new doctor with school loans to pay off. He has to have a couch, doesn't he? He can't sit on the floor."

"Hmmm."

Joan returned to her oatmeal, but her mind wasn't on the newspaper anymore. Was this an answer to her problem? Having a doctor next door might relieve Mom's worries, especially if he worked nights. That meant he'd be at home during the day. Surely a physician wouldn't mind checking in on his elderly neighbor every so often.

She could almost hear Mom's argument. "He'll be asleep during the day. He could snore right through a disaster and never even know it happened."

Besides, brand-new doctors can't claim their time as their own. Probably not a good idea to rely on him being there every day. Still, having a doctor right next door in case of an emergency was a big relief. And maybe Joan could pay one of the teenagers in the neighborhood to drop by in the afternoon, just to make sure everything was alright. The twins who lived three doors down seemed like nice girls. Gram would love having someone to talk to and stuff with cookies.

Across the table, Gram scooped the last of the Cheerios out of her bowl, ate them, and then wiped her spoon dry with her napkin. As she wiped, the set of her jaw became firm, like a woman with a mission.

She set the spoon on the table beside her bowl.

She dropped her hand to her lap.

She reached up again to turn the handle around to point toward Joan.

She dropped her hand to her lap.

Half a breath later, she picked the spoon up and turned it so the handle pointed toward her again.

Joan watched as she repeated the arranging of her spoon twice before relaxing against the back of the chair with a deep sigh. A shadowy fear settled in Joan's stomach. Though she usually ignored Gram's quirks, this was one she hadn't seen before. And this was different than alphabetizing or organizing. In light of her conversation with Allie, and her worries since then, she couldn't keep quiet.

"What was that all about?"

"What?" Innocent blue eyes stared across the table.

Joan waved toward the table. "That business with the spoon."

"Oh, nothing." Flashing a smile, Gram lifted a shoulder. "Just fiddling, that's all."

Her actions hadn't looked like nothing. If Mom had been in the room, she would have leapt on Gram's fiddling and pointed out that most people didn't compulsively shuffle their silverware. She would say this was one more reason they needed to "do something about Gram."

Joan banished those thoughts with a quick shake of her head and picked up the newspaper. What was the harm in rearranging a spoon?

The next morning Joan came out of the basement bathroom she shared with Mom, dressed for work on what she knew would be a busy Saturday. Head lowered, she nearly collided with her mother in the hallway. Mom worked three-on-three-off, but had been pulling extra shifts at the hospital for several months since they were shorthanded. Dressed in wrinkled blue scrubs, her eyelids drooped behind her brown-rimmed glasses, and her wavy blonde hair looked as though she had run her hands through it a couple dozen times too often. Half a head taller than Joan's five-six, her normally erect back slumped forward.

"Oops. Sorry, Mom." Joan peered at her face. "You look beat."

Her mom covered a huge yawn with pink manicured nails and gave a weary smile. "I am beat. I feel like I could sleep for a week. Thank goodness I'm off until Monday."

Joan hesitated. Now would be a good time to talk since Gram was still asleep. When Mom started to step around her, Joan put a hand on her arm. "Listen, I've been thinking about our conversation the other day."

Caution stole over Mom's features. How many times had Joan seen that expression? She suspected Carla Sanderson didn't know what to make of her middle daughter. Allie and Tori had inherited their mother's vivacious personality, her love of chatter. Joan had always been the quiet one, more like Daddy.

"You mean the one where you hung up on me?"

Joan let her gaze drop. "Yeah, that one. I'm sorry."

Mom patted her shoulder. "It's okay, honey. You were

busy, and I shouldn't have called you at work. I didn't mean to upset you."

"I just . . . I just wondered what you're planning to do." She tugged at the hem of her blouse, looking anywhere but into her mother's eyes. Why did she find it so difficult to come right out and tell Mom what she was worried about? She never had any problem talking to Daddy . . . before he left. "You know. About Gram."

Mom shook her head and sighed. "I'm not planning anything."

"Then you're not going to put her in that new nursing home in town?"

"You mean Waterford? It isn't a nursing home. It's an assisted living center."

A knot of dread settled in Joan's gut. "So you've looked into it."

Mom leaned against the doorjamb, removed her glasses, and rubbed her eyes. "No, I haven't. But a couple of the oncology patients have been released to the nursing program there. The doctors speak highly of the place."

A feeling of near-panic threatened to clog her throat. Mom actually talked to people about it. "Gram doesn't need a nurse."

"I didn't say she did. But you've got to admit she has slipped in the years since Grandpa died."

"So she alphabetizes things." Joan ran a hand over her ponytail, smoothing every hair into place. "So what? She's not dangerous, not to herself or to anyone else."

Mom shook her head. "I'm not talking about her kooky alphabetizing habit. She's weaker, more frail, and her eyesight isn't what it used to be. And she forgets to take her blood pressure medicine half the time. If we weren't here—"

"But we are here."

Mom gave her a tender smile. "You won't be here forever, honey."

"I'll stay as long as Gram needs me." She lifted her chin.

"I know you would, but that's not healthy, and Mother doesn't want you to give up your life for her." She pushed off the doorjamb and stood up straight. "Can we continue this conversation later? I'm so tired I can't think straight."

Joan didn't want to talk about it later. She wanted Mom's promise now, right this minute, that she wasn't going to force Gram out of her house and into a nursing home. Or an *assisted living center*, either.

But Mom did look tired, exhausted even. And besides, Joan didn't want to push her into a corner with an argument. "I guess so."

Mom put her arms around Joan, and Joan returned her embrace while fighting a sense of impending doom. She didn't feel better after the conversation. In fact, she had practically confirmed that Mom was thinking about sending Gram somewhere else to live.

As she headed down the hallway toward her bedroom, Mom said over her shoulder, "Wake me up in three days."

Joan stood looking at the bedroom door long after Mom closed it, lost in thought. She was right about Gram getting forgetful. But that didn't mean she needed to be put away in a home.

Joan would just make it a point to be sure Gram didn't forget anything important.

~ *3* ~

Joan turned onto Elmtree Drive, her Nikes striking the pavement with an even *thud-thud*. Bright sunlight blurred her vision. She reduced her pace for the last stretch of her five-mile run, regulating her breath for the slowdown, and glanced at her watch. 7:30. Plenty of time to get cleaned up before Sunday school. A trickle of sweat slid from her temple down to her jaw, and she brushed it away with her hand. Her mind felt clear, energized by her run.

She continued her deceleration and slowed to a brisk walk as she passed the Faulkners' house, thankful for the spray from their misplaced sprinkler on her hot face. Gram would say they were wasting money watering the sidewalk, but their flowers certainly liked the water and rewarded them with a sweet-scented rainbow carpet along both sides of the walkway leading to their front door. The grass became notably dingier as she crossed the property line separating the Faulkners' yard from their neighbor's, the Hendersons'. She glanced toward the front window, noting the charcoal-gray cat perched regally on the windowsill inside. Its head turned to watch her pass, as it did every morning.

She caught sight of someone heading toward her, a man walking a dog. Or, to be more accurate, a dog pulling a man, straining against its leash as it ran back and forth from one edge of the sidewalk to the other. When the dog caught sight of Joan, it tugged with renewed purpose until it gave a strangled cough. The guy winced as his arm jerked forward, but kept his grip on the leash.

"Don't blame me if you choke," he scolded the dog, who ignored him and kept up the effort to get at Joan.

She stopped a few yards from the eager dog. It didn't look dangerous, but she knew better than to approach a strange animal without caution. Its ears perked forward and its tail wagged nonstop. Sure, a wagging tail looked like a friendly gesture, but pit bulls wagged their tails too. She certainly didn't want to be a topic for the morning headlines:

DANVILLE WOMAN MAULED BY CRAZED DOG

Keeping a cautious eye on the animal, she asked, "Does he bite?"

"Trigger?" The man gave a snort of laughter. "More likely he'd drown you in slobber. But he does jump, and those claws can do some damage." He extended his arm to show her a long red scratch.

"Looks painful." Her gaze rose to his face. Stubble darkened a strong jaw, and greenish eyes smiled at her beneath long, brown lashes. Wavy dark hair brushed at his collar and curled gently over the tops of his ears. Joan suppressed a grin when she saw the dog also had longish curly hair covering his ears. Some people really did resemble their pets. She took a slow step forward, her hand outstretched to the excited animal.

"His name is Trigger? Like half-cocked?"

The man grinned, giving her a glimpse of straight, white teeth. "No, but that fits too. He's named after Roy Rogers' horse. Take a look at those paws. They're as big as hubcaps. I figure by the time he's full-grown, he might be roughly the size of the original Trigger."

Laughing, Joan took another step toward Trigger, which put her hand within sniffing range. The dog's wet nose and tongue investigated her fingers. Still straining at the leash, he rose up on his hind legs, his big puppy paws waving in the air.

"Down," she said in a firm voice. She dropped her hand, palm open toward the sidewalk, and squatted. When Trigger followed her motion, she rubbed his silky ears. "Good boy."

"Hey, you're good with dogs. Do you have one?"

Joan shook her head and allowed the excited animal to lick her hand. "No, but I used to. He died of old age a couple of years ago. He wasn't this big even fully grown, though."

"Trigger's only four months old, and he's already forty pounds. I'm afraid he's going to be a monster."

"What breed is he?"

"My sister calls him a Heinz 57. Fifty-seven different breeds, from what we can tell. I think there must be a good percentage of Great Dane in the mix, though."

Joan cocked her head to examine Trigger. His big snout and the shape of his head did resemble Scooby-Doo, though his spotted brown fur was longish and wavy.

"He looks like he might have some poodle in him too. Did you get a look at his parents when you got him?"

The man dropped down onto his haunches, and Trigger took advantage of the slack in the leash to push forward, knocking Joan on her rear end and covering her face with doggie slobber. Probably licking off the salty sweat. She laughed and pushed him back with a hand on either side of his head as the man tightened the leash.

"Whoa, Trigger. Leave the pretty lady alone. You're making a bad first impression."

Startled, Joan looked up to see another flash of white teeth. Pretty? She was sweaty from her run and without a drop of makeup, and this guy called her pretty? She lowered her gaze quickly to the dog again, rubbing his ears and hoping the sudden heat in her face wasn't obvious.

The man roughed the fur at the top of the dog's tail. "I didn't see his parents. I got him from a shelter. Actually, my sister got him from a shelter and gave him to me. My name's Ken Fletcher, by the way. I moved into the neighborhood yesterday."

Of course! The doctor. Joan looked up long enough to give him a brief smile. "Welcome to Elmtree Drive. I'm Joan Sanderson, your next-door neighbor."

"Joan Sanderson! Just the lady I've been hoping to meet. Your grandmother tells me you can hook me up with some furniture."

She hid a grimace. What else did Gram tell him? That she

was single and desperate, maybe? "I can, but we specialize in rentals, not sales."

He shrugged. "I'm renting the house. Might as well rent furniture too. Besides, I don't have a lot of money. This guy eats half my paycheck."

He yanked on the leash. Trigger, his eyes half closed as Joan massaged the soft skin at the base of his ears, ignored the tug.

"Does your sister live nearby?" Joan nearly bit her own tongue. She didn't want to offend him by prying into his personal life. "I mean, so she can help you train your dog."

Ken shook his head. "'Fraid not. She was hoping I would land a job close to her, but the hospital here is exactly what I want. Plus, there are several smaller hospitals nearby, so I'm hoping to pick up some extra money working at a couple of those. Small-town emergency rooms should be quite a change from Cincinnati, where I did my residency."

"My mom is a nurse at the hospital. Carla Sanderson. Have you met her?"

He squinted as he considered. "I don't think so. But I've only been here a week, and the names run together. I'm still trying to remember where the bathrooms are, and keeping a low profile where the nurses are concerned."

"Why is that?"

His eyebrows shot upward. "Your mother works at the hospital and you don't know? Nurses run everything, of course, and they aren't impressed with brand-new doctors. My goal is to amaze them with my skill when I'm seeing a patient and keep out of their way the rest of the time."

Joan laughed. She had heard Mom mention a new doctor or two in less-than-flattering terms. But the nurses wouldn't have a problem with this guy. He didn't have the arrogance of some of the physicians Mom complained about. "Sounds like a wise plan."

Joan glanced at her watch, and then scratched Trigger's ears with vigor before getting to her feet. Ken did the same.

"I need to get going. It was nice meeting you, Ken. And Trigger too. He's a great dog. I think your sister picked a good one."

"Karen told me he'd be a good way to meet women. She said, 'Chicks dig dogs.'" He flashed a boyish grin and locked eyes with Joan. "Looks like she was right."

With a shock, Joan realized he was flirting with her. Her face heated again. She had never been good at flirting. That was Tori's department. Something stupid always managed to come out of Joan's mouth, something that made her writhe in remembered agony for days afterward. She broke their gaze by bending down to give Trigger's head a final rub. With any luck he would think she was flushed as a result of her run.

Straightening, she gave Ken what she hoped was a carefree smile. "Come by the store and we'll get you fixed up. Abernathy Sales and Rental, over in the Danville Manor Shopping Center on the bypass."

"I'll be there this week. Sitting on the floor is giving me a stiff back." He stretched his shoulders backward, and Joan looked away from the sight of firm chest muscles visible beneath his clinging T-shirt. Yeah, he worked out. No doubt about it.

"Nice meeting you, Ken." She addressed Trigger. "You too, big guy."

"It was great meeting you, Joan. I'll talk to you later."

She dipped her head as she walked past him toward home, ignoring Trigger's disappointed barking at her departure. After a moment the barking stopped, and she heard the scrabble of claws on concrete as they continued on their way. As she turned into her driveway, she risked a look. Ken walked backward down the sidewalk, watching her. He lifted a hand in a friendly wave when she looked up. Blushing to the hair roots, she returned the gesture, ducked her head, and jogged up the front steps, escaping into the house.

When the front door to Joan's house closed, Ken continued down the sidewalk with Trigger. He could hardly keep the grin off his face. This town was looking better all the time. He'd landed a great job working in his specialty, found the perfect rental house with a fenced yard for the dog his sister saddled him with, and ended up right next door to a gorgeous girl.

"I wasn't sure about this neighborhood, but so far I like the way things are shaping up."

Trigger turned his head, an ear perked at the sound of Ken's voice for a fraction of a second before he resumed his wild attempt to run in four directions at once.

"You know what, boy? Karen was right. Joan liked you, maybe even more than she liked me." He gave a playful

45

tug on the leash. "You might actually have earned your keep this morning."

Women had been pushed to the back burner for a while now. Med school absorbed all his time, so the only girls he saw during those four years were other busy med students. Then his residency was unlike anything he'd ever imagined. Who would have thought a person could live through three solid years of such a frantic pace?

Besides, dating required money. He owed tons in student loans, though he had begun to make a dent in the mountain of debt. He should have them paid off in another . . . ten years or so. He grimaced at the thought.

Trigger pulled him down the sidewalk while his thoughts wandered to work. The pace was slower here, for sure, but that didn't mean he had much downtime. This ER was a busy little place, busier than he would have guessed, and of course they kept a much smaller staff. Many nights during the past two weeks he found himself rushing from patient to patient with barely enough time to gulp down a cup of coffee, just like in the big Cincinnati hospital. Different cases, though. He hadn't seen a stabbing or drug overdose yet. Nothing more serious than a fractured bone or appendicitis. And that was fine with him.

Now if he could just find a church. But as low man on the totem pole, he'd probably work most weekends, which made hunting for one difficult. Did Joan Sanderson go to church? He hoped so. Maybe he could finagle an invitation to go with her. And then maybe he'd take her out to lunch afterward . . .

Trigger paused in his mad pace to sniff at a bush. The dog circled a few minutes, nose to the ground.

The door of the house they stood in front of burst open, and a woman in a bathrobe stepped out onto the porch. She glared at him across the lawn. "I hope you're planning to clean up after your dog."

Ken pulled a wadded-up plastic grocery bag out of his pocket. He held it above his head for her to see. "Yes, ma'am."

"Well." Her scowl softened a fraction. "See that you do, then." The front door closed with a bang.

"C'mon, Trigger." Ken pulled the dog away from the interesting-smelling patch of grass. "Let's go home. You've got a whole yard of your own to sniff."

~ *4* ~

The organist had begun the prelude by the time Joan found Gram outside the seniors' Sunday school room and walked with her into the sanctuary. Their noses were assaulted by the startling clash of old lady perfume and gentlemen's cologne that almost overpowered the musty odor of hymnals. A smiling usher in a dark suit led them down the center aisle to the fourth row. Her face impassive, Joan groaned inwardly. She preferred a pew toward the rear, where she could blend into anonymity in the sea of worshipers. Sitting in the front seemed so . . . showy.

As they crab-walked into the empty space in the center of the pew, the choir filed into the sanctuary through a doorway in the loft. Joan got Gram settled with a tissue and a hymnal before scanning the green-robed figures for her mother. Mom said singing in the church choir and her weekly bowling league were all that kept her sane after the hectic pace of her job at the hospital. Joan found her in her accustomed place among the altos, second row center. Mom caught her eye with a smile and a slight nod of acknowledgment.

Joan opened the bulletin and reached for her own hymnal. She marked page 167 with a blank visitor card and let her gaze travel down the morning's order of worship to find the next hymn. If only everyone would take the time to find the songs before the service began. All that noise when people shuffled through the pages disrupted the service, and Joan disliked disruption.

The bulletin announced that they would hear from a guest speaker this morning, a woman. Joan searched the platform for an unfamiliar face. Rev. Jacobsen sat in his accustomed place on a bench behind the pulpit. No one sat beside him.

There. On the front pew sat an unfamiliar African American couple.

"Rev. Jacobsen isn't speaking this morning." Gram pointed toward the bulletin. "I wonder who Mary Alice Sachs is."

"I don't know, but I'm guessing that's her."

Joan dipped her head toward the couple. They sat facing the front, alone on the first pew. As she watched, the man leaned sideways to whisper something, and the woman nodded in agreement. With a flash of guilt, Joan noticed that no one spoke to them or introduced themselves. Of course, Rev. Jacobsen would have made them feel welcome, since he had obviously invited this woman to speak. And surely the greeters stationed by the door welcomed them when they arrived. That was the greeters' job, to welcome visitors. But it would be nice if someone in the congregation introduced themselves too.

Perhaps she should . . .

But no. The organist was nearly finished, the choir was in place, and people had stopped filing into the sanctuary. With a rush of relief, Joan decided she would speak to the visiting couple *after* the service. If she had time.

The organ music ended on a triumphant chord that reverberated through the sanctuary, and Rev. Jacobsen stood to welcome them as he did every Sunday. As the congregation followed the order of worship, Joan relaxed into the familiar sequence of events. First a hymn, then a prayer, then announcements, then another hymn before the offering.

The minister waited until they had settled themselves comfortably in their pews to introduce the visitors. "Today we have special guests." The overhead light turned his scalp red beneath his thinning gray hair. "Robert and Mary Alice Sachs have recently returned to the States from a three-month mission trip to Afghanistan. I heard Mary Alice speak at a district meeting a few weeks ago and asked if she would come and share her message with you. I know you'll make them feel welcome."

When Mrs. Sachs walked from the front pew up the stairs to stand behind the podium, Gram shifted in her seat. Joan patted her hand and gave her a smile before turning her attention toward the front. She knew how Gram felt. Any change in their regular Sunday morning routine was . . . disruptive.

"Thank you, Rev. Jacobsen, for allowing me to fill your pulpit this morning." The woman's low voice flowed like honey from the podium, melodic and rich. She nodded in the minister's direction and flashed a set of teeth that battled with the white blouse she wore beneath a dark purple suit jacket. "I want to tell you today about a God who is *real*. I know he's real, because I have lived in a place where his is the only hand that kept me from torture and death. I have seen his power displayed in ways that leave no doubt that this God we serve takes an active role in our everyday lives, if we let him."

The woman spoke for forty-five minutes. Joan sat fascinated along with everyone else as she told of wonders like those in the Bible happening every day during their mission. She described healings and miraculous escapes. When they had no food, she said God fed them. Tears glistened in her eyes when she spoke of changed lives among the orphans they went to serve when the children encountered this miraculous God.

Sitting in the pew, Joan's mind was transported to that far-distant land. What would it be like to do something so exciting, something that made an impact in other people's lives? But nothing like that ever happened here, in sleepy little Danville, Kentucky. Certainly not in her life. Still, she knew the same God as Mrs. Sachs. Why, then, did he choose to be so evident in this woman's life, but not in hers?

As Joan bowed her head during Rev. Jacobsen's closing prayer, that question hovered on the edge of her thoughts. When the organist began to play the final hymn, Gram dropped her hymnal and Joan's thoughts refocused. As the congregation stood, Joan stooped to pick up the book, her mind already turning toward the afternoon. Tori, Allie, and Eric were coming for dinner. A glance at her watch told her that the service had already run over by fifteen minutes. They'd have to hurry to get home before the others arrived.

The oniony aroma of Gram's meat loaf filled the house and teased Joan's rumbling stomach. From her seat in the recliner, she reached toward the coffee table for the Sunday comic section as soon as Allie laid it down.

"Dinner's almost ready," Gram announced from the kitchen doorway. "We can eat as soon as Tori gets here."

Joan tore her eyes off Beetle Bailey. "Do you need any help?"

"You can put ice in the glasses."

Joan reached for the lever to lower the recliner's footrest, but Mom came up the stairs from the basement bedrooms at that moment. She had changed from her church clothes into a long peasant skirt and a loose-fitting blouse that hung from her bony shoulders as though she had forgotten to remove the hanger before putting it on. She waved a hand at Joan as she passed through the living room on her way to the kitchen.

"I'll do it. You visit with your sister and Eric. Tell them about our guest speaker this morning."

"Guest speaker?" Allie looked at Joan over the top of the entertainment section.

"A missionary. You should have heard the stories she told, about living in danger and miracles and all that."

"Hmmm."

Allie looked back down at her paper. Church was a sore subject in the Sanderson family. Eric, who was not a Christian, had relented enough to agree to a church wedding, but had not set a foot through the door in the three years since. After the wedding, Allie came regularly for a while. Then she skipped a Sunday or two. Within a few months she had stopped coming completely.

"By the way, have you finished *Passion on the Ocean*? You've had it two weeks."

Joan grimaced and shook her head. "I can't get through it. Honestly, I don't understand how you can read those bodice rippers."

Allie dropped her hands, the newspaper wrinkling in her lap. "They're well researched, and usually historically accurate."

Joan gave a snort. "Maybe some are, but the writing is so bad in that one I didn't notice the research."

"All English majors think they're book critics." Allie stuck her tongue out at Joan.

"Don't let her fool you, Joan." Eric winked at his wife. "She likes the rippling muscles."

"Speaking of that, I want to get a look at this doctor." Allie tossed the paper onto the coffee table and twisted around to kneel on the couch, resting her arms on the backrest so she could peer through a crack in the white curtains covering the front window. "Eric, do something to make him come outside."

Eric's eyes remained fixed on the television screen. "You want me to ring his doorbell and run away?"

Joan laughed as her big sister rolled her eyes. Allie had

found her perfect match in the even-keeled 9-1-1 dispatcher. His quiet manner and steady approach to life countered Allie's exuberance, and a moment of watching them together left no doubt that he adored his lively wife. A good thing since, according to Allie, his dark good looks attracted women like a bag of chips on a beach full of seagulls. Eric had slipped into the lives of the Sanderson women shortly after Grandpa's death, a comforting male influence. And he was good with a toilet plunger too.

"So you say he's cute?" Allie caught Joan's gaze with raised eyebrows.

"I didn't say, but yeah, he was okay." If you were into gorgeous.

"Where's he from? Where did he go to medical school? And most importantly, does he have a girlfriend?"

"I don't know. I didn't ask for his life story. I just talked to him for a minute." Joan returned to Beetle Bailey.

"A minute is more than enough time to acquire all the pertinent information. If I had been there, I'd have found out all that *and* how much he makes." Allie turned back to the window. "Let's see. We know he has a dog. That's probably why he's renting a house instead of an apartment. He drives a red Ford Probe, older model."

"Nineteen ninety," said Eric, without looking away from the TV.

Joan looked up at him. "How do you know the year?"

"It was in the driveway when we got here." He shrugged. "I noticed. Ohio plates."

Allie turned, her face alight. "Hey! Eric could run his license plates. That'll tell us if he has a record or anything."

"I am not going to run his plates," Eric said in a voice that left no room for argument.

She showed him her lower lip in a quick pout, then raised her head to shout toward the kitchen. "Tori just pulled in the driveway."

The arrival of the youngest Sanderson sister caused a flurry of excitement. Joan stood with the rest of the family on the landing inside the front door to greet her with bear hugs and cries of "welcome home!" Though she lived only thirty-five minutes away and visited often enough that her arrival shouldn't cause such a stir, people couldn't help but get excited when the baby of the family showed up.

Like Allie, Tori Sanderson exuded energy. She stood only five foot three and had inherited her mother's thin frame without the gangly height. Her bright golden hair was the envy of blondes everywhere, and her elfish features and infectious grin had drawn attention from the first moment she toddled into the public eye.

Joan watched as Mom, first in the reception line, embraced her baby and exclaimed over her new designer jeans. Tori hugged Gram next, and the older woman's face brightened with delight. Next Tori stooped to place both hands on Allie's belly before hugging the mama-to-be and her husband.

Self-pity stabbed at Joan. When was the last time someone greeted her with such enthusiasm? In fact, when was the last time someone greeted her at all? She never went anywhere and, therefore, never came home to a reception line like this one. Maybe she should leave too, just go off on her own and let Gram and Mom fend for themselves.

That's what Tori had done. She hadn't worried about her family when she found that apartment in Lexington.

Because Tori knew she was leaving everything at home in competent hands. *Her* hands.

"Joan!" Tori nearly knocked Joan off balance with her enthusiastic hug. "It's so good to see you. I've missed you. When are you going to come spend the night with me, like you promised?"

Ashamed of her feelings, Joan returned Tori's embrace. "I mean to, but you know how it is."

"No, I don't." Tori stepped back but didn't release her grip on Joan's arms. "And I don't care how it is. You need to come to Lexington for a weekend. We'll rent chick flicks and have a sleepover and stay up all night talking about our older sister."

"Hey!" Allie sniffled, injured. "You have to be nice to me. I'm pregnant."

Grinning, Tori threw her arms around Allie's neck and squeezed. "Just kidding, Allie-gator, you know that. You can come too. We'll have a Sanderson Sister Sleepover."

"Let's do it! And soon, before the baby comes."

Allie and Tori hugged again, bouncing on their toes, and then as one turned to Joan. Each of them extended an arm to pull her into a three-way hug. Joan joined them, touching her dark head to their blonde ones, hearing a sister giggle in each ear.

"The Sanderson Sisters, together again!" Allie announced.

"We're in trouble now," Eric mumbled, turning back toward the living room and his ball game.

"Dinner's almost on the table," Gram announced.

"I'm starving." Tori raised her nose and sniffed. "I don't know what it is, and I don't care, as long as it isn't pizza or fast food."

"I can't believe you eat junk and stay so skinny." Allie shook her head, her arm still around Tori as she propelled her through the living room toward the kitchen. "It's not fair. What are those jeans, size two?"

Joan fell in behind them. That's the way it had always been—Allie and Tori plowing ahead, arm in arm, chattering like a pair of squirrels while she, the quiet one, trailed behind, a black jelly bean in a basketful of Easter eggs. Trying to match words with either of her sisters was too exhausting to even consider. Neither of them could talk without hand gestures and, usually, a full pantomime. The entertainment they provided was worth sitting back to watch.

After dinner the women shoed Eric into the living room as they took their accustomed places in the cleanup assembly line. They had a dishwasher, but it was rarely used. Gram and Mom scraped the leftovers into plastic containers. Allie stood with her arms sunk to the elbows in soapy water, handing the clean, rinsed dishes to Tori for drying. Then they passed to Joan, who moved around the familiar kitchen without thinking, storing the dishes in the places they had occupied for more years than the girls had been alive.

"Hey, look!" Allie leaned over the sink, straining her neck to see out the back window. "It's the doctor next door."

The towel stopped swiping the white china plate as Tori

turned a round blue gaze toward Joan. "There's a doctor next door?"

"There sure is," said Allie. "And get a look at him. What a hottie."

Joan placed the plate she held onto the stack in the cabinet while Tori shoved Allie away from the sink and stood on tiptoes to see outside. If only Ken had stayed in his house. He was part of *her* neighborhood, and she had been the first to meet him, to play with his dog. She had dibs.

"Hottie is right." Tori spoke without turning from the window, her voice warm with appreciation. "When did he move in?"

"Yesterday," Mom said. "He came to work at the hospital two weeks ago. I haven't met him yet, though."

"He's a nice young man," Gram added.

She placed a lid on the plastic bowl of leftover mashed potatoes and pressed in the center. When the lid didn't seal, Mom reached over and snapped it shut. Then she snatched it up and put it into the refrigerator with a single movement, leaving Gram standing beside the empty counter. Irritation flashed through Joan. That brisk, no-nonsense manner probably made Mom a good nurse, but did she have to be so abrupt at home?

"C'mon, you guys. Let's go introduce ourselves." Tori tossed the dishtowel at Allie, who caught it midair.

"Alright. Hey, Eric." She raised her chin and shouted toward the living room. "I'm going outside to meet a good-looking doctor. You'd better come along so he doesn't sweep me off my feet."

"Unless he's into instant fatherhood, that's highly un-likely." Tori gave her sister's belly a pat. She turned a questioning gaze toward Joan. "You coming?"

Joan hesitated. Though she'd like to talk to Ken again, the thought of trailing along while her lively sisters gawked and flirted did not appeal to her.

She shook her head. "You go ahead, and I'll finish up here."

Eric came into the kitchen in time to follow Tori and Allie through the back door. Joan stepped into the place Allie vacated and plunged her hands into the hot, soapy water. Through the window she saw Ken on the other side of the chain-link fence that separated his yard from theirs, throwing a tennis ball for Trigger. The delighted dog raced after the ball as it sailed through the air, and skidded to a somersaulting stop when he caught up with it. Ken looked up as Tori called a greeting.

Joan rinsed a clean plate and stood it in the rack to drip dry. She should have gone outside. She could have introduced Ken to her sisters and Eric, and listened as Allie extracted all the personal details of his life. So why was she inside, watching through the window?

Mom picked up the dishtowel and started drying the dripping plate. "You don't seem all that impressed by our new neighbor."

"Why do you say that?"

"You just don't." She set the dry plate on the counter and reached for the next one, stealing a sideways glance at Joan. "Don't worry, honey. The right man for you will come along soon."

A warm flush crept up Joan's neck. Did Mom think she was desperate for a guy? Well, she wasn't! Ever since Roger dumped her . . . she winced . . . everyone treated her like the family spinster. She was sick of it. She didn't *need* a man to make her happy.

Of course, an occasional date would be nice. And who wouldn't want to go out with a handsome doctor?

Oblivious to Joan's irritation, Mom's gaze fixed on the scene outside. "Would you look at her operate?"

She didn't have to ask which *her* Mom referred to. Following her mother's gaze, she saw petite Tori leaning gracefully on the fence. As she watched, Tori tilted her head sideways toward Ken and flashed her ready dimples.

When she saw Ken's answering grin, Joan's insides knotted.

~ 5 ~

"And why he is talking to me for the way I raise my daughter? Because he sent a check maybe three or four times?" Rosa's dark eyes flashed as an angry finger sliced through the air. "He no is telling me what to do."

Seated at her desk, Joan glanced over last month's P&L report as the woman ranted. Rosa didn't mention Tiffany's father often, but when she did, Joan had learned to stay out of the way of her fiery Latin temper. Normally she begged Joan to help her improve her English, because she was so eager to be accepted in the country she'd adopted seven years ago when she moved from Mexico. But her mood today made Joan keep her mouth shut. When Rosa got really angry, she lapsed into Spanish, and Joan remembered enough from her high school and college classes to be thankful she couldn't understand it all.

The store was quiet today, unusual for a Monday. The heat was probably keeping people indoors. Or driving them to the swimming pool, maybe. On her way to work this morning, she noticed a line at the public pool, waiting for the gate to open.

Rosa paced in front of the counter, her black hair whipping in the air at every turn. "Tiffany no will talk to him again. He made her cry."

He made that sweet little girl cry? Joan jerked her head upright and sucked in an outraged breath. "What did he say to her?"

"That he has no time to visit this summer. He is going somewhere else to work." She stopped pacing and slapped a hand on the desk. "I say *good*! We no need him anyway."

"*Don't* need him," Joan corrected, despite her better judgment.

"We *don't* need him anyway." She flashed a quick smile of thanks.

Poor Tiffany, her heart broken once again. How many times had her father promised to visit? Tiffany hadn't seen him since he left for Nevada two years ago, a third of her young lifetime. She couldn't possibly even remember what he looked like anymore.

Joan struggled to picture her own father. If she didn't have the family photo albums to refresh her memory, she was sure she wouldn't be able to draw up a mental image of him. At least Tiffany's father called every so often. Joan hadn't heard from hers in thirteen years, not since Mom threw him out.

Rosa's feet abused the cheap carpet. "He say why spend money on piano when our families are hungry in Mexico. I say they are not hungry because he sends them money, more to them than to me. I send money when I have extra. He say I have more extra without piano lessons."

The tirade ended as quickly as it had begun when Rosa stomped around the counter and threw herself into the empty chair beside Joan. Her shoulders drooped. "You think Luis is right? You think piano lessons are . . . *cómo se dice* . . . not useful?"

The last thing Joan wanted to do was get involved in a fight between Rosa and her estranged husband. She tore her gaze away from the intensity in Rosa's face and looked down at the report. "I don't know, Rosa."

"Joan." Rosa pronounced Joan's name in half a syllable, the J a touch softer than someone who spoke English as a native. Her tone forced Joan's eyes to her face. "Do American girls take piano lessons?"

Rosa's determination to give her daughter an upbringing as American as possible influenced every decision concerning the child. Even Tiffany's name had been chosen to brand her as a thoroughly American girl.

Joan gave a hesitant nod. "Some do."

"Then my Tiffany do too." She raised her chin. "And when Luis calls the next time, I will tell him—"

The door alarm interrupted the details of the terrible things Rosa intended to tell Luis. Grateful, Joan rose from her chair and headed toward the front. When she caught sight of the customer who stood just inside the store, her heart thudded in her chest.

Ken stepped into the store, the cool air bringing instant relief from the sticky heat outside. He looked around, letting his vision adjust to the fluorescent light after the glaring sunshine. The odors of furniture polish and new fabric were a welcome change from the antiseptic of the hospital. He spotted two people coming toward him.

There she was! He shoved his hands into his pockets as she approached. "Joan Sanderson, just the lady I wanted to see."

She looked different from the girl he met on the street yesterday morning. More professional. Her ponytail looked more severe, tighter. Or maybe it was the suit. Or the way she studied him through slightly narrowed eyelids as though appraising his credit worthiness. Whatever the difference, he felt a little intimidated by this new version of the girl next door.

Where was Trigger when he needed him?

"Ken." She held out her hand. "Good to see you again."

A shy smile softened her lips when her eyes captured his. The momentary awkwardness fled as he returned the gesture. This was more like it. "You too."

Her hand felt cool in his, and soft. A faint blush stained her round cheeks as he squeezed gently. Or was that her makeup? Whatever, the color set off the sparkle in her eyes and made him want to stare. She pulled her hand away, her gaze sliding to the woman beside her.

"This is my associate, Rosa Garza. Rosa, this is Dr. Ken Fletcher. He just moved to town and needs some furniture."

Rosa, a petite Hispanic woman, aimed a wide grin up at him as she clutched his hand and pumped it up and down a few times. "Nice to meet you."

"Sorry about the clothes." He gestured at his wrinkled hospital scrubs. "I just got off work and thought I'd stop by before I go home and rescue Trigger from the back porch."

Joan dismissed his concern with a wave. "You look fine."

The door behind him opened, and he stepped out of the way as a woman entered.

"Good morning." Joan greeted the woman, and then turned an expectant look on Rosa.

Good. For a minute Ken thought Joan might hand him off to the other woman, but it looked like she would wait on him herself. Rosa gave him another wide smile and stepped around him to greet the new customer. He followed Joan a few steps into the store.

"So, what can I show you today?"

"Everything." He grinned. "My sister is coming to visit next Sunday and my house is empty except for my desk. That's the only piece of furniture I own."

A crease appeared between her eyebrows. "You've been in the house several days. What are you sleeping on?"

"A sleeping bag." He arched his back to stretch stiff muscles. "And it's making me feel like an old man."

Hands on her hips, Joan cocked her head to deliver a sideways look. "You're a doctor. You should know better! Come on over here. We'll start at that side and work our way across the store."

He followed her past a display of dinette tables. "Hey, where were you yesterday? I met your sisters."

"Oh, I was inside." She zigzagged between two formal

dining room sets and stopped at the first of a row of bedroom displays. "I was in the middle of something."

He stood beside her and ran a hand over the gleaming headboard. Ornate carvings decorated the rich wood and rose to a graceful peak in the center like a crown. A matching nightstand and a huge wardrobe-thing stood sentinel on either side. Not really his taste. "This is nice. How much is it?"

She picked up a yellow tag and pointed. "That's the monthly rental, and that's the rent-to-own price."

He gave a low whistle. "I know I'm a doctor and we're supposed to be rolling in dough, but I'm up to my eyeballs in debt. Do you have anything cheaper? And maybe a little less, uh, fancy?"

That seemed to please her. He felt like he'd passed some sort of test when she grinned and jerked her head toward the back of the showroom. "I started you out at the high end. Come on back here."

"Do you make a commission on what I rent?" He teased as he fell in beside her.

Her lips twitched. "Of course."

"I'm in trouble now."

They passed several displays and stopped before an unpretentious set with a woodlike finish. Ken crossed to the matching nightstand to pick up the yellow tag. "Now this is more like it."

"I thought you'd like this one."

"Karen will say it's too plain, but she'll get over it." He plopped down onto the bed and bounced. "Feels great." Stretching out, he closed his eyes and settled deeply into the pillow. "Really great. Mind if I try it out for a couple of hours, just to make sure it's the one I want?"

"That depends. Do you snore?"

He opened an eye to find Joan standing at the foot of the bed with her arms crossed, watching him from beneath arched eyebrows.

"A little," he admitted. "Especially if I'm tired."

"In that case, yes, I mind. Get up, Dr. Fletcher. You're not finished shopping yet."

With an exaggerated sigh, he sat up and swung his feet to the floor. "Okay, furniture lady. Lead on."

Actually, he didn't feel tired at all. He felt energized following Joan around the store. This was fun, picking out furniture with her, trying to draw out the quick smile that ignited her eyes. She guided him next to a series of living room displays. He selected a sofa and lay down on it, his head resting on the padded arm.

"I like this one. And it looks nice too. My sister will approve."

"You're supposed to sit on it, not lay on it."

"Except when Karen and Jordan are here. Then I'll be sleeping on it."

"Jordan's her husband?"

"No, he's my nephew. Neal has to work, so it'll just be Karen and the kid next week." He sat up and extended his arms across the back. "I want you to meet them. After all, I met your sisters."

Joan's head dipped. "I'd like that."

"Good." Ken reached for the yellow tag and did a quick calculation. "I'll take the sofa and the chair and the end table. But I can get by without a coffee table for a while."

"Done. Now what about the dining room?"

"Actually, I thought I'd just get some bar stools. There's a wide counter in the kitchen."

Her eyebrows rose. "Your sister won't mind that you don't have a properly furnished dining room?"

He laughed. "I've given you a bad impression of Karen. She's really great. In fact, she's a lot like your sister Tori, energetic and funny and beautiful. Smart like Tori too, and she has a heart of gold. I admire her more than anyone else I know."

For the briefest of moments, Joan's features became immobile. Then the corners of her mouth lifted in a smile that failed to light her eyes. "I can't wait to meet her. We've got some bar stools over here." She walked away and left him sitting on the sofa.

What did I say? Surely she wasn't jealous of Karen. Some women were like that, though. Didn't want to hear a guy say anything nice about another woman, even a relative. Ken had no patience for people like that. Spending time with someone who insisted on being the center of attention was just plain tiring.

But Joan didn't seem like that sort of woman. He probably just read her wrong.

He got up off the sofa and followed her, but their easy banter had turned cold. She was all business as he selected four stools and filled out the rental application. Try though he might, he couldn't coax a genuine smile back to her face.

His furniture deal settled and delivery arrangements made, he stepped outside into the hot sunshine. As he walked toward his car, he shook his head. He must have been wrong about her. The last thing he wanted was to get involved with a jealous woman.

❧

Joan stood behind the counter, Ken's application in her hand. She watched him get into his car, close the door, and pull out of the parking lot.

He liked Tori.

The knowledge burned in her stomach like she had swallowed a lemon. Why was she surprised? Of course he liked Tori. Everyone did. She was everything he admired, like he said. Fun and pretty and smart and . . .

Her throat tightened. Who would choose Plain-Jane-Joan over Perky-Pretty-Tori?

Nobody, that's who.

~ 6 ~

Joan closed the car door and walked across the driveway toward the front porch, her step slow. The morning might have started out dead, but the afternoon brought a steady stream of customers that kept her and Rosa running. She rejected the thought that Ken's huge sale, the first of the day, had brought her good luck.

She glanced at his empty driveway. What sort of shift did he work? He seemed to always be gone whenever she was at home. She could ask Mom . . .

Not a good idea. Knowing Mom, she'd feel the need to drop a few hints like Gram had. Besides, he was a nice guy, but he was interested in Tori, not her.

She pushed the front door open, stepped inside onto the landing, and inhaled. Supper smelled heavenly. Gram said this morning she planned to make lasagna, and Joan detected the spicy odor of tomato sauce. Her stomach gave an expectant rumble.

"Gram, I'm home."

From the direction of the kitchen, she heard a soft sob. Her heart stuttered. "Gram?"

Joan threw her purse to the floor and dashed through the living room. She catapulted through the doorway and stopped.

The oven door stood open, and heat poured into the room. A mound of browned mozzarella and long ribbons of pasta formed an untidy lump in the center of the tiled floor, midway between the oven and the counter. Splatters of thick tomato sauce covered the floor and cabinets, and left a red trail where chunks slid down the lower half of the refrigerator. In the middle of the mess sat Gram, surrounded by shards of glass and the splattered remains of supper. Hands resting motionless in her lap, shoulders wilted, her chin trembled as she surveyed the wreckage.

Joan's pulse thumped in her ears. "Are you alright?" With an effort, she kept her tone even. "Are you hurt?"

Her grandmother drew a shuddering breath, and then raised a tear-streaked face to Joan. "I dropped it. I was taking it out of the oven like I've done a thousand times, and I dropped it." A sob broke her voice, and she lowered her head to cover her face with her hands.

Joan's heart twisted at the misery in Gram's voice. She stepped across the room, careful to avoid the worst of the mess, and pushed back a shard of glass before dropping to her knees beside her grandmother. Placing an arm around the shuddering shoulders, she pressed her cheek against Gram's wrinkled one.

"As long as you're okay, it's not a big deal. People drop things all the time."

"Not me." The old woman peeked between her fingers

71

at the mess and sobbed. "I couldn't hold on to it. It wasn't that heavy. But it slipped right out of my hands."

Joan squeezed her shoulders. "Is your arthritis bothering you today?"

Gram lowered her hands and held them before her. She turned them over, studying them as though they belonged to someone else. Joan looked at the wrinkles, the dark purplish age spots, the swollen knuckles. They were the hands of an old woman, not as strong as they had once been.

"All that food wasted." Gram shook her head, her expression tortured. "Children starving in Africa and look what I've done. I'm old and useless."

"It was an accident." Joan took Gram's hand in one of hers and pressed gently. "It could have happened to anybody."

Gram speared Joan with a mournful blue gaze. "I promised Carla lasagna when she got off work."

Joan's mouth went dry. What would Mom say when she found out about this? Would she say this was one more reason Gram couldn't be left at home alone?

Joan got to her feet and bent to assist Gram. "Then we'll make another one. She won't be home before morning, so we've got all night."

Doubt clouded Gram's features as she struggled to stand. Joan forced a confident smile to her face. "Come on. Let's get this cleaned up, and then I'll take you out for a hamburger and a milkshake before we go to the grocery store."

Joan retrieved a plastic garbage bag from beneath the sink and knelt to scoop the mess into it, keeping a furtive eye on Gram. She moved slowly, picking up shards of the broken baking dish with care and placing them one at a time in the trashcan. Her hands trembled. She looked older tonight than she had this morning. Sick fear settled over Joan. Should she talk to Mom about this incident? She shied away from the idea. No reason to act like this was a big deal.

Gram disposed of the last big chunk of glass and turned a worried face toward Joan. Tomato sauce splattered her blouse and skirt and also a streak of white hair.

Joan lifted a tender smile toward her. "Why don't you go get cleaned up? I'll take care of this."

She gave a single nod and disappeared down the hallway. Joan listened to the shuffle of her shoes on the carpet, and the soft click of her bedroom door.

Uncertainty clenched her throat. What if she was wrong? What if Gram really was too old and frail to be home alone?

She shook her head to clear it. No. If Gram had Alzheimer's or dementia, Joan would be the first to admit that she needed to be someplace where people would look after her 24/7. But she didn't. Her grandmother was perfectly rational and capable of taking care of herself. She was just getting on in years, that's all. She'd spent a lifetime caring for others and had earned the right to grow old gracefully in her own home.

If Joan had to stand up against Mom and Allie and her entire family to protect that right, she would do it.

For the fifth time in as many minutes, Joan rolled over in bed and wiggled on the mattress to find a comfortable position. Fatigue dragged at her limbs, but her mind refused to release her to sleep. Counting didn't work, though she had paraded entire herds of sheep and cows and a bunch of other barnyard animals across the dark stage inside her eyelids. She'd tried every relaxation technique she knew, to no avail. She even tried reciting "The Rime of the Ancient Mariner" in her mind. When she was in school and had to memorize Coleridge's entire work, that never failed to put her to sleep. But now she only managed to get as far as "The ship was cheered, the harbour cleared." There were a bunch of verses between the harbour and the albatross, but she couldn't remember how to get there.

The clock's face glowed 2:47 in vile red numbers. With a disgusted jerk, she tore the sheet away and got out of bed. The only thing the poem had done was make her thirsty with thoughts of "Water, water, everywhere, nor any drop to drink."

She padded up the stairs, the thick carpet cushioning any sound her bare feet might have made. A seashell nightlight illuminated the kitchen with a dim yellow glow. The overhead light might wake Gram, so Joan left it off. She opened the cabinet and scanned the contents for her favorite mug. The collection had grown over a lifetime, a mishmash of sizes and colors. Some bore slogans, like "World's Greatest Mother," and some came from the conferences Grandpa used to attend. Everyone in the family had their favorite. Joan moved Mom's blue mug out of the way and pulled out the one with a flock of dancing pink flamingos in polka-dot swimsuits. She filled it from the faucet and, standing by the counter, sipped at her water.

No wonder she couldn't sleep. This had been a difficult day, and not just because of Gram's lasagna episode. Rosa was in a bad mood after her fight with Luis, so Joan felt like she had to tiptoe all day or risk setting her off on a tirade. And then they had a couple of customers who were poor credit risks. As the manager on duty, the responsibility of delivering the bad news that they didn't qualify fell on Joan. She hated that, hated seeing the embarrassment and disappointment in their eyes. They didn't often turn people away at Abernathy's, so two in a single day was hard.

Joan gulped a mouthful of water. And then there was Ken's visit. She reached into the cabinet to reposition a coffee mug, trying not to remember the harsh disappointment that gripped her like a fist when he talked about Tori. Of course she wasn't surprised at his choice. And she would never in a million years let on that she thought anything more of him than a friendly neighbor with a dog. But here, all alone in the dark kitchen, she wouldn't lie to herself. For a little while, like half a day, she actually thought Ken might be the guy to fill the empty place in her life that Roger left.

"Well, that's not going to happen, so I need to get over it."

Somehow the sound of her own voice speaking the words that had whirled through her brain a million times in the hours since she went to bed brought a sense of relief. She stacked the blue mug neatly on top of another one. Okay, so she was attracted to the guy. Who wouldn't be? He was gorgeous, smart, with a good sense of humor. But he liked her sister better than he liked her. It wasn't the end of the world. Her attraction would fade eventually. She could handle Ken as a brother-in-law. And having a doctor in the family would be great. She turned a stoneware mug so its handle faced sideways. Hopefully she could find a decent-looking guy to take her to the wedding so she didn't look like the spinster sister.

Joan laughed at herself as she emptied her mug and set it in the sink. Look at the path her thoughts had traveled. Tori and Ken had just met. They'd barely spoken to each other, and here she stood, planning their wedding.

Besides, who was she kidding? She didn't want a brother-in-law she was attracted to. That was just wrong. She wanted Tori to find a nice guy, sure, but somebody brotherly. Like Eric.

And, however unlikely it was to happen, she wanted Ken for herself.

She turned away from the sink, reaching to close the cabinet door as she did so. Her hand froze. The mugs lined the shelves in neat rows, arranged by color, their handles pointing the same way at exactly the same angle in military-like precision.

Stunned by the realization of what she had done, Joan couldn't make her feet move. She had stood here in the middle of the night and organized the mug cabinet. And the worst part was that it felt *good*, like she had accomplished something worthwhile. She'd be able to sleep now.

Standing in the dimly lit kitchen, a deep horror stole over her. Gram's kooky organizing quirk was hereditary!

"Dr. Fletcher, you've got a customer."

Ken swiveled the desk chair toward the nurse standing in the doorway. "Thanks, Debbie."

She slid a thin folder across the desk and disappeared. Ken rubbed his eyes. Bad enough to work the midnight shift, but sitting in this closet-sized office while he filled out endless reports on the computer was enough to lull anyone to sleep. Good thing he wasn't claustrophobic.

He opened the folder. A ten-year-old male with a laceration on the bottom of his left foot. Immunizations up-to-date, compliments of the health department. Vitals all good. Weight a little light for his height, but in the acceptable range. The responsible party was his mother. Ken closed the folder and left the office. He walked past the row of empty hospital beds to the one across from the nurses' station. The curtain had been pulled closed for privacy. He took a breath and arranged his features into a pleasant expression before stepping through the curtain.

The boy sat unmoving in the middle of the hospital bed, as though afraid to soil the crisp white sheet. His shaggy dark hair looked like it hadn't been washed, or even combed, in days. A fresh pressure bandage, no doubt compliments of Nurse Debbie, wound around one filthy foot. The kid's chin rose as he threw a defiant glare toward Ken. But Ken detected a hint of fear buried in his tough-guy stare.

"I'm Dr. Fletcher. And I'll bet you're Michael."

The boy didn't respond, just stared. Ken shifted his gaze to the woman who sat in a hard plastic chair beside the bed. She looked like she could stand a shower too, and some clean clothes. He took a step toward her, his hand extended, and kept the smile on his face though he nearly flinched at the sharp odors of cigarette smoke and sour alcohol that rose from her. She looked maybe twenty-five. Surely not old enough to have a ten-year-old son.

"You're Mrs. Lassiter?"

Her grip was timid, as though she wasn't accustomed to shaking hands. "I'm not married."

"Ms. Lassiter, then." Ken grinned at the boy. "But you're this big guy's mother, right?"

The kid rolled his eyes and looked away. Okay, too old to be called a "big guy."

"Yeah, that's me."

Ken kept his hands behind his back as he bent over the boy's filthy foot. "So, Mike, I see you've got a battle wound here. Mind if I take a look?"

One edge of the boy's mouth twisted. "That's why we're here."

Smart-aleck kid. Ken swallowed a sarcastic response, and crossed to the sink against the wall to wash his hands. Both sets of eyes followed him. He pulled on a pair of examination gloves and unwound the bandage. As soon as he pulled the gauze away, blood seeped from a two-inch wound. Deep. Broken glass, probably. Ken had seen a couple like this in Cincinnati. He glanced at the boy's face.

"Want to tell me what happened?"

"I stepped on a busted bottle." His voice was tight. "Didn't see it in the grass."

"How long ago was that?"

78

His mother spoke. "About half an hour ago. I brought him straight here, soon as I saw it."

Ken glanced at the clock on the wall. 2:47. "Out kind of late, weren't you?"

The boy shrugged. Ken kept his gaze on the wound but saw the woman bristle out of the corner of his eye.

"We fell asleep in front of the TV." She sounded defensive. "Michael must have got up and went outside without me knowing."

Passed out was more likely, considering the smell of her breath. His jaw tightened as he bit back a disapproving response. "Mike, can you move your ankle up and down, and wiggle your toes?" He did, which brought a fresh flow of blood. Ken blotted the wound with a clean Steripad. "Good. Now I'm going to push on your foot, to see if I can feel any glass still in there." He caught Michael's eyes with his and held them. "It might hurt a little."

The boy's throat convulsed, though his expression did not change. He lifted a shoulder.

The nurse had already attached a portable magnifying lamp to the bed rail. Ken swung it into place and watched the wound as he probed. The gash looked clean, the edges neatly sliced. He found no evidence of glass still inside. Michael stiffened a couple of times, but not a sound escaped those tightly clamped lips. A tough guy, huh? Well, better that than a screamer. Ken had seen older kids lapse into hysterics in similar situations.

The initial examination complete, he flipped off the lamp and lowered the arm, then perched on the edge of the bed.

79

He spoke to the mother. "It's deep, but he's lucky. If the glass had cut the extensors, he would have needed surgery to repair the damage." He swung his gaze to the boy. "We'll stitch this up, and you're going to have to stay off of it for a day or two. And it's important to keep the area around the wound clean."

"What are you going to do to me?" His voice wavered, and he clamped his mouth closed as though irritated he had allowed his fear to show.

Ken blotted the wound once again, and spoke matter-of-factly. "First we're going to spray on some anesthetic to numb it. Then I'm going to give you a shot."

The boy's eyes widened. "I don't like shots."

He gave a sympathetic shake of his head. "Neither do I. Unfortunately, you're going to get two, one in your foot and a tetanus shot in the arm."

"In my foot?" Michael didn't bother to hide the alarm in his voice. "You mean in the cut?" His voice rose in pitch until he almost shouted the last word.

"Shut up," his mother snapped. "It's your own fault, you little idiot. If you'd stayed in the house like you were supposed to, none of this would have happened. Stupid little . . ." She ended with an obscene exclamation that made her son flinch.

Ken felt his own lips tightening. He'd seen parents berate their kids for getting injured before, but that didn't make it easier to witness. He ignored the woman and placed a hand on Michael's leg. "I won't lie to you, it might hurt. But only for a few seconds, and then you won't feel a thing. When the area around the wound is good and numb, the nurse is going to wash it. Then I'll stitch it up and you can go home."

Michael studied him while a pleasant female voice from the speaker in the ceiling paged Dr. Anoush. Ken kept his face impassive. Finally, the boy nodded.

"Good." Ken stood. "Let me get the nurse and we'll get started. You'll be home before you know it."

He slipped through the curtain and crossed three steps to the nurses' station where he outlined the treatment plan to Debbie. While she assembled the necessary equipment, he stepped into the tiny office to type his notes into the boy's file. They returned together to the examination room, Debbie's white sneakers squeaking on the polished floor.

"Okay, Mike, are you ready?"

The kid didn't look as brave as he had a few moments before. His eyes were glued to the stainless steel tray Debbie carried, the one with two hypodermic needles on it.

"Look," the mother interrupted, "how much is this going to cost me? I'm not working right now, so I can't afford a big bill."

Ken bit back a sarcastic comment about the cost of cigarettes and alcohol as compared to the health of a child. Instead, he picked up the chart and studied the admission form. "Says here Michael is covered by the Kentucky Child Health Insurance Program."

Debbie spoke up. "They'll handle all costs above the deductible you already paid. We get a lot of patients with KCHIP. They're good."

The woman nodded. "Do I have time to go outside for a smoke?"

81

A look of pure panic crossed Michael's face. The boy quickly replaced it with the belligerent expression he customarily wore, but Ken felt his own jaw clench. Some people shouldn't be allowed to have children.

"I'm afraid you'll need to stay in the room while we treat your son, Ms. Lassiter."

The woman folded her arms across her chest, red fingernails clutching her forearms. "Fine. Can we get on with it, then?"

Ken put on a fresh pair of gloves and picked up the topical anesthetic. "Okay, Mike. I'm going to spray your foot with this. It won't hurt a bit."

Michael nodded, and watched closely as Ken sprayed the wound. His foot jerked as the cold spray hit and the sharp smell of antiseptic filled the air. "It kinda tickles."

Ken grinned up at him. "I told you it wouldn't hurt."

They waited a few moments, and then Ken caught and held the boy's eye. "Okay, now we're ready for the first shot. Have you ever been stung by a bee?" Anxiety creased the kid's forehead as he nodded. "It's going to be something like that, but only for a few seconds. Then it will go completely numb."

The muscles in Michael's cheeks bunched as his jaw clamped shut.

"You can scream as loud as you want. There's nobody else in the emergency room right now, so you're not going to bother anybody. Understand?"

Michael gave a single nod. His mother rolled her eyes and turned her face toward the wall.

Debbie handed the syringe to Ken and stepped up to the

bedside. "Hold my hand, honey. It helps if you squeeze something."

The boy clutched Debbie's hand in both of his, screwed his face up, and said to Ken, "Okay. I'm ready." Then he shut his eyes tight.

Ken administered the injection as quickly as he could. As the needle entered the tender flesh, Michael's scream pierced the air and echoed down the hallway. The scream ended in a string of curses that made his mother's sound like Sunday school talk. Thankfully, Debbie's face remained impassive as she returned the boy's white-knuckled squeeze.

"All done." Ken set the syringe in the tray and smiled at Michael. "It'll go dead any second now."

The boy's face cleared slowly, creases falling away as his crushing grip on Debbie's hand relaxed. "It already is."

"Good. We'll give that a few minutes to get things good and numb before we start stitching that cut." He looked at Michael's mother. "Can I talk to you for a moment?"

He left the room without waiting to see if she would follow. He'd seen plenty of kids like Michael in Cincinnati, good kids who needed a strong positive influence in their lives before they started trying stupid things to look cool in front of their peers.

The woman's expression looked a lot like her son's when he first arrived—belligerent. She stood with her arms crossed, her purse slung across one shoulder, and refused to look him in the face.

"Ms. Lassiter, do you know what your son was doing outside the house so late at night?"

"Hey, it wasn't my fault." She tapped a sandaled toe. "I

knew I was going to get blamed for this. I can't watch the kid every minute, you know."

"Granted. But surely you have rules about when he has to be home at night."

"He was home. I told you, he slipped out after I fell asleep. It's those kids he runs with. They're bad news."

Ken kept a firm grip on his patience. "Maybe if you explain to Michael why you think they're bad news, and that you don't want him to hang out with those kids anymore, he'd listen to you."

She gave a blast of humorless laughter. "Are you for real?"

"I just think—"

"I don't care what you think. It's easy for you to stand there and tell me how I should act. You're not there every day, you don't know what our life is like. Your job is to take care of that cut and butt out of our business. So why don't you do that and get off my back?"

Ken stared after her as she stomped away. True, he didn't know what their life was like. He only knew his heart twisted in his chest when he thought about that ten-year-old boy running around the streets with a gang of kids at two o'clock in the morning. Where would Michael be in five years? In three, even?

There were so many kids like him in Cincinnati. But somehow in a big city Ken expected to see street gangs and all the problems that went with them. Gunshot wounds, knife fights, drug overdoses. He never thought about those same things happening in a smaller town like this one.

Should he report her for child abuse? There was no

indication that Mike had been abused, none of the typical signs like bruises or broken bones. Neglect, maybe? He shook his head. She would just stick to her story that he snuck out of the house after she was asleep. And it was probably the truth.

Maybe he was overreacting. After all, a ten-year-old who stepped on a broken bottle in the middle of the night was a far cry from a street thug. With a sigh, he headed back toward the examination room to stitch Michael's wound.

~ 7 ~

Joan drizzled fat-free dressing across her salad while beside her Allie piled chicken wings on a plate already full of fried fish, mashed potatoes, cheesy macaroni, and yeast rolls.

"I love this buffet." Allie balanced a final wing on top and licked her lips. "They have the best rolls."

Joan eyed the mountain of starch and grease her sister was about to consume. "You know, you really should eat something healthy every now and then."

Allie answered by balancing her plate in one hand while grabbing an apple off the buffet table with the other. She scowled. "There. Something healthy. Are you satisfied?"

Joan shook her head, laughing, as she led the way back to their table. "Don't come crying to me when you want to fit into your pre-baby jeans and you can't get them past your pudgy knees."

Allie set her plate down and tried to slide into the booth. She pushed the table toward Joan a few inches so her bulging belly would fit. Scooching into the center of the bench, she looked so funny Joan couldn't help laughing again.

Allie glared across the table. "Okay, no making fun of

the pregnant lady. You'll give me a complex. Instead why don't you tell me what's bothering you today?"

Joan pulled a napkin out of the dispenser and handed it across the table. "What makes you think anything is bothering me?"

"Because your voice sounded funny when you called this morning. And because I usually have to pry you out of that store for a lunch break, so if you call me for lunch, something must be bothering you." She leaned forward. "Is it Gram?"

Their drinks arrived. Thankful for the interruption, Joan peeled the paper off her straw and gathered her thoughts as Allie sent the server back for more lemon slices. She had worried about her midnight mug-arranging episode since the moment her eyes opened yesterday morning. But now that it was time to talk about it, she couldn't find any words that didn't sound lame. Maybe she should just ignore the whole thing. After all, what did she expect Allie to do?

"Maybe I just wanted to get away from Rosa's constant griping about Luis for a while."

Chicken wing in hand, Allie gave her a shrewd look. "You never could lie to your big sister. Come on, out with it."

Joan heaved a sigh. "Okay, so maybe something is kind of bothering me. It's not a big deal, really. It's just that . . . ," she toyed with her fork, "I'm afraid I might be going crazy."

Allie's forkful of mashed potatoes paused halfway between her plate and her mouth. "Why do you say that?"

Joan speared a piece of lettuce. "Because the other night I got up at two in the morning to rearrange the coffee mugs."

Allie's face remained impassive, probably a technique she'd learned from her college counseling classes. At least she didn't laugh. Joan couldn't take Allie laughing at her right now. Not about this.

"You mean rearrange like the way Gram rearranges."

It wasn't a question, but Joan nodded anyway. "Exactly that way. Only Gram would have alphabetized the mugs somehow. I just arranged them so they were all facing the same way. You know, so they were neat."

"And how did you feel?"

Joan rolled her eyes. "I felt like an idiot organizing the cabinets at two in the morning, that's how I felt."

"No, I mean did you feel compelled to do it? Did the thought of the coffee mugs in disarray keep you awake and nag at you until you couldn't stand to leave them alone? Did they . . . ," she raised her eyebrows, ". . . call to you?"

"Of course not." Joan shoved the lettuce in her mouth, chewed with vigor, and swallowed. "I wasn't thinking about them at all. I couldn't sleep, and I went to the kitchen for some water, and just fiddled with them while I was drinking." She paused, and then confessed the worst part. "I didn't even realize I was doing it. I did it automatically, like my brain was keeping me occupied so I wouldn't notice what my hands were doing."

Allie fell silent for a moment as she took a few thoughtful bites. Joan tried to concentrate on her salad, but she wasn't hungry. She felt a little foolish for scheduling a lunch to talk about something so stupid, but for some reason she wanted—no, needed—her sister's opinion.

"Well, I don't think you're going crazy." Allie made her pronouncement matter-of-factly, like a diagnosis.

"You don't?"

"No, I don't. But I do think you're bored."

"Bored?" Joan shook her head. "I'm so busy I barely have time to do anything."

"Busy with what?" Allie cut a bite of fish and dunked it in a puddle of tartar sauce. "You work all day long at a dull job—"

"Hey!" Joan's back stiffened. "I like my job."

Allie cocked her head. "Don't give me that. You do not. You might like aspects of your job, but in general you're bored by it. Then you go home and sit in that dull, boring house with Gram."

Joan bristled. "Gram is not dull and boring."

"No, but she's old." Allie leaned as far forward as her belly would allow. "She's in a different stage of life, Joan. You're twenty-five. You can't live like you're eighty. You need to get out and do something."

"Like what? Join Mom's bowling league? There's *so* much going on in this town." The bitterness in her voice surprised her. She stabbed at a cherry tomato with her fork.

"I don't know." Allie shrugged. "Lexington is only a forty-minute drive, and there's lots to do there. Take salsa dancing lessons, anything to get you out of the house." She grinned. "How about dating that cute doctor next door?"

Joan looked away. "Not an option."

"Why not? He's absolutely gorgeous, and he's a doctor, for cryin' out loud. I'll bet you could get him to ask you out."

"Actually, I think he's interested in Tori." Joan picked up her water glass and put the straw to her lips, trying to ignore the stab of jealousy she felt at that admission.

Allie's brow creased. "Are you sure about that? He seemed friendly with her the other day, but he definitely wasn't falling all over himself."

"He came into the store Monday and told me how much he enjoyed meeting her. And I know she likes him. You saw her flirting with him on Sunday."

Allie waved a hand. "That doesn't mean anything. Tori flirts with everybody. Besides, if she knew you were attracted to the guy, she'd back off."

Something in Allie's tone set her teeth on edge. Did she think Joan could only get a guy if there was no competition? That she could only have someone else's leftovers? She set her glass down a little harder than necessary. "What do you mean by that?"

Allie looked up from her plate, startled. "By what?"

"You think Tori has to back off in order for me to have a chance with a guy?"

"I didn't say that!"

"But you thought it, didn't you?"

Allie tossed her fork onto the table. "Maybe I was wrong. Maybe you are going crazy. You're imagining things." She stopped, and a slow smile spread across her lips. "I know what's wrong with you. You're jealous. You like this doctor and it's eating you up because you think he has a thing for your little sister."

Joan raised her chin. "I am not jealous."

"I think you are. And you should do something about

it." She grinned. "Set a goal for yourself, Joan Sanderson. Get the doctor to ask you out instead of Tori."

Joan's jaw went slack. "You're the one who's insane."

"No, really. This is exactly the goal you need. And it's completely achievable."

Remembering Ken's glowing description of Tori in the store Monday, Joan wasn't so sure. "But if he likes tiny blonde babes, why would he want to go out with me?"

Allie dismissed that with a wave. "Men don't know what they like. They rely on us to tell them. And you're going to convince Dr. Gorgeous that he likes tall, athletic, beautiful brunettes."

Could she really make Ken interested in her instead of Tori? Allie's confidence gave her a flicker of hope. "But what if Tori is interested in him?"

As a kid, they'd had their fair share of struggles, but never over anything more serious than the use of the family car. Going after a guy her sister liked felt . . . wrong. Unnatural.

Allie didn't seem to think so. "Then you'll have a little competition. But don't worry, you've got the home court advantage." She giggled. "This is going to be fun!"

Joan wasn't so sure, but she couldn't deny feeling a spark of excitement that caused the corners of her mouth to twitch upward.

For the rest of the day, Joan's thoughts whirled as she replayed the conversation with Allie. She let Rosa handle the few customers who came into the store while she sat in the tiny office beside the loading dock in the back and tried to concentrate on her monthly inventory report.

She had never gone after a guy before. Through high school, college, and beyond, she dated Roger. Their relationship was so comfortable neither of them had to be the aggressor. In the months since they broke up, she hadn't gone on a single date. Maybe because she hadn't been asked out on one.

Well, except for the guy who tore tickets at the cinema, the one who looked like he could use a stint in rehab. He asked her out, but Joan refused. She wasn't interested in a fixer-upper boyfriend.

She bounced a pencil eraser on the desk. Ken definitely didn't fall into that category. But he would be a challenge. Especially if he was attracted to blondes instead of brunettes . . .

Stop. She refused to think that way. Tori might be more experienced when it came to dating, but Joan had some things going for her too. Ken called her pretty the day they met. She was healthy and fit, not an ounce of flab anywhere. She had a good job.

No, Tori had a good job. Ken had a good job. Joan had a boring job. Scratch the job angle.

She slid the pencil across the surface of the desk with a finger. What did she know about Ken? He owned a dog. If she made friends with Trigger, would Ken take notice of her? The idea rolled around in her head, sparking her interest. She could start carrying dog treats in her pocket. That way when she happened to bump into Ken walking his dog, or maybe in the backyard . . . No, stupid idea. What kind of dopey girl walks around with dog treats in her pocket? Plus, every dog in the neighborhood would be after her. She'd become known as the Pied Piper of Dogville. Imagine the newspaper headlines. She shuddered.

But she could offer to help train Trigger.

Joan rocked backward in her desk chair. That idea had possibilities.

Brrring. Brrring.

The phone pierced the silence of the small office like a claxon and caused Joan to jump nearly out of her chair. Goodness, she was edgy today. She took a breath and blew it out before she picked up the receiver. "Good afternoon, Abernathy's."

"We have a situation."

Allie sounded serious, but Joan detected a touch of humor in her voice. She relaxed.

"What situation?"

"The competition has made the first move, and it's a good one."

She could only mean one thing. "Tori?"

"Exactly. She just called and told me she's coming to dinner at the house tomorrow night, and she has instructed Gram to invite Dr. Gorgeous. She wants me and Eric to come too, so it'll look like a big family gathering."

Joan's grip on the telephone tightened. "Did you tell Tori that I—"

"Of course not. If I tell her you've got a thing for the guy, she'll back off, and I want this to be a fair competition.

You need to see that you can compete with the best and win. You've got the right stuff, Joan Sanderson!"

Joan couldn't help laughing. "You sound like a football coach."

"I feel like one."

"Wait a minute." Joan shook her head. "He leaves for the hospital before I get home, and works all night. He won't be able to come to dinner."

"Not tomorrow. Thursdays are his days off. Tori had Mom check his schedule."

"Mom checked his schedule for Tori?" Joan fought to keep her voice calm. She remembered the look of pride on Mom's face as she watched Tori flirt with Ken through the kitchen window.

Don't get upset. Mom doesn't even know I like the guy. If she did, she wouldn't choose sides. Would she?

"Yeah, Mom," said Allie. "But don't worry. I'm in your corner. Now, I'm going to call in sick tomorrow. Can you take the day off?"

"Whatever for? You said he's coming tomorrow night."

"That only gives us twenty-six hours to get ready! We need to make effective use of the time."

"Actually, I've already got an idea to get on Ken's good side." She told Allie about the offer to help with Trigger.

"That's your big idea? Tori will show up for dinner wearing size two designer jeans and you're going to offer to pick up his dog's poop?" Allie's snort blasted in her ear. "We've got more work ahead of us than I thought."

Well, yeah, put like that it sounded lame. Joan shifted her weight in the chair. "I just figured if I could—"

"Don't figure. You've got to get with the program, girl, and you obviously need my help. Take a vacation day tomorrow and we'll go shopping."

Indecision seized Joan. The memory of Tori's clothes on Sunday forced a mental review of her closet. The results were not promising. She grabbed the computer mouse and checked tomorrow's schedule.

"I can't take the whole day, but I could probably leave at two when Pat gets here for the evening shift."

A heavy sigh sounded in her ear. "Okay, if that's the best you can do. Pick me up at home as soon as you can."

~ 8 ~

Ken pulled the Probe into the driveway. With a cupped hand he shielded the clock display on the dashboard from the bright morning sun. 9:47. They'd had a rush just as he prepared to leave work at 6:30, and he ended up staying to help out. He hoped he didn't miss the furniture delivery scheduled for this morning.

He shut off the engine and rubbed his eyes. That new bed would feel good.

The door to the house next door opened, and Joan's grandmother came outside. She descended the front stairs leaning heavily on the handrail, but the minute her feet hit the ground, she made a beeline across the grass in his direction.

"Ken, yoo hoo, Ken!" An arm waved above her head to get his attention.

"Hello, Mrs. Hancock." Ken got out of the car and closed the door. "How are you this morning?"

"Fine, thank you." She halted a few feet in front of him and peered into his face. "You look tired."

"I am. You'd think I would get used to staying up all

night after a couple of weeks, but some shifts are tougher than others. I'm so happy to have a day off. I intend to sleep through most of it."

"I hope I can convince you to wake up long enough for dinner tonight. Carla and all my granddaughters will be here."

Dinner with Joan and her sisters? Two days ago he would have jumped at the chance, but now he wasn't so sure. He'd done some thinking about it, and decided maybe he'd be better off concentrating on finding a church instead of a girl. Besides, churches were great places to meet women who shared his commitment to his faith.

On the other hand, he couldn't deny he liked Joan. Another chance to talk with her might be a good idea.

Mrs. Hancock tilted her head, her blue eyes twinkling. "We're having pot roast and homemade yeast rolls."

Ken's stomach answered with a rumble that made them both laugh. "I think that's a yes."

"Good!" She clapped her hands together. "Dinner is at 6:30. Come early, though, so we can get to know you better."

"Thanks, I will."

The old woman turned away looking pleased, and Ken headed toward his house. He whistled under his breath as he turned the key in the lock. A family dinner sounded great. He'd get the chance to see Joan in her natural habitat. You could tell a lot about a woman by watching her interact with her family.

"You look incredible." Allie leaned back against the headboard and balanced a glass of lemonade on her belly. "Those jeans are awesome."

In the middle of her bedroom, Joan swiveled to examine herself from the side view in the full-length mirror on the closet door. "They ought to look good, for the price I paid."

They'd spent the afternoon on a whirlwind shopping expedition, where her sister forced her to buy designer jeans, a double-draped Banana Republic silk jersey, and a pair of strappy sandals that cost more than any shoes Joan had ever owned, all from different stores in the mall. The cost of the clothing Joan wore on her body right now could probably buy an Italian villa.

"They're True Religion, silly. Of course they're expensive."

Joan shook her head. "The CKs would have been fine. In fact, the Levi's were great. The only difference I could see in any of them was the price. I doubt if Ken will even notice the brand."

"Ken doesn't have to notice." She sipped from her glass. "You'll know what you're wearing, and the knowledge will boost your confidence."

There might be something to that. Joan swiveled again and admired the rear view. She'd never been much of a clotheshorse, but she had to admit she looked good in these. Plus, the afternoon had been fun, trying on the outrageously expensive clothes Allie selected. And then letting Allie do her makeup too. It was almost like the dress-up parties they loved when they were kids.

She couldn't get used to wearing her hair down, though. This was a totally different look from her usual tidy ponytail. Good, but more . . . breezy.

"You look great," Allie repeated. "Ken's going to drool all over himself when he sees you."

"I don't know about that." Joan turned a look on her sister. "Tori will probably show up in a sequined ball gown or something."

Allie raised her eyes to the ceiling. "Sequins? No way. She'll be draped in designers from head to toe. But don't let that get you flustered. You can take her. Have some confidence."

Joan clicked her expensive heels together and gave a mock salute. "Yes, sir!"

Allie glanced at her watch and sat up. "We don't have much time. Tori will be here in half an hour, so let's practice some flirting."

Joan cocked an eyebrow. "Practice flirting?"

"Yes, silly." Allie rummaged in her duffel bag and pulled out a thin stack of papers. "Tori is an expert, so you need to make sure you're on top of things." She shuffled through the pages as she talked. "Keep in mind that 55 percent of the impression you make on someone is based on your appearance and body language, 38 percent on your style of speaking, and only 7 percent on what you say. So what you say doesn't matter that much, as long as you look good saying it."

Joan dropped onto the bed and peered over the top of the papers. "Where in the world did you learn that?"

Allie looked up. "I googled it."

"They actually have stuff on the Internet to teach you how to flirt?"

"Tons. Now pay attention. We don't have much time so we'll focus on body language for now. Eye contact is extremely important. The longer you maintain eye contact, the stronger the signal you're sending to the guy."

Joan frowned. "What sort of signal am I sending?"

"That you're interested in him, that you find him attractive. That's what flirting is all about, signaling your attraction to a guy and letting him know you'd like to move the relationship forward. But you've got to be careful with eye contact. It's very powerful."

"Powerful? Oh, come on." Joan twisted away from her sister on the bed.

"I'm serious. If you hold your target's gaze too long too soon, he'll either think you're a stalker or you want to jump into bed with him, and obviously you don't want either of those. So the trick is to go gradually. When you talk to him, make eye contact. Just for a moment, like a second or so, and then look away. Then look back again. If he meets your eye a second time, he's returning your interest."

"This is ridiculous." But in spite of herself, Joan was interested. She nodded toward the papers. "What else does it say?"

"Proximity is important. Don't invade his personal zone right away. Picture him standing inside a hula hoop."

The image of Ken with a plastic pink-and-white-striped circle around his waist made Joan giggle. "What size hula hoop? Regular size, or one of those giant ones we had when we were kids?"

Allie glared. "If you're not going to take this seriously, I won't bother trying to help you. Now, if you're talking to him face-to-face, stay outside his hula hoop. Gradually inch closer and watch his body language. If he leans away from you, or if he folds his arms or anything like that, you're coming on too strong."

Joan's giggles dissolved. This was all so confusing. "So is it better to sit beside him or across from him at dinner?"

"I've taken care of that already." Allie looked up from the papers. "Gram is going to seat him at the end of the table, with you and Tori on either side. Your job is to keep him leaning toward you, even when Tori is talking. His shoulders should be turned toward you, or you could try to get him to shift his body toward your side of his chair."

"How am I going to do that?"

Allie threw her hands up in the air. "That's what I'm telling you. Now, let's talk about touch."

Joan's throat felt raspy. She leaned across the bed and grabbed Allie's lemonade. "I have to touch him?"

"Not too soon," her sister commanded. "When his body is oriented toward you, and when he's consistently making eye contact with you, then you can very briefly touch him on the arm to emphasize a point. Watch his reaction, and if he doesn't back away from you, do it again a few minutes later. But whatever you do, keep it brief. Touching his arm for more than a second or two is a bold move. And stay away from his hands. Hands are too intimate for this stage."

"Hands are intimate?" Joan gave a helpless wail. "I'll never remember all this."

"Of course you will. Most of this is intuitive, you do it without realizing it. Flirting is the natural order of things. You're just like the peacock, showing off your beautiful feathers to attract a mate."

"The colorful peacock is a guy," Joan reminded her. "The girl peacock is supposed to sit back and watch the guy strut."

"He'll never strut your way if another girl peacock grabs his attention first."

Joan threw herself backward on the mattress. "It's no use. I can't do this stuff. I'll feel like an idiot."

"Yes, you can. Now stand up." Allie nudged her with a toe. "We're going to practice hair flipping."

Joan heaved a sigh and rolled off the side of the bed. "I have to flip my hair? You mean like in *Legally Blonde*?"

"Exactly like that. A woman's hair is one of the most attractive features to a guy."

Joan moaned. "Then I'm doomed. Tori's hair is perfect."

"No," Allie corrected, "Tori's hair is short, gelled, and stylish. She can't flip her hair because it's cemented into place by expensive salon products. Your hair is perfect for flipping. Now watch this."

Allie leaned forward so she was not touching the headboard. She arranged her blonde hair in front of her shoulders, and then tossed her head with a rolling motion. Her hair flipped expertly behind her back. She ended the gesture by making eye contact with Joan, and grinned. "Now you try it."

Ignoring a rising sense of panic, Joan turned toward the

mirror. She arranged her hair, and then imitated Allie's gesture. Not only did her hair flip behind her shoulders, the silver that dangled from her earlobes shimmered with the effort. "Hey, that looked pretty good."

"Not bad." Her sister nodded and heaved herself off the bed. "Not bad at all. You keep working on it and I'll go upstairs and see if Mom and Gram need any help. I'll leave this here for you to read later, when we're ready to move to Phase Two." She set the papers down on the nightstand and left the room.

Joan spent a few moments in hair flipping practice. Then she let her gaze sweep over her reflection in the mirror. Nerves tickled her stomach. No wonder she was no good at flirting. There was so much to master. She'd probably be a total flop at the body language thing, but at least she looked good. What did Allie say? That was 55 percent of flirting. The way the silky fabric of the jersey draped from both shoulders to cross at her waist accentuated her lean body. The milk chocolate color made the brown of her eyes look deeper, or maybe that was the mascara Allie had layered on. And the shoes were awesome. She turned a heel to admire them. The clothes did give her a measure of confidence, but she would never admit that to her older sister.

The bedroom door burst open and Allie rushed in, flushed with excitement. "Ken just left his house. I saw him through the window. He'll be here any second."

The doorbell rang, and Joan's stomach flip-flopped. She grabbed for Allie's hands and tried to fight the panic that rose in her throat. "I can't do this. I'm too nervous!"

103

"Oh, yes, you can." Allie lifted her chin into the air. "You're ready, girl. Now go up there and do your thing."

Allie squeezed Joan's hands, and Joan returned the gesture gratefully. Then she dashed out of the room and up the stairs to the front door with her sister close on her heels. Gram came out of the kitchen, but Allie waved her away. "We'll get it, Gram."

Joan stood on the landing for a moment, took a deep breath, and relaxed her shoulders. Then she put a smile on her face and swung the door open.

On the front porch, Ken drew a breath to say something and then froze, his lips open. His gaze swept to her feet and then came back to her eyes. A thrill coursed down Joan's spine as he held the eye contact for much longer than the brief second Allie prescribed as a starting point. Remembering Allie's instructions, she looked away, a shy smile on her lips, and then glanced back at his face.

"Hi, Ken."

"Joan. Hi." His throat convulsed as he swallowed. "You look, uh, very nice this evening."

"Thank you. Please come in." She stepped back to allow him to enter, and then closed the door. "You remember my sister?"

Joan gestured toward Allie, who stood watching with a wide grin. She stepped forward and stuck her hand out. "Nice to see you again, Ken. Come on in and have a seat."

When Ken caught sight of Gram standing in the kitchen doorway, a genuine smile lit his face. He advanced toward her, his hand extended.

"Mrs. Hancock, thank you again for inviting me. I realized about half an hour ago that I should have offered to bring something."

Gram took his hand in one of hers, and patted it with the other. "Nonsense. You're our guest tonight. We're glad you could join us."

Gram looked particularly nice this evening as well. She wore a print dress that she normally reserved for church, and had put on lipstick and powder. Her eyes twinkled as she smiled at Ken.

Mom stepped out of the kitchen. She advanced toward their guest with an outstretched hand. "Dr. Fletcher, we haven't met. I'm Carla Sanderson."

"Please call me Ken." He shook her hand. "It's nice to meet you. I understand you're an RN at the hospital."

"That's right. I'm up on four, in Transitional Care." Mom released his hand, and her glance slid down to the landing. Her eyes widened when she caught sight of Joan. "Joan, you—" She stopped. Judging by the look on Mom's face, she must think her middle daughter looked pretty good tonight. Hopefully she had sense enough not to comment on it in front of Ken. It would be beyond embarrassing to have her mother make a big deal about a few new clothes and a little makeup.

Mom's forehead dipped in silent acknowledgment of the changes in Joan's appearance, and then she looked back at Ken. "Please come in and have a seat. We're just finishing up in the kitchen. Tori and Eric should be here soon."

Joan exhaled, relieved. Allie stepped in front of her and

walked backward into the living room, using her body as a shield as she gave a huge grin and a thumbs-up.

"We'll eat as soon as everyone else gets here," Gram told them.

Joan went to stand near Ken, careful to keep a distance of about two feet between them. "Would you like something to drink? Some iced tea, maybe, or water?"

"Iced tea sounds great, thanks." He didn't move away from her, which, according to Allie, was a good sign.

"I'll get it," Allie said. "You guys sit down and talk."

A lump of nerves lodged in her throat. About what? Talking must be covered in Phase Two.

"Thank you, honey." Gram led the way to the sofa as Mom and Allie disappeared into the kitchen.

Ken caught Joan's eyes once more before following her. Despite the nervousness, her insides sang. Allie was right. That eye contact was powerful stuff.

Gram sat in the center of the sofa and motioned for Ken to sit beside her. Joan hesitated, debating the best position. Gram had him closed in on the left, so she selected a place on the love seat, on the end nearest Ken.

"So how do you find the house?" Gram asked. "It was empty for such a long time before you moved in, I hope it didn't smell musty."

"I haven't noticed any smell." Ken shrugged. "It's actually a lot more comfortable now that I have a bit of furniture." He looked toward Joan, a smile curving the corners of his mouth.

"Oh, it was delivered, then?"

"Just this morning. The living room stuff looks great.

And the bed is so comfortable." He leaned against the sofa to stretch his back. "I had the best five hours of sleep this afternoon I've had in years."

Allie returned and set a glass of iced tea on the coffee table in front of Ken, and one in front of Gram. She looked at Joan. "Would you like something?"

Joan shook her head. "No, thanks, I'll wait for dinner."

Behind Joan's back, the front door opened.

"Anybody home?" called Tori's voice.

Allie looked over Joan's head, her eyes going wide. Joan's stomach fluttered. Let the games begin.

~ 9 ~

Joan stood and turned in time to see Tori enter the living room. Allie had been right—she wasn't wearing sequins. But she might as well have been. She looked like she'd just stepped off a Paris runway in a two-piece black suit with a sleek narrow skirt and bead accents. A lacy red camisole peeked between satin-trimmed lapels. Ken got to his feet, his eyes fixed on her little sister.

Tori walked with a confident stride. She tossed her purse, an expensive-looking one Joan had never seen, onto the floor beside the recliner before crossing the room toward Ken. Taking Ken's hand in her right one, she then covered it with her left. Joan glanced at Allie. Hands were intimate? If so, Tori was practically making out with Ken right there in front of them.

"It's so good to see you again, Ken." She tilted her head and swept her gaze upward, an adorable dimple creasing her cheek. "I'm glad we have the opportunity to get to know you a little better."

To Joan's great displeasure, Ken's smile for her sister was

108

as warm as it had been for her a moment before. "You too. You look very nice."

Tori looked down at her suit. "You'll have to forgive me for not changing before I came. I got caught up at the office and didn't have time to run by my apartment."

Joan wanted to grunt her disgust. No way Tori wore clothes like that to the office. Staring at the skirt, Allie's eyebrows arched.

Joan couldn't take her eyes off their clasped hands. *Let go of him, for cryin' out loud!*

The handclasp finally broke apart when Mom came into the room from the kitchen. She took in Tori's new outfit with a slight widening of her eyes, then crossed the room and caught her youngest daughter in a hug.

"It's always good when I get to see my baby twice in a single week." She released Tori and looked toward Joan and then Allie. "I love having all my girls together."

Tori hugged Allie, and then turned to Joan. She stopped, staring. Maybe it was Joan's imagination, but she didn't think her little sister looked entirely pleased.

"Wow, Joan, you look great." She tilted her head to examine Joan's clothing. Her jaw dropped. "Are those True Religion?"

Heat threatened to flood Joan's face. Trust Tori to recognize a designer brand. The last thing she wanted was for Ken to know she bought new clothes just for tonight.

"Yeah, I've had them a while." Technically, a *while* could be any amount of time, so two hours counted as a *while*. She smiled toward Ken. "I've just needed a reason to wear them."

Tori's eyelids narrowed a fraction. She looked like she was about to say something else when Mom broke into the awkward moment.

"Eric will be here any minute, and then we can eat. Tori, do you want water or iced tea with dinner?"

Tori tore her eyes away from Joan with obvious effort. "Water's fine."

Gram stood. "You young people sit here and talk while I get things on the table. No, no." She waved away Joan's offer before it was spoken. "Carla and I can handle it. You girls entertain our guest."

Joan looked toward Allie, who was trying to communicate something with eyebrow flashes and nearly imperceptible nods. Too late, Joan realized what instruction she was being given. Tori stepped around the coffee table and took Gram's place beside Ken. Allie rolled her eyes and dropped into the recliner.

"So," Tori said as they all settled into their seats, "how do you like Danville?"

Ken turned on the sofa, displaying the back of his head to Joan. Anxiety tightened her jaw. She had to do something to make him shift his body toward her.

"I think I'm going to like it. It's definitely different than Indianapolis."

"Indianapolis." When Joan spoke, Ken turned politely her way. Much better. "I thought you were from Cincinnati."

"That's where I did my residency, but Indianapolis is where I grew up."

Tori asked, "And do you have family there?"

When Ken turned back to answer, Joan ground her teeth. Tori made it impossible to keep him facing this way.

"My sister and her husband and my nephew live just outside the city, not far from where we lived as kids. They're both attorneys."

Two attorneys and a doctor in the family? His parents must be thrilled. Joan spoke again. "The only thing I know about Indianapolis is what I see on the sports channel. Are you a racing fan?"

He turned toward her again. At the rate his head was whipping back and forth, the poor guy was going to need a chiropractor before the evening ended. Joan made eye contact and smiled.

"I'm not." He shrugged. "Actually, I've never even been to the speedway."

Tori giggled, a charming sound. And a bit practiced, to Joan's ear. "Just like most Kentuckians have never been to Churchill Downs or seen the Kentucky Derby in person."

This time when Ken turned toward Tori, she leaned sideways slightly. Definitely inside his hula hoop. Joan threw a quick glance at Allie, who was chewing on a fingernail as she watched the two on the couch.

Behind Joan, the front door opened and Eric announced his arrival with a cheerful, "I hope supper's ready, because I'm starved."

"There's my knight in shining armor." Allie heaved herself out of the recliner and hurried to meet Eric on the top step.

He kissed her and then bent over to speak to her belly. "How are my girls today?"

The corners of Ken's mouth curved into a tender smile as he watched the couple. He rose from the couch and rounded the coffee table with his hand extended toward Eric. Maybe it was her imagination, but he seemed eager to escape the sofa.

Eric shook it. "Good to see you, Ken."

"Thanks. You too."

"Wow!" Eric caught sight of Joan and Tori. He stood with his mouth agape, his gaze volleying between them. "Would you look at you two? What's the special occa—ouch!"

Allie smiled sweetly up at her husband as though she had not just elbowed him in the ribs. She announced to the room, "I think dinner is on the table."

"It is indeed," sang Gram from the dining room. "Come on, everyone."

As Ken followed Allie and Eric around the partial wall that separated the living room from the kitchen and dining area, Joan reached over and picked up his untouched tea glass.

"Nice outfit," Tori whispered, one eyebrow higher than the other.

"Yours too," Joan answered. "The dress code at your office must have changed drastically."

Joan returned her little sister's stare. After a moment, Tori gave a single, nearly imperceptible nod. The competition had been acknowledged. Nerves tickled the pit of Joan's stomach. Why did she have to look so good in that black suit?

"Are you girls coming?" Gram stood waiting in the doorway.

"On our way." Joan skirted the coffee table on one side as Tori went around the other. In the dining room, Ken stood behind his chair at one end of the table, Eric at the opposite end, waiting for the ladies to be seated. Tori went to sit on Ken's right. Joan placed the tea glass in front of his plate and stood before her own chair on his left.

"Thanks." He nodded down at her.

He's not smiling. Do something! Do the hair thing.

Joan made brief eye contact with him and tossed her head with the gesture she had practiced. Her hair flipped expertly behind her shoulder, and her earrings dangled.

A crease formed between Ken's eyebrows as he returned her smile with a polite one of his own. Somehow Joan didn't think the gesture had the effect she'd hoped for. He didn't lean away from her, but he didn't seem all that enchanted by it, either.

On the other hand, across the table Tori's eyes were perfect circles. And Allie gave her an approving nod. Seated beside Eric, Mom stared, her eyebrows disappearing beneath her bangs.

Gram crossed the short distance from the kitchen counter to place a basket of steaming rolls in the center of the table. She was in her element entertaining a guest for dinner. Thank goodness Joan hadn't seen even a hint of weird behavior tonight, no alphabetizing, no fork fiddling.

She sat in the chair between Joan and Mom and beamed at everyone as the men also took their seats. "Now we're ready. Ken, would you be comfortable asking the blessing?"

"Absolutely."

He bowed his head, and everyone else did likewise.

"Dear Heavenly Father, thank you for new friends, and for this evening of fellowship. We ask that you guide our conversations, and that they'll be pleasing to you. We thank you for this food and ask your blessing on it, and on the hands that prepared it. In Jesus' name, Amen."

"Amen." Mom reached for the rolls and offered the basket to Eric. "Ken, you sound as though you're no stranger to prayer. Do you go to church?"

"Yes, ma'am, since I was a boy."

"We'd love to have you join us sometime," Gram said. "We go to Christ Community Church, down by the college."

Ken's eyes brightened. "I'd like that. I've been meaning to find a church here in town, but so far the job has kept me pretty focused."

"What about this Sunday?" Tori held the platter of roast and batted her lashes at him while he took a piece. "We usually leave around 9:45 to get there in time for Sunday school."

Joan wanted to roll her eyes. Tori hadn't gone to church with them in months!

"That sounds great."

He offered Joan the roast, and she took her time selecting a piece. When she finished, she placed the platter in front of Gram where it started, her mind whirling. She had to say something to keep him turned in her direction. "Where do your parents live, Ken?"

He lowered his eyes to his plate and shook his head. "They don't. They were killed in a car accident when I was a kid. It's just my sister and me."

He looked so sad Joan felt a flash of sympathy. They had

something in common. She'd lost a father too, though not to death. And while she didn't always get along with her mother, she couldn't stand the thought of losing her. She touched his arm briefly. "I'm so sorry."

He looked up and caught her gaze with his. "Thanks."

Joan looked away and saw Allie's wide grin. What? Oh! She'd touched his arm. That was one of the things Allie told her to do. She'd done it automatically, out of sympathy, but apparently it was the right move. She straightened in her chair. Maybe Allie was right. Maybe some of this stuff was instinctive.

"So you're an orphan?" Tori's voice dripped sorrow. "That must have been so hard for a teenage boy."

As she spoke, Tori placed a hand on Ken's other arm and kept it there. She had skipped the brief touch phase and gone straight for the long touch. A bold move, even for her. She must be feeling uneasy with the competition. The thought made Joan happy, and she took a sip of her water to hide her smirk.

As Tori's hand continued to rest on his arm, Ken's smile suddenly seemed pasted on. He nodded, and then leaned back in his chair. He reached for his napkin with that arm, which forced Tori to release her hold. Joan cast a triumphant glance toward Allie, who returned it.

"So tell me about your church," he said as he picked up his fork. "What sort of service do you have?"

"Oh, it's really traditional." Tori's voice sounded too bright, as though she realized her mistake with the arm thing.

Gram nodded. "We're old fashioned, but that's the way I

like it. None of that newfangled music for me." She peered at Ken. "I suppose you like that loud stuff?"

Ken laughed. "My church back home is pretty contemporary. Drums and guitars and everything."

Joan tore a bite off her roll. "If anyone brought a drum into our church, they'd be playing to an empty house." Ken gave her a startled glance, and she shrugged. "Most of the congregation is elderly."

"As long as the focus is on God," Ken said, "the style of the music is irrelevant."

An awkward silence fell on the table. Ken must be pretty religious. Something about the way he spoke reminded her of Mary Alice Sachs, the missionary lady. Joan shifted in her seat, and noticed that Tori seemed intent on her plate. At the other end of the table, a glance passed between Allie and Eric. Time to change the subject, before Eric went off on a tirade about churches being a leech on society. That always upset Gram.

Allie rescued the conversation. "So, Ken, how does our little hospital here compare to the one in Cincinnati where you did your residency?"

"It's a lot smaller, of course. But that's alright with me. The staff is great, especially the nurses." He smiled toward Mom. "I think once I get used to the procedures I'm going to like it. I've had my share of crises in the past three years, so I'm looking forward to treating small-town emergencies."

"Trust me," said Eric, "you'll get your share of shootings and stabbings. We've even had some gang activity in the past few years."

116

"That's right, you're a dispatcher." Ken bit into his roll.

Eric nodded. "I'm the one who sends them your way."

"Actually," Ken said, "I treated a kid the other night who seems to be hanging with a rough crowd."

"Oh, please." Tori shook her head. "Danville doesn't have near as much crime as Lexington, where I live."

"Really? So why do you want to live there?"

Ken turned his head to look at Tori, but as he did so he leaned away from her. Which meant he was leaning toward Joan. Thrilled, Joan cast around in her mind for one of Allie's gestures. A hair flip didn't seem appropriate at the moment. And she couldn't risk an arm touch after Tori's disastrous attempt.

A hint of pink colored Tori's cheeks as she gazed at him with round blue eyes. "Because of everything a bigger town has to offer. Malls and museums, the opera house."

"I miss having those things nearby," Joan admitted, and Ken turned to face her. She leaned ever so slightly toward him, her eyes locked onto his.

His gaze dropped to his plate, and he leaned away. Drat! She'd invaded his hula hoop. Frustration turned the good food to acid in Joan's stomach. She'd never master this flirting thing. The only consolation was that Tori didn't seem to be having any better luck with him than she was.

"I like this town," Gram said. "I hate to see it grow any bigger. If I want shopping malls and museums, I'll have Joan or Carla drive me to Lexington."

Ken turned a smile on her. "You and I are in complete agreement, Mrs. Hancock. That's why I chose Danville."

117

Gram leaned toward Ken, which meant she leaned near Joan. She tilted her white head and displayed a dimple to rival Tori's. Seated between them, Joan saw her make eye contact with Ken.

"Please call me Grace."

Ken's smile deepened, and he leaned forward in his chair as he spoke. "Yes, ma'am, Grace."

A blush colored her cheeks and she looked down coyly, then back up at him. Joan's jaw slackened. Gram was flirting with Ken! And judging by the look on his face, he liked it. She looked at Allie, whose chin dropped to her chest as she slowly shook her head from side to side.

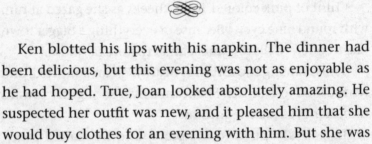

Ken blotted his lips with his napkin. The dinner had been delicious, but this evening was not as enjoyable as he had hoped. True, Joan looked absolutely amazing. He suspected her outfit was new, and it pleased him that she would buy clothes for an evening with him. But she was acting strangely. And what was going on between her and Tori?

"Grace, that was a fantastic dinner. I could get addicted to those rolls."

"They're my specialty." The old lady grinned. "Whenever my husband and I had a spat, I always made rolls for him. He loved them, and that was my way of letting him know I was ready to make up."

Ken stood when Gram did and picked up his empty plate. "I can't imagine anyone wanting to spat with you."

Her eyes twinkled at him. "You are a smooth talker, young man."

Beside him, Joan stood abruptly, and Tori did likewise.

"You're our guest," Joan said as she took the plate from his hands.

"That's right," agreed Tori. "You go into the living room with Eric and watch a boring old ball game or something while the women clean up."

She batted her eyelashes as she cleared his bread plate and utensils. Ken returned her smile politely, and stepped backward so she had a clear path to get to the kitchen. She held his eyes as she walked by.

Tori was cute, without a doubt. But what a little flirt! Ken had never felt comfortable around girls like her. He always felt a little sorry for women who needed to behave so outrageously to get a man's attention. He much preferred easygoing girls, ones who were maybe a touch shy.

Just then Joan returned from setting a stack of plates on the kitchen counter. She walked over to him and stood so close he got a whiff of her hair. She smelled good. None of that fake perfumy stuff, but a clean, sporty smell. Smiling, she tossed her head, which sent her hair flying over one shoulder. Discomfort settled in Ken's stomach. A different gesture than her sister, but it felt the same as Tori's eyelash batting. The smile on his face went stiff as he edged sideways away from her and escaped to the living room where Eric had claimed the recliner and the remote control. Until tonight, he had gotten the impression that Joan was a confident, no-nonsense sort of girl. But that sure wasn't coming through tonight. Who was the real Joan Sanderson?

"What is going on between you two?"

Mom's voice was low enough not to be heard over the television by those in the living room, but a note of concern came through loud and clear. Joan picked up the platter of pot roast from the table and placed it on the kitchen counter. Beside her, Tori grabbed the broccoli casserole and did likewise.

In front of the sink, Allie turned on the faucet. "Pretty obvious, isn't it? They're making a play for the same guy."

"They're making fools of themselves." Mom gave them each a stern look. "You've made the poor man so uncomfortable he looks ready to bolt."

"Well, it's Joan's fault," Tori hissed, her blue eyes narrowed to slits.

"Shhh!" Joan pointed toward the living room. "He'll hear you!"

Allie wore a wide smile as she squirted detergent into the water. It looked to Joan like her older sister was getting a little too much enjoyment out of the show. Whereas Gram, who stood looking from one of them to the other, had deep worry lines creasing her forehead.

"Outside," Mom whispered in a voice that brooked no argument. "Both of you."

Joan found herself being shooed through the back door, Tori right behind her. Moist evening heat slapped her in the face, a shock from the air-conditioning, as the cloying odor of Gram's rosebushes replaced the yeasty smell of rolls inside the house. Mom followed them onto the wood deck and closed the door. Joan turned to find Tori glaring at her, arms folded across her chest.

"Don't you dare try to blame this on me." Joan pointed a finger in her sister's face. "This is your fault for being such a little flirt."

Tori slapped a hand to her chest. "My fault? You're the one who horned in on my dinner."

"Horned in? I live here, remember? You're the one who practically stalked the guy to find out when he had a day off so you could play like a princess in a happy family scene."

Her eyes slitted. "Yeah, well, you're the one who bought True Religion."

"Like you didn't go out and buy that?" Joan shielded her eyes from the setting sun as her gaze dropped to Tori's suit. "It's so new it still smells like the mall."

Tori's chin shot into the air. "For your information, this didn't come from the mall. It came from a very exclusive shop downtown that you can't even afford to walk into."

Joan gasped an outraged breath. "Oh no? Well, maybe I've got too much sense to spend my money on an outfit that makes me look like Professional Barbie."

Tori's arms dropped to her sides, her hands clenched into fists. Her chest heaved as she drew breath to fire back a retort when Mom stepped between them.

"Girls, that's enough."

"But she—"

"Mom, you don't—"

"I said that's enough."

Mom's glasses magnified the sternness in her stare,

commanding their silence. Joan folded her arms and looked out across the backyard.

"Honestly, with three girls so close together in age, I expected you to fight over boys when you were younger. But look at you! Grown women acting like immature children."

Joan tightened her lips and heard Tori give an injured sniff.

"Now," Mom continued in a level voice, "I want you to discuss this like adults. It appears that you're both interested in Dr. Fletcher. Obviously he won't date you both. He's too much a gentleman for that. So how are you going to handle this situation?"

Tori spoke first, her tone one of calm reason. "I think Joan should back off."

Joan sucked a breath through her nose and matched her sister's tone. "I think Tori should go back to Lexington where she belongs."

"It was my idea to invite him to dinner."

Joan leveled a stare at her sister. "I met him first. I have dibs."

Tori's chin shot upward. "You weren't even interested in him. You didn't go outside to talk to him last Sunday."

"Maybe I didn't want to make too big a deal out of him because I was afraid you'd jump in and try to monopolize him." She raised her eyebrows. "Which you did."

Mom heaved a loud sigh. "This is getting us nowhere. Tori, are you really interested in Ken, or is he just an attractive man you'd enjoy passing the time with?"

Tori's gaze dropped to the ground as she considered Mom's

question. Joan watched, tension building in her stomach as she waited for the answer. *Say no. Please say no.*

"It's hard to tell, because I barely know him. But . . . ," Tori gave a slow nod and locked eyes with Joan, ". . . I might be."

Her mouth dry, Joan felt like crying. It wasn't fair. Tori could date any guy she wanted.

"Joan?" Mom forced her to look her in the eye. "What about you?"

She didn't trust herself to speak. Was she interested in Ken? She thought of the way her stomach flip-flopped earlier, when she gazed into his eyes. Swallowing, she nodded. As she did, Tori's shoulders drooped and she turned away.

Mom shook her head slowly. "You girls are going to have to work this out on your own. But I want you to remember one thing." She paused, and continued only when both girls were looking at her. "You are sisters. Family. Please don't let this come between you."

She turned away from them and went inside the house. Joan stared out over the backyard, the awkward silence between her and her sister almost a physical barrier. So much for Allie's comment that Tori would back off if she knew Joan was interested. The fierce jealousy she'd felt inside watching Tori flirt with Ken faded as she struggled to think of something to say. What would make Tori decide to leave the handsome doctor to her? She couldn't think of a thing. But neither did she want to watch a romantic relationship develop between Ken and her little sister. The thought twisted her insides.

Tori broke the silence, though she didn't look Joan's way. "I wish you'd told me you liked him last weekend."

Joan paused a moment before answering. Time to be honest, both with Tori and with herself. "I guess I was afraid to admit it. That way if he wasn't interested in me, I wouldn't have to feel like an ugly duckling."

Tori's head jerked toward Joan. "An ugly duckling? You are *not* an ugly duckling. You're a beautiful woman." She paused, then went on grudgingly. "And you look amazing today, by the way."

Warmth washed through Joan. "Thanks. So do you."

Tori grinned. "Even though I look like Professional Barbie?"

Joan returned the grin. "Sorry about that. I didn't mean it."

"Yeah, I'm sorry too. Especially for the crack about the expensive shop."

Joan shrugged a shoulder. "It's probably true."

They both fell silent for a few moments. Then Tori said, "Listen, what if we promise to stop acting like maniacs and just be ourselves? We'll let Ken choose."

Joan considered that suggestion. Just be herself? What a relief, not to have to watch for body language and remember to count how many seconds they made eye contact.

On the other hand, what if Ken asked Tori out first? Could she handle that? Well, she'd have to. What choice would she have?

But lightning might strike. He might ask her out first. And how would Tori like that?

"So if he expresses an interest in one of us, the other one will back away?"

Tori nodded. "Agreed."

She forced a grin. "Although judging by the look on his face at dinner, I doubt if he's interested in either of us at the moment."

"I don't know what came over me." Tori shook her head. "It was like I couldn't stop myself. I probably blew my chances."

"Oh, I don't know." Joan twisted the knife in her own gut. "He likes you. He told me so at the store the other day."

She looked up, eyes wide. "Really?"

Joan nodded and tried to ignore a sudden tightening in her throat. She took a deep breath. "So, are we okay?"

Tori stepped forward and enveloped Joan in a hug. "Of course we are. Sisters first, right?"

"Right." Joan returned her sister's embrace, then pulled back and smiled. "I guess we should get back in there."

They entered the house together, arm in arm. In the kitchen, Mom turned a concerned frown their way. It turned into a smile when she caught sight of them. "That's what I like to see."

Joan went into the kitchen, and Tori peeked around the wall into the living room.

"Hey! Where's Ken?"

"He had to leave." Gram wiped the dishtowel across a wet plate. "He seemed in a hurry."

Allie turned from the sink to give them both a disgusted look. "Way to go, girls. You scared him off."

~ *10* ~

"Luis is coming!"

Joan looked up from her seat behind the sales counter as Rosa ran from the front door through the store, her black mane flying behind her. "He is? What made him change his mind?"

Rosa collapsed across the counter, her face inches from Joan's. "He say he cannot stay away from his family anymore." A grin stole across her face. "He is missing Tiffany and me too much."

"Well, of course he is." Joan placed her hands over Rosa's and squeezed. "I'm so glad. When will he be here?"

"Next week. He take the Greyhound bus." She stopped, and then corrected herself. "He *will* take the Greyhound bus. And Señor Rodriguez says he has work in the kitchen while he is here. Oh, Joan." She straightened and clasped her hands beneath her chin. "Maybe he will stay this time. Maybe we will be a real American family together."

Seeing the longing in Rosa's face, Joan hoped so. She had to admit, she couldn't wait to meet the infamous Luis. After years of hearing Rosa talk about him, she'd built a mental image of a big, strong construction worker type with a loud voice and a pushy, domineering manner. He'd have to be tough to stand up to Rosa's fiery temper.

Rosa hopped down from the counter and came around the corner. She shrugged her purse off her shoulder and dropped it into the bottom drawer. "Your dinner was good?"

Joan swiveled away in her chair to shuffle the stack of customer invoices she'd been folding. She could kick herself for telling Rosa about Ken coming to eat with them last night, but she was so nervous yesterday morning the news exploded out of her almost on its own. "It was okay."

Rosa leaned forward, the long necklace she wore brushing the desktop. "You have a date with him, yes?"

Joan slid a stack of window envelopes and the folded invoices toward her. "Here. Stuff. No, I don't have a date with him."

Rosa peered at her, but Joan kept her gaze fixed on her hands as she worked. After a moment, Rosa patted her shoulder. "You no worry. He will ask you soon."

Joan's spirits rose at the confidence in her tone. "*Don't* worry, not *no* worry." She risked a sideways glance. "You think so?"

"*Don't* worry." Rosa amended, then nodded. "He likes you. I watched him look at you when you showed him furniture."

Yeah, well, Rosa didn't see him when he got his first look at Tori last night. For most of the night Joan had tossed in her bed, unable to clear her mind of the image of Ken and Tori's clasped hands. Or Tori's adorable dimple and Ken's smile as he gazed down into her face. True, he hadn't seemed all that crazy about either one of them as the evening wore on. And his sudden departure did seem suspiciously like an escape. But as Allie said, looks counted for a lot. And Tori did look awesome.

When sleep finally came, Joan dreamed she was walking down the center aisle at Christ Community Church on a white satin runner strewn with rose petals. Dressed in a tux, a smiling Ken waited for her at the altar. But when she got to the front of the sanctuary, a swell of music made her turn to look behind her. Tori stood in the doorway, dressed in white lace and carrying a bridal bouquet. As her little sister glided gracefully down the aisle, Joan looked at her own outfit and saw that she wore an old pair of ripped jeans and flip-flops. When Tori reached the front, she shoved the bouquet into Joan's hands and whispered, "Gosh, Joan, at least you could have worn the True Religions to my wedding."

Shaking off the dream, Joan folded another invoice and added it to the pile in front of Rosa. She had another chance, though—church on Sunday. True, Tori planned to be there, but they'd both promised to be on their best behavior.

She had one day to figure out what her best behavior should be.

❈

"We need to debrief."

Heart pounding, Joan whirled around in the desk chair.

Allie leaned against the doorjamb of the tiny back office, her arms folded across the top of her belly.

"Don't sneak up on me like that!"

She stepped into the room and lowered herself awkwardly into the hard visitor chair tucked between the desk and the wall. She kicked her shoes off and flexed her swollen toes with a sigh. "Why do you sit there with your back to the door? It would give me the creeps. You should get a couple of those delivery guys to turn the desk around for you."

"There's no room in here. I'd have to crawl over the top of it to get to my chair." Joan rocked backward and fixed her sister with a fearful look. "Was last night as big a disaster as I think it was?"

"Not at all! True, the guy escaped as soon as your back was turned, but you had some very nice moments. He practically drooled all over himself when you opened the door."

"Yeah, till Tori showed up looking like a model."

"That outfit was unexpected." Allie shook her head. "I figured she'd go chic casual, not elegant professional. But don't worry about that. Somehow Ken doesn't strike me as the kind of man who's impressed with suits. You did fine."

The knot in Joan's stomach relaxed a fraction. "He does seem more like a jeans guy, doesn't he?"

"Absolutely. And that's why I've got our next step all planned out. I did some surfing through the online catalogs on my lunch break, and I have the perfect outfit picked out for Sunday. Our baby sister will choke on her bubble gum when she gets a look at you."

Joan cocked her head and gave Allie a hard stare. "You seemed to enjoy the evening quite a bit. A little too much, in fact."

Her eyes went round. "Who, me?"

"Yes, you. If I didn't know better, I'd think you staged the whole show for your exclusive enjoyment."

A grin stole across Allie's face. "You two were pretty funny. You blushed like crazy every time he looked your way. And I've never seen Tori so discombobulated. One look at your jeans and she started acting like a runner-up in a beauty pageant."

Joan answered Allie's grin with one of her own. "She did, didn't she?"

"Which is why we're going to follow up with something completely unexpected. If we can keep her flustered, she'll spend more time worrying about you than trying to impress Ken. Are you up for another trip to the mall tomorrow?"

Joan caught her lower lip between her teeth. She couldn't take off work on a Saturday. She was scheduled to open the store. And she already spent more on clothes this week than the past year. But she didn't have a thing to wear on Sunday, not anything that could hope to look good next to Tori's wardrobe.

She glanced at the clock on the corner of the desk. "It'll have to be late. I can't leave work until four."

Allie heaved an exaggerated sigh. "Just how I wanted to spend my Saturday night. Fighting the mall crowd." She brightened. "I know. Let's go to that new Mexican restaurant. I heard their fried ice cream is to die for."

Ken opened the back door to let Trigger out onto the screened porch. Dog toys littered the floor beside a big fluffy bed and a huge tub of fresh water. A doggy door allowed free access to the backyard. Standing in the doorway, Trigger turned mournful eyes up at him and then looked away, ears and tail drooping.

"Sorry, boy." He squatted down on his haunches and rubbed the dog's neck. "I wish I could leave you inside, but you can't be trusted. You've got some pretty bad habits, you know."

He tossed a couple of chewy treats onto the bed. He'd learned in a dog training book to always give a treat when leaving for work in order to establish positive feelings about the regular routine. Trigger seemed to get the routine part, but the positive feelings were slow in coming. As though he knew he had no choice, the dog slunk through the doorway, a picture of dejection, and dropped onto his bed. He ignored the treats as he cast a last reproachful glance at his master. Guilt pricked Ken as he looked down into the woeful canine face.

"Hey, a guy's gotta work. I can't stay home and play with you all the time. You've got a huge yard to run in, tons of toys, a cushy bed, and your very own room. You're living in dog paradise."

Trigger didn't appear to appreciate his good fortune. He rested his head on his paws, eyes never leaving Ken as the door closed.

Ken bolted the latch and peeked through the curtain.

"Terrific. Now I get to feel guilty while I go to work to save lives. Thanks, Karen."

He went into the bedroom to retrieve his bag. When he passed his desk, his gaze fell on the single sheet of paper he'd printed out. Directions to Mike Lassiter's apartment. He couldn't get that boy out of his mind. What kind of place did he live in? And how about the kids he ran with? His mother said they were "bad news," but that could mean anything.

Ken picked up his bag and slung it across his shoulder. Something about Mike's tough-guy attitude niggled at Ken's thoughts. Ten was a critical age, so easily influenced for good or for bad. He got a glimpse of the boy's relationship with his mother at the hospital, and it didn't look good. Did Mike have any positive influences in his life?

He stared at the printout in the center of the desk. All these questions refused to go away, so yesterday morning Ken copied down the address from the hospital file and printed the directions off the Internet. The Lassiter apartment wasn't too far from here. If he hurried, he had time to drive by before he went to work. Just to take a look, to satisfy his curiosity.

Snatching up the paper, he crept to the back door and peeked through the curtains. And smiled. The chewy treats were gone, and Trigger was playing out in the yard with a stuffed cow. Ken watched as he whipped the toy back and forth violently, then tossed it up into the air and pounced on it when it hit the ground. The picture of a happy pup.

Chuckling, Ken left through the front door. He tossed

his bag into the passenger seat as he slid behind the wheel. Weird how the mutt weaseled into his emotions so quickly. He and Karen didn't have dogs growing up, because Mom always said animals were too much work. Turns out she was right. But since Trigger came into his life, he was starting to see why people were willing to take on the responsibility. Having the lively pup around took the edge off of the loneliness that haunted his off-work hours. In the past few weeks, he realized that dogs really could be man's best friend.

And, as Karen said, chicks dug them. He shook his head, remembering the meeting with Joan on the sidewalk. He had actually considered asking her to help him train Trigger. She seemed to like dogs, and she knew how to make them behave. But after spending a little more time with her last night, Ken wasn't sure what he thought. Things got uncomfortable when Tori showed up. There was something weird going on between those two. Maybe he'd better just stick to the dog training book.

He drove to Main Street and turned left, following the directions on the paper.

And what about the way the conversation froze last night when he mentioned God? Eric's face had hardened and Allie looked uncomfortable. Funny, he always heard Kentucky was smack-dab in the middle of the Bible Belt, where church was a big part of everyone's lives. But he was finding out that, just like anywhere else, some people here attended church out of habit more than anything else. He couldn't understand that. His faith had been such an important part of his life since his teenage years.

A couple more turns and Ken found the apartment complex he was looking for. It was about what he'd expected, ten or twelve faded brick buildings with uniform rows of shutterless windows. Broken-down chairs and rusty bicycle parts littered the concrete stoops before each dirty white door. He rolled down the window for a better look. Heat overpowered the air conditioner in an instant, and a rancid odor stung his nostrils when he drove by an overflowing trash dumpster. A few nice cars were parked in the lots that ran between the buildings, but most of them were beat-up and some even had duct tape and plastic in place of missing windows.

Between the last two buildings, a group of six or seven young people loitered around a graffiti-covered landscaping rock that bordered a broken-down playground. Beyond it, a basketball goal hung at an unusable angle from a busted backboard. Ken downshifted into second and drove slowly, scanning the boys' faces. He caught sight of a familiar shaggy head and put on his brakes.

"Hey, Mike," he shouted out the window.

All heads turned in his direction. They were young teens, Ken guessed, bored and up to no good. A couple wore dingy T-shirts with a strange-looking symbol sketched on the chest in bold black lines. One kid looked right at Ken as he defiantly puffed a cigarette. Ken let his gaze slide over the boys and come to rest on Mike, the smallest and probably the youngest of the group by several years.

Mike stared at him a moment, and then his face brightened with recognition. He tossed his head in a gesture of greeting. "What's up, Dr. Fletcher?"

The boy wore a pair of ragged tennis shoes. Hopefully he was keeping his stitches bandaged and clean. "Just passing by. How's the foot holding up?"

Mike glanced at one of the other boys before taking a few steps toward Ken's car. He limped noticeably. "It's okay. I stayed off of it until today, like you said. It ain't bleeding or anything."

Ken nodded. "Good. You coming back next week to have the stitches removed?"

He crossed the rest of the distance to the car and spoke in a low voice. "I don't know. My mom says we don't need to pay no doctor. She can take stitches out, no problem."

Ken read uncertainty in the boy's expression. His mother probably could handle removing a few stitches, but the wound really needed to be inspected to make sure it had healed properly and wasn't infected.

"Tell you what," he said. "I'll come back here about this time next Thursday. It won't cost your mom a penny, and I'll just make sure everything looks good. How's that sound?"

Relief cleared the creases from the boy's forehead. "Sounds good."

Over Mike's shoulder, Ken saw a couple of the older ones watching, their expressions suspicious. He looked back at Mike and spoke in a low voice. "You stay out of trouble, okay?"

The boy grinned, a gesture so infectious Ken couldn't help returning it. "You bet, Doc."

He turned and limped back toward his gang. Ken watched

his retreating form for a second, then put the Probe into first and rolled away. He liked that kid. If only there was something he could do to help him.

The sun had set Saturday night before Allie deposited Joan in her driveway. This shopping trip was even faster than the first, thanks to Allie's preplanning on the Internet. If she hadn't insisted on sitting through an hour-long waiting list to get a seat at the new Mexican restaurant, they would have been home well before dark.

Joan got out of the car and reached into the backseat for her bags.

"You're going to look great tomorrow," Allie commented. "Like you just stepped off the cover of a magazine in that Maggy London dress. The dark red color is totally you."

"At least I didn't have to take out a loan to pay for it." Joan slammed the door closed, then leaned in through the open window. "Are you coming with us to church to witness the spectacle?"

"I don't think so, but don't worry. We'll be here for dinner when you get home."

Joan hesitated. Allie never went with them anymore. Gram had commented on it more than once, and Joan knew it bothered her that her oldest granddaughter had apparently given up on religion since her marriage.

"You sure?" She grinned. "I could use my coach and fashion consultant's support."

"You'll do fine." Allie shifted the car into reverse. "Just

be sure to study the flirt facts I printed out for you. And try not to invade his hula hoop too soon."

Joan stood on the sidewalk and watched as the car backed out of the driveway. She knew why Allie wouldn't go to church in the morning. Eric. Oh, he'd let her go if she wanted to, but she probably felt awkward leaving him at home. They didn't have much time off together, what with his erratic schedule as a dispatcher. But Joan couldn't help wondering what would happen when the baby was born. Would Allie insist on raising her daughter in the church, as she had been raised? And how would Eric feel about that?

When Allie's taillights disappeared around the corner, Joan stepped up the three concrete stairs and pushed open the front door. The lamps in the living room created soft pools of yellow light by which Gram and Mom both sat reading.

"Hey, I'm home."

Gram looked up from her book, her forehead betraying deep worry lines. "You're awfully late."

Mom glanced at the clock on the mantle. "It's only ten o'clock, Mother."

Joan draped the bag containing her dress across the back of the recliner before dropping onto the seat. "You didn't have to wait up for me."

"Looks like you found something to spend some money on." Mom nodded toward the bag. "Is that for tomorrow?"

A wave of heat assaulted Joan's cheeks at the knowing look her mother gave her. "Yeah. Allie helped me pick out a new dress."

Mom held her eyes for a long moment, then her lips twitched. "I can't wait to see it."

"Guess what we did this afternoon." Gram continued before Joan could venture a guess. "Carla took me to visit Myrtle Mattingly. She has the nicest apartment at that new place out on the bypass. What's it called again?"

She turned a questioning look on her daughter, who answered without taking her eyes off her book. "Waterford."

Ice formed in the pit of Joan's stomach. Mom took Gram out to the assisted living center?

"That's it! Waterford. My goodness, what an elegant place. Chandeliers that sparkle like diamonds, real paintings on the walls, and carpet so soft you feel like you're walking on a cloud. And you should see the dining room. Myrtle says it's like eating in a fancy restaurant every night."

Joan clutched the arm of the recliner as she cast around for something to say. She didn't want Gram within ten miles of that place. How could Mom do this the minute her back was turned?

"Myrtle's apartment is nice. Just three rooms, but they're big. And she has a patio with a flower garden outside. Her own microwave and refrigerator and sink too, in case she wants to heat something up instead of going down to the dining room." Gram's white hair waved as she nodded with enthusiasm. Then her brow creased. "But I thought she had too much furniture in there, didn't you, Carla?"

"Oh, I don't know." Mom shrugged. "She had a lot, but as long as she's comfortable, that's all that matters."

Joan couldn't sit still any longer. She stood abruptly,

drawing surprised glances from both Gram and Mom. "I'm tired. I'm going to bed."

She didn't wait for an answer but scooped up her shopping bag and fled down the stairs, aware that both women stared at her retreating back. In her bedroom, she tossed her purchase onto the bed and turned to close the door. Very carefully.

Then she let her anger boil.

Mom did this on purpose! She waited until Joan was out of the way for an evening and then took Gram out to *that place*. She probably called in advance and told them to spiff the place up so they'd make a good impression.

Was Allie in on it? Maybe Mom gave her the assignment of taking Joan out of town so she could drag Gram out there and parade her around.

Joan flung herself onto the bed beside her dress bag and covered her eyes with her arm. No, of course Allie wasn't in on it. She wouldn't do that. And maybe Mom didn't either. Gram's friend probably called and invited her over. She would have asked Joan to take her if she'd been here. There was nothing secretive about a friendly visit.

Calm down, girl. I'm getting paranoid. This is only a big deal if I make it one.

A knock sounded. "Joan, may I come in?"

Mom.

"Uh, yeah." Joan scooted to the edge of the bed and stood as the door opened. She did not look at her mother but instead scooped up her bag and crossed the room to hang her dress in the closet.

"Are you alright? You look upset."

Joan slid the closet door open with extreme care. Slamming it would antagonize her mother and force an unpleasant confrontation. "I'm fine. I'm just tired, that's all."

Mom crossed the room and sat on the edge of the bed. "You're sure?"

Joan chewed on the inside of her cheek. Should she confront Mom, accuse her of trying to plant the idea of an assisted living center in Gram's mind? Joan's anger wilted under her mother's blue stare, magnified through the lenses of her glasses. She forced a smile. "I'm sure. Want to see my new dress?"

Chicken! Coward!

"Absolutely."

Relief saturated Mom's voice. Maybe she didn't want a confrontation any more than Joan did. Joan felt the last of her anger slip away, though a gnawing worry remained. She ignored it, and slid the dress out of its protective plastic bag.

"Oh, my." Mom gasped. "That is gorgeous."

Joan held the hanger up to her neck and clutched the faux-wrap waist to her own. "Do you think so?"

"I do." Mom stared admiringly. "Did it cost a million dollars?"

"Well," Joan admitted, "it wasn't cheap. But the jeans I bought the other day make this look like a bargain."

She laughed. "I figured that. I don't know a thing about clothes, but Tori sure seemed impressed."

Tori. Joan sobered at the reminder of her beloved competition. She slipped the bag back over the dress and hung it in the closet. Silence stretched into the awkward range as Joan took her time spacing the hangers evenly on the bar, casting about in her mind for something to say. Talking to Mom had never been easy.

"Well." Mom stood. "I just hope you girls don't let this doctor come between you. Trust me, there isn't a man alive who's worth that."

"Not even Daddy?"

Mom's hand froze inches from the doorknob. A blank expression overtook her features, but Joan saw the muscles in her throat constrict. She took a slow breath, then without looking up, grabbed the knob and twisted it open.

"Especially not him."

When the door closed behind her, Joan's pounding heart roared in the silence of the room. Mom never discussed Daddy, not once in all the years since she threw him out. Joan and her sisters learned to keep their mouths shut rather than see the fury flare in Mom's eyes when his name came up.

While this couldn't exactly be called a real conversation, it was more information than Joan had ever gotten from her mother.

Odd, though. For once, Mom didn't look angry at the mention of her ex-husband. That frozen look on her face had been kind of . . . sad.

~ 11 ~

"Look at this." Mom shoved the newspaper across the breakfast table and tapped on a picture in the Sunday Calendar section.

Joan scanned the brief article beneath the heading *Missionary to Speak on Work in Afghanistan.* "Hey, it's that woman from last Sunday."

Gram looked up from her oatmeal. "What did she do?"

"She's going to speak in Lexington on Wednesday night," Mom explained. "She must be visiting several churches in the area to raise money for that orphanage she told us about. I bet she'll give the same talk we heard."

Joan read the article a second time. Nothing new here, just a brief description of Robert and Mary Alice Sachs and their work for children orphaned by the fighting in the Middle East. As she scanned the bare facts, Joan felt something stir inside her. She found herself trying to read between the lines to catch a little of the fervor the missionary woman exhibited last week.

"We had her first." A hint of complaint colored Gram's

tone. "Why didn't the paper print an article about our church?"

Mom lifted a shoulder. "Because nobody called the paper and asked them to. That church in Lexington is huge. They probably have a staff member who writes press releases and things like that."

Gram nodded and scooped the last bite of oatmeal into her mouth. She set the spoon down on the table, put her hand in her lap, and then started to reach for it again. Joan watched without turning her head. Gram stopped herself, her fingers hovering for a moment above the utensil as she looked across the table where her daughter sat absorbed in the newspaper. She dropped her hand, and because Joan was seated beside her, she saw Gram clasp it firmly in the other one beneath the table.

Without looking up, Mom asked, "Mother, did you take your medicine this morning?"

"I . . ." Gram's face went blank. "I think so." Her forehead creased. "No, I don't think I did."

Mom caught Joan's gaze across the table for a split second, then her eyes turned toward her mother. "That's why we have that daily pill reminder. Check and see if the Sunday morning space is empty."

"Of course!" Gram's expression cleared. "What a good idea someone had when they came up with that thing."

Joan looked down at her bowl, ignoring her mother's unspoken *I told you so*. So Gram forgot. So what? Like she said, that's what the reminder box was for.

She stood and tightened the belt on her bathrobe before taking her dishes to the sink. Gram followed, and took the

143

bowl from her hands with a smile. "I'll wash these. You go have your shower."

A swarm of hummingbirds seemed to be darting around behind her breastbone as, forty minutes later, she donned the dark red Maggy London dress. The sweeping skirt fluttered as she moved, and the gathered side ruching accented her trim waist. Soft fabric crisscrossed her chest to form a flattering V-neck. She frowned at her reflection. Was it too low-cut for church? She twisted back and forth, watching the movement with a critical eye. No, she didn't think so. As long as she didn't bend over and touch her toes in front of Ken, it should be okay.

Honestly, this was the nicest dress she had ever owned. If nothing else, this little competition with Tori had certainly improved her wardrobe.

As though thoughts of her sister conjured her appearance, Tori's voice echoed down the stairs. "Hello? Where is everyone?"

"Down here," she shouted in answer. She slipped the earrings Allie selected into her earlobes, stepped into her shoes, and stood back to examine the finished product as her bedroom door opened.

"I'm a little early. The traffic was lighter—" Tori stopped, her eyes going round. "Wow. Where did you get that?"

"Nordstrom." Joan twirled to demonstrate the effect of the full skirt. "What do you think?"

"I think you're cheating." Tori's lower lip stuck out in a pout. "We agreed to be ourselves, remember?"

Joan decided to ignore the insinuation that being herself wouldn't allow her to wear a nice dress. Instead, she cocked her head and examined her sister's dress, a dark blue military-style button-up with shoulder epaulets and a belt at the cinched waist. She wore tights instead of pantyhose under the short skirt, giving her a sexy little-girl look that only someone as tiny and gorgeous as Tori could pull off.

"I don't remember seeing that before." Joan tried to filter a sudden flare of jealousy out of her tone. "Is it new?"

Pink stained Tori's fair cheeks as she looked down. "Well . . ."

"I thought so." Joan glanced at her reflection once more, to reassure herself that she looked good too. Good enough to take Ken's attention away from her adorable little sister? She ran a hand down the gathered fabric at her side and allowed a faint smile to steal onto her face. Maybe.

"I thought I heard Tori's voice." Mom stepped through the doorway, stopping to stare when she caught sight of them. "My goodness. You both look beautiful."

Tori dimpled and pirouetted. "Do you like it?"

"A lot." Mom's gaze slid to Joan, registering approval. "And that's a gorgeous dress too, honey. You two look like you're ready for a homecoming dance, not church."

Tori stepped up to stand beside Joan, and together they turned toward the mirror. Their reflections stared back at them, two completely different women, two completely different styles. One dainty and petite, the other tall and athletic. One blonde, one brunette. One stylish and fashionable, and one . . . Joan grinned. *Two* stylish and fashionable.

Mom stepped up behind them, taller than either one.

Tiny lines at the corners of her mouth strained her smile. Joan remembered her words last night. She was worried that Ken would cause a rift between her girls. Seeing the determination on Tori's face, and feeling a matching sensation in herself, Joan couldn't deny the possibility.

Mom put a hand on each of their shoulders and gave a gentle squeeze. "When you two walk into the room, Ken Fletcher won't know what hit him."

⸛

Not only Ken Fletcher, apparently.

Sitting in the pew between Gram and Ken, Joan felt the imaginary heat from a dozen pairs of eyes boring into the back of her head. If she wondered whether she had achieved her goal in the looks department this morning, all she had to do was catch the eye of any man under the age of ninety. Being the focus of unconcealed male admiration was a new experience for her, and not at all unpleasant. Not that she was interested in anyone here. Most of the guys her age were friends of Roger's. Blech.

Unfortunately, the dress didn't seem to have the desired effect on her target. After an initial compliment, Ken's attention had been focused elsewhere since they stepped through the door of Christ Community Church. Joan's only consolation was that he appeared equally unimpressed by Tori. And her baby sister didn't like it one bit.

In fact, at the moment he had apparently forgotten about the two beautiful babes flanking him in the pew. Instead, he seemed intent on memorizing Rev. Jacobsen's every word. She had never seen anyone pay such close attention to a sermon. He even removed a thin notebook from his Bible cover when the service began, and appeared ready to take notes. So far, though, he hadn't written anything beyond the title of the sermon in a typical doctor's scrawl—practically unreadable.

Joan leaned backward to look at Tori behind Ken's head. Her sister met her gaze and raised one eyebrow as though to say, "What gives with this guy?"

Joan had no answer.

Sunday school had been . . . interesting. To be sure, the Sanderson sisters made a splash when they walked through the door with the hottest young doctor in town. A simultaneous sigh rose from the throat of every female in the room, and Brittany Daniels dropped the lipstick she was applying. A few male eyeballs popped as well, and Ryan Adams tripped over his own feet and spilled his coffee when he jumped up out of his chair. Joan felt like part of the Tremendous Trio, even though she suspected Ryan was staring at Tori and not her.

Mr. Carmichael taught from a lesson book, the one used by every church in their denomination in the entire district. This week's lesson was about the importance of finding a place of service in the local congregation. They'd settled into their chairs, and Joan was trying, as always, to figure out whether Mr. Carmichael's hair was a wig or just a really bad dye job, when Ken raised his hand to ask a question.

Every head in the room swiveled in their direction. Mr. Carmichael stopped midsentence and stared, dumbfounded.

No one ever interrupted him to ask a question. It wasn't *that* kind of Sunday school class.

That Ken wasn't impressed with Sunday school had been obvious from his polite expression while Mr. Carmichael fumbled to come up with an answer to his question about spiritual gifts. He remained silent through the rest of the class.

At least the sermon was pretty good this morning. Joan cast a furtive glance sideways, trying to gauge from the look on his face what Ken thought of Rev. Jacobsen. Faint creases appeared between his brows. Could be concentration. Or maybe disagreement.

At the front of the sanctuary, Rev. Jacobsen signaled the wrap-up of his message by intoning, "In conclusion . . ."

During the two-minute summarization of his points, Gram reached for her hymnal, as did many others in the congregation. Ken looked around, his lips tightening. Joan followed his gaze. Very few people were paying any attention whatsoever to the minister. She felt slightly embarrassed when Ken slipped the notebook back into his Bible cover with a soft sigh. Apparently he hadn't heard anything worth writing down. Judging by the bland expression on his face, he wasn't any more impressed with the worship service than with Sunday school.

Her grip on the songbook tightened. Why did she feel like she was being judged by the quality of the church she attended? And like she had been found wanting?

The car ride back to the house was awkwardly quiet. Ken had opted to ride with them and leave his car at home, which thrilled Joan at the time but now didn't seem like such a good idea. She needed some time alone to gather her thoughts. Instead, she sat squashed against the door in Mom's Camry, acutely aware of the heat Ken's thigh generated where it touched hers in the tight quarters of the backseat. And painfully aware that his other thigh was generating similar heat for Tori.

"So, Ken," Tori asked, cocking her head prettily, "what did you think?"

Ken wet his lips and kept his eyes forward. "It was . . . nice," he said in a voice that meant the exact opposite.

"Was it very different from your church?" Mom asked.

Ken gave a brief smile. "Very. My home church in Indiana is much less formal. Chairs instead of pews, the words to the songs projected onto a big screen. We don't even have a choir."

Up front in the passenger seat, Gram turned her head. "Oh, I wouldn't like that. I love a good choir."

"Our pastor's messages are different too," he went on. "Much less, uh, polished, I guess. But he speaks from the heart, and he really makes me want to live out my faith."

Joan and Tori exchanged a glance, and then Tori turned her head to stare out the window. Joan felt awkward, uncomfortable. Live out his faith, he said. What exactly did that mean?

She looked out the window as the car pulled onto Elmtree Drive. No doubt Mrs. Sachs knew what that meant. The missionary and Ken, though they had never met, shared something, some kind of real connection to God.

It was a little scary.

Gram changed the subject just as the silence in the car threatened to become uncomfortable. "I hope you'll join us for Sunday dinner. We're having a chicken and rice casserole, one of my specialties."

Mom steered the car into their driveway as Ken answered. "Thanks for the invitation, but my sister will be here in a couple of hours, and I've got a ton of paperwork to get done before she arrives."

And that, as they say, is that.

Disappointment settled on Joan like a physical wave. All that effort, all that money for clothes, wasted. He wasn't impressed enough with either of them to want to stay for lunch. She exchanged another glance with Tori, whose eyeballs swept upward before she turned away.

The car glided to a stop, and they all got out. They moved as a group toward the house, pausing at the front porch to say goodbye to Ken.

He nodded first at Gram, and then Mom. "Thanks for the invitation, ladies. Maybe next time I can stay for lunch."

"You're welcome anytime." Gram patted his arm.

He glanced at Tori. "It was nice seeing you again."

"You too, Ken." Her smile was polite, but not, Joan noted, at all flirty.

His gaze shifted to Joan. Maybe her imagination was working overtime, but she thought his smile deepened as he gazed into her eyes. Her pulse did a rumba and she forgot to count how many seconds he held the eye contact. It was a long time, though.

"See you soon?"

She swallowed. "Sure."

Then he was gone, crossing the grass toward his house. As he reached his front door, Eric's pickup pulled into the driveway and parked behind Mom's car. Allie jumped out of the passenger side and crossed to the place where they stood waiting. She dipped her head in the direction of Ken's place just as his door closed. "Did you girls scare him off again?"

Mom laughed. "No, I think he was properly impressed with both your sisters. Unfortunately, our church didn't seem to thrill him."

"He's used to a different style of service." Gram defended him loyally. "He didn't feel comfortable with ours. I could tell."

"I have an announcement," Tori said as Eric joined them. She looked at Joan, her eyebrows high. "You, dear sister, can have him. I'm out."

Joan ignored Allie's jubilant glance. For some reason, she didn't feel the triumph she thought she would at Tori's declaration. Winning by concession wasn't the same as being chosen.

"Why?" she asked, narrowing her eyelids.

Tori shook her head. "Frankly, I'm not interested in going out with a religious fanatic, even if he is a doctor. The next thing you know he'll be inviting us to a snake-handling service or something."

She gave a delicate shudder as Eric let out a belly laugh.

Unease stirred in Joan as she followed her family into the house. She glanced next door. Ken was definitely more religious than any of the Sandersons. Did she want to get mixed up with a fanatic, even a gorgeous one?

151

Ken sat at the desk in his bedroom, his full focus on the computer screen, when the doorbell rang. Trigger leaped up from the floor beside Ken's bed and ran from the room, barking.

A familiar voice echoed through the house. "Anyone home?"

"I'm in here, Karen."

He clicked the Save button and exited the software. His back ached as he stood and stretched sore muscles. The past three hours had been spent transcribing his rather terse treatment notes. If he was going to make a habit of bringing work home, he should probably spring for a real desk chair instead of the lopsided white plastic one he rescued from the dumpster at his last apartment.

"Down, you monster!" From the sound of her voice, Karen didn't think much of Trigger's enthusiastic greeting. "Ken, get in here and call off your mutt."

Ken jogged down the short hallway. He stopped just inside the living room, laughing at the sight of his sister, halfway through the doorway, trying to hold an excited Trigger at bay. The dog stood on his hind legs, supported by Karen's restraining hand on his chest. Nineteen-month-old Jordan, laughing with delight, twisted on his mother's hip to grab at the dog's flailing front paws.

"Don't just stand there." Karen's green eyes threatened death if he didn't move quickly. "Rescue us!"

Ken hauled Trigger off by the collar and set him down on the floor. He held on for a minute and said, "Down," in a deep tone like the book instructed. They'd worked on this command. At the sound of his voice, Trigger's muscles relaxed a fraction. When Ken released the collar, the dog rushed once again toward the newcomers, tail wagging like crazy, but at least he kept all four paws on the floor.

"Gosh, look how that mongrel has grown! What are you feeding him, elephant food?"

"Hey, don't call my dog a mongrel. You picked him out, after all."

Ken grinned at his sister. Her dark hair was a little longer than the last time he saw her, and her skin glowed with a healthy summer tan. She looked good. Happy. And his nephew had grown at least a couple of inches in the past month.

He enveloped them both in a hug. "Glad to see you, sis. You made good time."

"Yeah, right after church we ran home and tossed every-thing into the car. The kiddo slept most of the way."

"That's good." Ken took the giggling toddler and swung him into the air. "Us guys can stay up all night together when your mama wimps out at nine o'clock."

"You laugh now, but just wait until 3:00 a.m. when you're begging him to go to sleep." Despite her insults about Ken's dog, Karen dropped to her knees and delighted Trigger with a few moments of roughhousing. When she stood, she looked with interest around the living room and beyond.

"Nice little place. When do you plan to unpack?" She nodded toward a stack of cardboard boxes piled against the wall in the empty dining room.

Ken settled his nephew on his hip. "Oh, that's a bunch of stuff from school. Textbooks, mostly. Someday I'm going to put some shelves in there and turn it into my office."

She nodded, then walked over to the couch and ran a hand across the arm. "I like the furniture. But it's too sterile in here. You work in a hospital. You don't have to live in one. Put some pictures on the wall, scatter some knickknacks around."

Trigger left her side and bounded over to stand in front of Ken, neck extended to get a whiff of the interesting creature he held. Jordan leaned forward, squealing with glee when the dog licked his hand. Ken held the squirming toddler in a firm grasp, ready to twist away if Trigger got too rough. He didn't think the playful pup would hurt a kid on purpose, but since this was the first time he'd been around anyone but adults, a little caution was in order.

"I don't have any knickknacks to scatter. And besides, if I tried it would just look like junk." He gave her what he hoped was an endearing smile. "Maybe you can help while you're here. You know, give the place a woman's touch."

Karen disappeared through the dining area toward the kitchen to continue her inspection. Her voice drifted back to him amid the sound of cabinets closing. "I was hoping you'd find a woman of your own to help with that. Any progress in that area?"

Ken knelt and placed Jordan on the floor, a warning hand on Trigger's neck, ready to grab hold of his collar if he got too rambunctious for the toddler. Amazingly, as though he sensed this was a youngster, the dog curbed his natural bouncy behavior and contented himself by bathing Jordan's face and neck in dog slobber.

"Depends on what you mean by progress." He raised his voice to be heard over the child's excited squeals.

Karen returned to the room at a jog, as he knew she would. "You met a woman?"

"Two, actually. Unfortunately, I don't think it's going to work out with either of them."

"Why not?"

"Well, they're sisters, for one thing."

She spread her hands. "So? That just means you can't have both of them. Pick one."

He gave her a cockeyed look. "Come on, Sis. Stop matchmaking. I thought you put Trigger in charge of setting me up with women."

Jordan became overly exuberant in his caresses, and Trigger whimpered when a misaimed slap hit him square on the nose. Ken put a comforting hand on the dog's head as Karen dropped cross-legged onto the floor and pulled her wriggling son into her lap.

"Be nice to the dog." She took a pudgy hand and guided it in a gentle rubbing motion across Trigger's head. "He's a good dog."

"Dog," Jordan repeated, and calmed his caresses so that Trigger nosed closer to him. "Good dog."

"Hey!" Ken sat up straight. "That was really clear."

"Yeah, he started a little late, but the kid's becoming a real talker." Pride stole into her voice. "He's in the eightieth percentile in height, and his doctor says he's way above other kids his age in agility and balance. I think he's going to be a basketball player, like his uncle."

Ken returned her grin. "Or a golfer like his dad."

"Maybe." She raised an eyebrow in Ken's direction. "Back to your love life. I'm not trying to play matchmaker, per se. I just want to see you happy with someone. If we had a mother, she'd be nagging you about finding a wife and supplying her with a houseful of grandchildren. I'm just filling in."

Ken gave her a tender smile and reached out to tuck a stray strand of hair behind her ear. "You've been the best big sister a guy could ever hope for. And a great nag too." He laughed and ducked away from her slap.

"Don't change the subject. Why don't you ask one of these women for a date?"

Ken sobered. "I don't know, Sis. They're both beautiful, and smart." He avoided her shrewd lawyer eyes. "I was really hitting it off with one of them, but when her sister showed up, they both started acting weird. Dressing like movie stars and batting their eyelashes, you know? And one of them kept flipping her hair around. Looked like she had a twitch or something."

"Hmmm." She shook her head. "You've never liked flirty women."

He brightened. "I did go to church with them this morning, though."

"And how was that?"

He shrugged. "It's not like our church back home."

She cocked her head. "Any chance I'll get to meet these sisters?"

"Maybe. One of them lives right next door."

Karen straightened. "Why didn't you say so? I'll scope her out for you."

At that moment, Jordan leaned forward in his mother's lap. Before either adult could stop him, he stuck out his tongue and returned Trigger's enthusiastic lick with one of his own.

"Aaaccckk!" Karen's scream as she jerked her son backward sent Trigger scurrying from the room with fright. "My child just licked a dog!"

❈

The opportunity for Karen to meet Joan happened sooner than Ken expected.

They had moved to the sofa, where they sat talking as they watched Jordan play with a toy on the floor before the big front window. Ken was relaxed, listening as Karen brought him up-to-date on all the news of their friends back home. He sat straight up when he saw movement in the Hancock-Sanderson front yard.

"Hey, there she is. There's Joan."

"Where? Let me see!" Karen jumped up and rushed to the window.

As they watched, Joan rolled a big trashcan from the corner of the house to the front curb in preparation for pickup tomorrow. As she set it in place, Karen ran through the front door. Ken stepped backward. He didn't want Joan to see him watching.

Why not? He shook his head. What was this, nerves?

Playing it cool, Karen didn't immediately make a beeline across the yard. Instead, she went to her car and opened the back door. Reaching inside, she pulled out an overnight bag and then stood. Her back was toward Ken as she faced Joan. He saw Joan look across the yard and then pause in her walk down the driveway back to the house.

"Mama?" Jordan's voice held a touch of uncertainty as he looked from the front door through which his mother had disappeared, to Ken.

"She's right outside, big guy. See?"

He swung the toddler into his arms and stood at the window, watching his sister talk to the girl next door.

❧

Joan set the trashcan in place at the curb and turned. This had been a gorgeous summer day, cooler than usual for August. For once the oppressive humidity was missing. She took a deep breath and filled her lungs with relatively moisture-free air.

Next door, a woman stepped out of the house and onto Ken's front porch. She trotted down the sidewalk toward a pearly white Lexus with gold trim. Joan didn't know much about cars, but this one looked almost new and extremely expensive. Tori would be impressed.

Heck, Joan was impressed.

"Hello, there," the woman called, catching sight of her.

Joan nodded. "Hello. You must be Ken's sister."

This pretty brunette with an oval face and straight white

teeth could be no one else. Even from a distance, she looked like a female version of Ken.

"That's right. I'm Karen Poulson. And you must be Joan."

Ken's sister knew her name? A flush of pleasure rippled through her. He talked about her to his family!

She crossed the yard, her bare feet prickled by freshly mowed grass. "Joan Sanderson. It's nice to meet you. Ken's mentioned you several times."

"You too. He was just telling me how kind you and your sister have been, inviting him to dinner and church. You've really made him feel welcome."

The pleasure deflated a bit at the mention of Tori, but Joan forced her smile not to fade. "We're glad to have someone in the house. It's been empty for over a year. And having a doctor nearby makes my grandmother feel safe."

Karen looked up and down the street. "Seems like a nice neighborhood. And what I saw of the town when I drove through looked charming. Have you lived in Danville all your life?"

"I have." A touch of embarrassment flooded Joan at the admission. To a successful attorney who drove a new Lexus and lived in a big city like Indianapolis, Danville must seem like a hick town. And Joan was just one of the locals who'd never managed to escape. Her and Frankie Belcher and a bunch of other boring people.

Except Allie. Allie wasn't boring.

"My older sister lives here too," she said. "She's expecting a baby next month. Danville is a great place to raise kids."

159

Enough babbling. What was she doing, trying to gain brownie points by attempting to convince Ken's sister that someone besides her thought Danville was a good place to live?

Karen's eyes lit. "Really? Is this her first?"

"The first for all of us." Joan smiled. "Ken told me you have a son."

Karen's face lit with motherly pride. "Jordan is nineteen months old. He's a rascal, that's for sure. He keeps us hopping. Takes after his daddy in that respect." An offhand expression overtook her features. "So, Ken tells me he went to church with your family this morning."

Interesting. Karen brought up church. Maybe she could find out from Ken's sister why he was so into this religion thing.

"That's right." She paused and caught Karen's eye. "I don't think he was overly impressed with the service, though."

A brief smile curved Karen's lips. "He did mention that it wasn't like ours at home."

Ours? So brother and sister attended the same place. Even more interesting. Maybe fanaticism ran in the family. "How so?" She gave an embarrassed shrug. "Christ Community is the only one I've ever known, so I don't really have anything to compare it to."

"Well, I haven't been to yours, so I only know what Ken said. It's pretty traditional?" She raised her eyebrows as she asked the question.

Joan shrugged. "I guess so."

"Our service is really contemporary. We sing worship songs for about thirty minutes—"

"Thirty minutes?" Holy cow! Didn't their throats get hoarse from singing so long?

Karen rolled her eyes in sympathy. "Sometimes it goes on a bit too long, in my opinion. But we sing a lot of choruses and modern songs, and I like them. Occasionally a hymn or two. Then our pastor speaks. He doesn't use notes or anything, just his Bible. He's a great preacher, really speaks from the heart."

Tori's comment burned in Joan's mind. Just how much a fanatic was Ken? She needed to settle that question right now. "When you say your service is contemporary, do you mean just the type of music? Or do you do . . . weird things?"

Karen's eyebrows rose. "You mean do we dance in the aisles and roll on the floor?"

Joan looked at her feet, away from Karen's direct gaze. "Yeah. Or handle snakes or anything like that?"

Karen laughed out loud. Joan looked up and flushed at the amusement she saw in her face. "Trust me, if anyone tried to bring a snake within five hundred feet of me, I'd be out of there in a heartbeat. I'm scared to death of snakes." She tilted her head, fixing Joan in a curious stare. "What would make you think that?"

Joan gave an embarrassed laugh and looked away. "Oh, no reason, really. Ken just talks a lot more about his religion than most people I know. There are some churches not all that far from here that are pretty 'out there,' and do some strange things in their services." She grinned and gave an exaggerated sigh of relief. "I was starting to worry about what kind of pets besides Trigger he might be hiding in that house."

Karen chuckled, then sobered. "Trust me, our church is completely normal. We believe in the Bible and try to do what Jesus teaches, pure and simple. No dancing, no shouting, nothing like that. I'm sure there are similar churches here."

"Oh, there are." Joan nodded. "Danville isn't that small. Some of the bigger churches even have both contemporary and traditional services. I'm sure Ken will be able to find one he likes." She grinned. "If he wants to drive out in the country, he might even be able to find one with snakes."

Karen shuddered. "Heaven forbid." She sobered and caught Joan's eye in an unblinking gaze. "So what about your church? What do you believe?"

Startled, Joan might have been flash-frozen. Was Karen asking about her church, or about her personal beliefs? Sure, it sounded like a question about her church, but something in that direct gaze of Karen's made the question seem more personal. This wasn't your typical small talk. Not, "What do you do for a living?" Or, "Where did you go to school?" Or even, "What toppings do you like on your pizza?" Just a very straightforward "What do you believe?"

Behind Karen, Ken's front door burst open. Feeling as though the cavalry had just ridden into view, she tore her gaze from Karen as a high-pitched wail pierced the peaceful late afternoon. Ken came through the door at a run, holding a screaming toddler at arm's length.

"There!" He shouted at the child as he ran across the grass toward them. "Your mama's right there. See? Quit crying."

Joan couldn't help laughing at the panic on his face as he thrust the child into his mother's arms. The crying slowed to a sniffle.

"He wouldn't stop," Ken said as Karen soothed the child. He looked up at Joan and spoke in a defensive tone. "I didn't do anything to him, honest!"

"There, there," Karen crooned. "Did mean old Uncle Ken scare you? Don't worry, Mama will protect you."

"I didn't do anything," Ken repeated. An injured expression settled on his face. "He used to like me."

Karen laughed. "Oh, don't be silly. He still likes you. He's just going through a clingy stage right now. He even cries if I leave him with Neal."

Joan peered at the red face resting on Karen's shoulder. Brown baby eyes peered back at her as he drew a shuddering breath through a slightly runny nose. "What a cutie. He looks like you, Karen."

"You should see him when he's not crying." Ken chucked a finger under the baby's chin. "He's the spitting image of me at that age."

Karen inhaled through her nose. "I think I detect the problem here. We need a new diaper, don't we, Jordan?" She turned a smile on Joan as she stepped toward the house. "It was nice meeting you."

Joan nodded. "You too, Karen. I hope you enjoy your visit."

She walked away, murmuring in a low voice into the toddler's ear. Ken watched her disappear into the house, and then turned to Joan. "So you got to meet my sister."

Joan's stomach fluttered as she returned his smile. "Yeah. She's great."

He exhaled a deep breath. "I knew you'd like her." He took a backward step. "Well, I guess I'd better get in there. See you later?"

"Sure."

She walked toward the house, pausing at the front door with her hand on the knob. Ken stood in an identical position on his own porch, watching her. He waved, then disappeared inside.

Funny, Ken seemed relieved that she and Karen had met. What was that all about?

His parents were deceased, and he was obviously very close to his only sibling. Could this have been a sort of "meet the family" test? Her stomach flip-flopped at the thought. If so, did she pass?

Doubt nibbled at her insides. Karen's last question had thrown her. She must have looked as confused as she felt, and those sharp lawyer eyes wouldn't have missed that. Thank goodness she'd been saved from answering.

She turned the knob and stepped across the threshold. Ken had been right about one thing. Karen was smart, like Tori. But as far as Joan could see, the similarity ended there. They didn't look a thing alike. Karen's tall frame and dark hair were completely opposite from petite, blonde Tori.

A thought caused Joan's foot to stop midstep.

In the looks department, Karen was more like her than Tori.

Was that good or bad? She had no idea, but for some reason the thought made her smile.

~ 12 ~

"Hi, Miss Joan." Tiffany shouted a greeting as she ran through the doorway into Abernathy's showroom Monday morning. "Mrs. Gonzales is sick."

"Hello, sweetie." Joan returned the little girl's enthusiastic hug. "Does that mean you're staying with us for the day?"

Rosa, following at a slower pace, searched Joan's face anxiously. "I cannot leave her at home by herself. She will be quiet. She brought books. See?"

Tiffany dropped her backpack to the floor and unzipped it to let Joan peek inside. "And crayons too."

Though Joan wasn't aware of any rule that prohibited having the child of an employee on the premises for the day, she doubted an active little girl running around the showroom while they were trying to close a sale would help business. Still, what could she do, send Rosa home? Cover the store alone until the two o'clock shift arrived? Joan didn't have the heart to do that. Rosa didn't hold down two jobs just for the joy of working. She needed the money.

But no way books or crayons would keep the active six-year-old entertained for an entire day. She grinned down at the dark-haired child. "Tell you what. Why don't you and your mom walk down to Video Vern's before we get busy and rent a couple of movies? You can watch them on the computer in the back office if you get bored."

"Alright!" Tiffany pumped her little fist into the air.

Joan fished some money out of her purse and pressed it into Rosa's palm. When the woman protested, she raised her chin. "My treat. I insist."

The anxiety melted from Rosa's features. "Thank you, Joan. *Eres muy simpatica.*"

Joan acknowledged the compliment with a hand squeeze. Eyes bright, Rosa spun away, embarrassed by her emotional lapse into her native tongue.

"Come on, Mama." Tiffany grabbed her mother's hand and pulled her toward the door, skipping with excitement. "Can I get *Mulan*?"

"Ai, Tiffany," exclaimed Rosa with a backward grin at Joan, "more *Mulan*? Why not something new?"

In the doorway, they passed someone coming into the store. Joan set her professional smile in place, and then felt her eyes widen when she recognized her customer. Karen Poulson, Ken's sister. A quick scan of the sidewalk outside the showroom window showed no sign of Ken and the baby.

"Good morning," she said, crossing the room to meet Karen halfway. "What a nice surprise."

"I escaped." Karen grinned. "Jordan got over being bashful and kept Uncle Ken up half the night playing. Worked out great, since Ken's adjusted to the night shift. I don't know what time they finally went to bed, but they're both still sound asleep." She looked over the furniture displays. "Ken told me he rented his furniture here, so I figured I'd come by and see what you have in the way of entertainment centers. He's got his television sitting on a dilapidated dining room chair that looks like it might disintegrate if you turn the ceiling fan on too high."

Karen didn't meet Joan's eyes as she spoke, and her smile looked a little tight. She hadn't come to look at furniture. But why else would she drive across town? Joan sucked in a breath as realization dawned. Karen was scoping her out! Interviewing, so to speak, a possible girlfriend for her brother. A flush of pleasure washed over her, followed by a fit of nerves. How in the world could she, manager of a small town furniture store, measure up to a doctor and a lawyer?

Her professionalism kicked in. She smiled and gestured toward the displays on the left side of the showroom floor. "We don't have too many to choose from, I'm afraid, but what we do have is over here."

She led the way, weaving through the furniture and stopping before a light oak piece. Karen examined it closely, then shook her head.

"That's too wide, I think. It would dwarf his little living room." Her gaze swept the room. "Hey, what about that corner one over there?"

Joan followed her to it. "The finish is slightly darker than the end table Ken picked out last week, but it's a nice piece."

"It is." Karen opened the double doors and peered inside. "And it's perfect for that room. It won't block the front window. I'll tell him he needs to come look at it."

She closed the doors carefully, then turned and faced Joan. "Actually, I had another reason for coming by today. I was hoping we could finish the conversation we started yesterday."

Joan's mouth went dry. Continuing that conversation was at the very bottom of the list of things she wanted to do today. She had spent all night *not* thinking about Karen's uncomfortable question, which was practically the same thing as thinking about it. Obsessively.

But the store was empty, so she had no way to gracefully excuse herself. Where were customers when you needed them? She gestured toward a nearby sofa, and then seated herself on the matching love seat.

Karen dropped onto a cushion. She caught Joan in a green gaze that looked very much like her brother's. "What I really want to know is, do you like my brother?"

Joan gave a startled laugh. "Excuse me?"

"You'll have to forgive me for being direct." She gave a slight shrug. "It's the lawyer in me coming out."

Maybe that's why this felt like a cross-examination. Joan shifted on the love seat. "Well, he's a nice guy."

"But?"

Joan gazed out the window into the parking lot. Just how honest should she be with this woman? Would everything she said be reported back to Ken? Probably.

Karen leaned forward, forcing Joan to look at her. "I'm sorry if I'm coming off as rude. I don't mean to be. But I think my brother likes you. Ken and I have always looked out for each other, and I just want to make sure he doesn't get hurt."

Ah, Karen was being the protective big sister, just like Allie had always been. A pain in the neck sometimes, but Allie could always be counted on to take up for her kid sisters. Okay, Joan could respect that.

"Ken is a great guy," Joan began, "but to be honest he's a little more . . . out there, when it comes to religion than my family is accustomed to. He's different, not like any other guy I've ever met. Obviously church is very important to him, but I'm not sure I'd be comfortable in a service like you described yesterday."

She nodded. "Our faith is important to us. We were both baptized as teenagers, after our parents died, and our church has been a huge part of our lives ever since."

Joan remembered the day of her baptism, all dressed up in white and standing at the front of the church with two other girls her age who had also just completed their confirmation classes. The minister dribbled water on their heads, and they repeated their confession of faith after him. Mom and Daddy and Gram and Grandpa sat in the second pew with Allie and Tori, all of them beaming proudly as the minister presented her with a white Bible, her name engraved on the cover in gold letters.

That was about a month before Daddy left. She swallowed against a dry throat and forced that thought out of her mind.

She flashed a brief smile at Karen. "Well, I'm a Christian too, but I don't talk about it the way Ken does."

"And he makes you a little nervous by being so out-spoken?"

Joan looked away. Actually, *both* of them were more outspoken than she was comfortable with. "A little."

The shadow of a smile tugged at the edges of Karen's mouth. Joan felt like a lab specimen being studied. The woman might as well have pulled out a magnifying glass. Finally she gave a single nod. "I think I understand."

Joan waited, expecting her to explain. In fact, Joan wanted to hear the explanation. Maybe it would help her understand the differences between them too.

Instead, Karen changed the subject. "You have to prom-ise me something." She leaned against the back cushion. "My brother would die of embarrassment if he knew I said he likes you." She gave a self-conscious laugh. "Actually, it is kind of high schoolish, isn't it?"

"Well, yeah." Joan relaxed against the back cushion. At least she acknowledged how strange this conversation was.

"Okay, so here's a question that's totally high schoolish. You didn't answer my question. Do you like him back?"

Suddenly immobile, Joan stared into Ken's sister's eyes. Did she like him? She'd nearly pulled her family into World War III over the guy. He was handsome and smart and kind. And over-the-edge or not, there was something fas-cinating about the way he displayed his religion so openly. No, it was more than religion. It was . . . well, whatever it was, she found herself interested and frightened at the same time. Part of her wanted to sit him down and ques-tion him, to find out why religion was so important to him. Another part wanted to run away so she didn't catch whatever it was.

But to admit that to his sister, who was as weird about religion as he was?

She licked her lips, shifting her glance to the silk plant on the coffee table between them. "He's a nice guy."

Karen grinned. "Good enough." She stood, and Joan did too. "I'll tell him to come in and look at that entertainment center."

Joan walked her to the door, as she would have done had Karen been a guest in her home instead of a customer in her store. "When are you heading back to Indiana?"

"Tomorrow. When Ken gets off work at the hospital, we're going to have breakfast together, and then Jordan and I will leave and he'll go to bed. I'll be glad to get home." She looked at the floor, a pretty blush appearing on her cheeks. "I know it's only been a day, but I miss my husband."

They reached the front of the store, and she paused with her hand on the handle. Her teeth caught her lower lip for a moment before she looked up.

"I like you, Joan. And I love my brother. I believe God helps us find the right relationships, so I'm going to ask him to show you and Ken what he wants for you."

She flashed a quick smile and fled. Joan watched through the glass as she slid behind the wheel of her Lexus. She liked Karen too, in spite of her direct manner and teenagerish questions. What an amazing thing to say, though. Did she honestly believe that God got involved in picking out dates, like some sort of cosmic dating service?

But as the Lexus pulled from the parking lot onto the

171

busy street, she knew Karen wasn't talking about only a date. She was talking about something way more permanent. Would God listen to those prayers?

A tickle in her stomach, Joan turned her back toward the door. She had too much to do today to deal with Karen or her blunt comments. She had invoices to key into the computer, and the inventory report to finalize, and . . . She'd better make a list to organize her thoughts.

Ken hovered over Jordan, not entirely sure the flimsy chair would withstand the toddler's energetic squirming. Karen brought a booster seat with her, but even that didn't provide enough height for Jordan to reach his food on the countertop, so they piled a few medical textbooks beneath it and secured the whole thing with bungee cords. So far the contraption seemed to be holding, but it looked way too easy to topple, and if anything happened to his nephew while in his charge, he'd never forgive himself. Where did Karen go, anyway? Her cryptic note, *Be back soon*, didn't give Uncle Ken much to go on.

Lifting his mug to his mouth, he bolstered himself with a deep, coffee-scented breath before he drank. Jordan fished another handful of soggy Cheerios out of his bowl and leaned sideways to feed them to a delighted Trigger. The boy giggled with glee as the dog licked his fingers more or less dry.

With a sigh, Ken wiped Jordan's hand with a wet dishrag for the fifth time. "Hey, kiddo, try to get some of those down your own throat too."

At least Trigger had behaved himself admirably during this visit. Though when Karen and Jordan left, he wondered if he'd ever be able to stop Trigger from begging for handouts during mealtimes. He'd worked hard on that before Karen's visit. But with two other dog lovers in the house, Trigger had taken advantage of the situation.

At the sound of the front door opening, relief wilted Ken's shoulders. This babysitting stuff was nerve-wracking.

"Mama!" Jordan began bouncing up and down in his booster seat when Karen came into the room, the palms of both hands slapping the counter. Ken rescued the bowl of cereal before disaster occurred, and then scooped the kid up before he tumbled to the floor.

"There's my sweet boy." Karen took the toddler from his arms and cuddled him, grinning at Ken. "And how's Uncle Ken doing this morning?"

"Great." Ken topped off his coffee from the pot. "We had a few anxious moments when we first woke up and found you missing, but we made it. Even managed to get a clean diaper on."

"Ah, diapering. Yet another skill I'm sure they taught you in medical school." She buried loud kisses into Jordan's chubby neck and then set him on the floor where he made a grab at Trigger's tail. The dog had learned a painful lesson last night and executed a skillful maneuver to keep the fascinating appendage out of harm's way.

"Where'd you go, anyway?"

"Oh, I decided to do a little shopping while you guys slept." She flashed a grin at him as she went to the counter and filled a coffee mug. "Furniture shopping."

173

Ken raised an eyebrow. Why wasn't he surprised? She was as nosy as a little old lady and seemed to have made getting to know Joan her objective for the trip. "Did you find anything you couldn't live without?"

She faced him, leaning against the sink as she cradled the mug in both hands. "I might have." She blew away the steam rising from the mug and took a cautious sip.

"Are you going to tell me about it?"

Karen shrugged. "Not much to tell, really." She swallowed another sip, eyeing him over the rim of the mug. "I think she likes you."

A touch of excitement pricked Ken's interest. "How do you know?"

"Just something she said. But apparently we both make her a little nervous with our talk about church."

"Talk about church? I certainly haven't had any theological discussions with her." Ken frowned. "If mentioning God makes her uncomfortable, I don't think she's the one for me. I've met plenty of women who think being a Christian means going to church every Sunday and acting nicely during the week. That's not what I want in a wife."

Karen laughed. "Who said anything about a wife? I just had a friendly talk with the girl who lives next door. What could it hurt to ask her out? Take her to get a pizza or something. Get to know her."

Ken shook his head. "I'm not sure that's a good idea."

"I like her, Ken." She stared into the mug for a moment. "This sounds nuts, but I think she's been hurt." She held up a hand. "Don't ask how I know, because I have no idea. She seems to be holding something back." She glared and pointed a finger in his face. "So don't you dare hurt her more, do you hear me, little brother?"

She whirled to follow Jordan and Trigger into the other room, leaving Ken alone to consider what she'd said.

A few moments later, he followed his sister into the living room, a sense of peace settled deep inside. He still didn't know if he would ask Joan out or not, but he felt positive that his life—and his relationships—were in God's hands.

Joan left Rosa with a customer in the showroom and went into the back to check on Tiffany. The little girl sat at the desk in the office, coloring intently while she twisted back and forth in the desk chair. The computer speakers played a lively Disney tune while a cartoon puppy wreaked havoc with some chickens on the monitor.

Joan dropped into the guest chair and peered at Tiffany's project. "Whatcha coloring?"

She slid the coloring book toward Joan. "Cinderella. She's trying on a dress that some mice and birds made for her so she can go to the ball and meet the prince."

"That was nice of them."

She pulled the book back and applied her crayon, shaking her dark head. "She won't get to wear it, though. Her mean sisters tear it up."

"How sad for her."

Earnest dark eyes looked up into Joan's face. "Mice can't really sew."

175

Joan swallowed back a chuckle and kept her face as serious as Tiffany's. "I didn't think they could. But it's fun to pretend, isn't it?"

Tiffany nodded and continued coloring. She was such a beautiful girl, with smooth, toast-colored skin and the same jet-black hair as her mother. Normally an energetic child, she had certainly been quiet this afternoon. Amazing what a few Disney DVDs could do to calm a kid down.

"So I hear your daddy's coming home tonight?" Rosa had asked for tomorrow off so they could spend the day together as a family.

Tiffany's slender shoulders moved in a shrug, but the crayon continued its soft swishing across the page. Odd reaction. The kid should be ecstatic to finally see her father after two years. She seemed indifferent. Maybe she was nervous.

Joan picked up a crayon and waited until Tiffany moved to make room for her. "I know he'll be happy to see you."

She bent her head farther over her work, hiding her face from Joan. "I guess. You can do that mouse if you want." She pointed toward the page.

"Thanks." They colored silently for a moment. "I bet your dad has missed you very much."

She looked up. "Then why didn't he come home before?"

Uh-oh. Joan had just entered forbidden territory. This was absolutely none of her business, and she should shut her mouth right now.

But Tiffany's question shot through her and probed at that aching place in her own heart. Why didn't he? Joan had spent several years dreaming up a thousand reasons for her own father's continued absence. She'd never considered that poor little Tiffany might have spent the past two years doing the same.

Tiffany's crayon hovered over the page as she waited for an answer. Joan shook her head. "I don't know, sweetie. But the important thing is that he's coming now."

Her thin shoulders drooped. "Who cares? He'll leave again, and Mama will cry."

The waxy smell of crayons rose from the box when she opened the lid. She slid the slender blue stick back inside and extracted a red one. Joan's heart twisted in her chest. Poor kid, so young to learn such a painful lesson. If she let herself become hopeful, she would only be setting herself up for more pain when Luis left again. Then her mama wouldn't be the only one who cried. Better not to hope at all than to make herself vulnerable.

Joan opened her mouth to say, "Maybe not," but she closed it again. Fathers couldn't be trusted. Who knew that better than she did?

Rosa floated through the door Wednesday morning, her eyes full of twinkles. She threw herself into an overstuffed chair near the sales counter and bestowed a happy smile upon Joan.

Leaning against the counter with her arms crossed, Joan couldn't help laughing at her rapturous expression. "I guess Luis got home safely."

Rosa nodded. "He has not changed. The same handsome Luis. Only stronger, more, how you say . . ." She flexed an arm and patted a bicep.

"Muscles," Joan supplied.

Rosa sighed and leaned back. "*Sí*. More muscles. He worked at the house yesterday fixing the door and the washing machine. My Luis, he can fix anything. Today he is washing dishes at the restaurant."

Joan hoped he spent some time playing with his daughter as well. She kept her voice carefully even. "Was Tiffany glad to see him?"

Rosa's face clouded as she straightened in the chair. "She

was glad, yes, but quiet all day. He brought her a gift, a necklace made from Indians of the West. She said thank you with good manners, but would not wear it." She shook her head. "I think she is shy from not seeing him for a long time."

Joan nodded. "I'm sure that's it. She was really young when he left."

Rosa's expression cleared. "He brought a gift to me too. See?"

She held up a pendant for Joan's inspection. An oval of blue-green turquoise dangled from the end of a silver chain.

Joan ran a finger over the cool, smooth stone. "It's beautiful."

She dropped it to her chest and kept it covered with a hand. A joyful smile curved her lips. "He say he miss us too much. He say . . . pardon, *says* families should be together."

"So he's staying, then?"

A line appeared between her eyebrows, and she looked away. "Maybe. Or maybe we go with him."

Go? She would consider leaving Danville, leaving Abernathy's, leaving her? Joan clamped her jaws shut. This was none of her business. Rosa had every right to move out West if that's what it took to keep her family together. Joan was only her employer, nothing more.

So why did she feel so hurt, so . . . offended?

She heaved herself off the counter and walked to the other side. Rosa stood and followed.

"He has a good job in Nevada, working construction.

He *says* they pay lots of money on big buildings in Las Vegas."

"Las Vegas?" Joan widened her eyes. "Are you sure that's a good place to take Tiffany?"

Rosa's hands gestured wide. "Luis says lots of families are there, lots of nice places to live, and good schools. Las Vegas is a good place to live, not like on television."

That was probably true. But it was sure to be a lot different than little old Danville.

"I'll miss you and Tiffany." Joan was surprised to hear her voice catch, and turned away to straighten a stack of papers. How embarrassing. She didn't want to get emotional on the job.

Rosa laid a hand on her arm. "We do not decide now. Luis will start work in three weeks. We will talk more."

Joan put down the papers and forced herself to smile at Rosa. "I'm sure you'll make the right decision."

Joan picked up the phone and dialed home. The clock read 4:30. Hopefully Gram hadn't started supper yet.

"Hello?"

"Gram, I'm going to be late tonight, so don't plan on me for dinner."

A short silence. "But I've got Salisbury steak in the Dutch oven. You like Salisbury steak."

"I know, but something's come up and I need to go to Lexington. Why don't you give Allie a call? Eric's working tonight, and she loves your Salisbury steak."

Another pause. "I guess I could do that." Joan steeled herself against the distress in her grandmother's voice. She knew how Gram hated having her schedule disrupted. "But what will you eat?"

"Don't worry about me. I'll pick something up on the way."

"Why do you have to go to Lexington on such short notice?"

Not a question she wanted to answer at the moment. She glanced toward the appliances where Pat, the store's assistant manager, was pointing out the features of an upright freezer to a middle-aged woman. The rest of the store was empty. "Oops, there's a customer, Gram. I've got to go. I might be late, so don't wait up. Love you. Bye."

She replaced the receiver quickly, before Gram could ask any more questions.

❦

The Open Bible Church didn't even look like a church. It looked like a convention center. The parking lot was divided into sections with names like "Love" and "Faith" so you wouldn't lose your car. At a church! What was this place, Six Flags Over Jesus? Joan parked in the Hope section and sat clutching the steering wheel, her stomach in her throat. A stream of people strode past her car up the walkway toward a huge modern building that looked like it had been designed for the twenty-third century, with a roof slanted at artistic angles atop a gigantic entryway. The building itself was octagonal, and not a stained-glass window in sight. No doubt that this was a church, though. The sidewalk split around an enormous white cross that reached toward the sky on the front lawn.

What was she doing here? She hated reruns. She couldn't even stand to see a movie twice. What was it about the missionary woman that made Joan want to hear her again?

She hated going anywhere new alone. Could she have convinced Allie to come with her? She shook her head. No, she didn't want to have to try to explain to Allie why she wanted to hear Mrs. Sachs again. She couldn't even explain it to herself, really.

Inside the building, a woman approached Joan with a friendly smile the moment she stepped through the glass doors. "Hello. I don't think we've met. I'm Sandy."

Her hand caught in a soft, warm grip, Joan whiffed a subtle scent of roses as she returned the smile. "I'm Joan. I came to hear your guest speaker."

"We're glad to have you visit with us. The sanctuary is right through there. Sit anywhere you like." She gestured at the nearest set of open double doors, through which Joan glimpsed rows of chairs. "Not as many people come on Wednesday nights, so we close the balcony so we can get cozy down here."

Cozy? In this colossal building? "Thank you."

Joan stepped through the doorway and stopped, her jaw slack. This was not a sanctuary. It was more like a . . . a concert hall. Six sections of plush chairs in long rows filled the gigantic room. The carpeted floor slanted downward toward a huge stage in the center, where an elaborate drum set stood surrounded by an assortment of band instruments. The polished surface of a huge grand piano gleamed in the bright lights. The only thing that made this look like a church was the large illuminated cross on the back wall. Giant speakers hung suspended from the ceiling all around the auditorium, and two huge white screens flanked the cross.

Was this what Ken and Karen's church looked like?

Trying not to gawk like a country bumpkin, Joan selected a row near the back. She slipped into a chair on the aisle, her stomach fluttering. If anything weird happened, if anyone started rolling on the floor or shouting or anything like that, she intended to make a quick exit.

The stream of people filing into the auditorium slowed to a trickle a few minutes past 7:30. Only about a third of the chairs were filled, she estimated, which was still probably several hundred people. Christ Community Church saw a crowd this big a couple of times a year, on Easter Sunday and Christmas Eve. They'd given up Wednesday night services during the summer several years ago because not enough people showed up to justify running the air conditioner.

A slip of paper peeked from the pocket of the seat in front of her. Joan pulled it out. A bulletin from last Sunday. Curious, she flipped it open. No order of worship, no list of hymns, not even a sermon title. Instead, she read through the announcements, prayer requests, and a list of activities going on in the church throughout the week. The list continued on the back page, with youth activities and Bible studies and meetings in the coffee shop. Coffee shop? She looked again. Yes, apparently this church had its own coffee shop and a bookstore too. She even saw a notice listing the times those establishments were open for business.

But obviously they didn't believe in punctuality. Joan had glanced at her wristwatch a dozen times when finally, at 7:36, a door she hadn't noticed at the side of the stage opened and a troupe of people filed onto the platform. Several of them made their way to the instruments, while four people around Joan's age carrying microphones arranged themselves across the front of the stage facing the congregation. Mr. and Mrs. Sachs followed a thirty-something man in jeans and a golf shirt through the doorway. They walked down a set of steps and sat in chairs on the front row, much as they had at Christ Community, while the man Joan assumed to be the pastor crossed to the center of the stage to stand behind a simple wooden podium.

"Welcome, church. Tonight we're going to suspend our regular Wednesday teaching so we can hear from a special guest. I'll introduce her in a moment, but first, let's begin with prayer."

Joan stood along with the congregation and bowed her head as the pastor led them in a lengthy prayer. When he said Amen, Joan started to sit down. She stopped when he went on with, "Now let's lift our voices as our praise team leads us in worship of our awesome God."

The gigantic screens came to life as the band launched into a lively tune. Joan didn't recognize the song, but everyone around her knew it. They all sang, though she couldn't hear anyone over the sound of the instruments and the voices of the singers with microphones. The tune was simple, easy to follow. Joan joined in on the second verse, reading the words from one of the big screens in a soft voice.

When the song concluded, Joan looked toward the pastor, expecting him to step back up to the podium and make announcements. Instead, the band changed keys and launched into another. Uh-oh. Were they going to sing for thirty minutes like they did at Karen's church? Joan glanced at her watch again. It would be after 10:00 before she got home at this rate.

But the music was great. No doubt that band rehearsed a lot more than Christ Community's choir, which only practiced once a week during the Sunday school hour. These singers sounded so good they could have been a professional performing group. Two trumpet players stood up and played a duet. People applauded when they finished. If anyone ever tried to applaud at Christ Community, they'd probably be escorted from the service.

The third song was slower. The singers all had their eyes closed, and two of them raised a hand high above their heads, as though reaching toward heaven. Many of the people around Joan did the same. Down on the front row, Mrs. Sachs had her head thrown back and both arms stretched into the air, like a little girl who wanted her parents to pick her up.

Joan read the words on the screen as the congregation sang them.

> You are worthy, Lord,
> You are worthy, oh my Father,

You are my life, my love, my heart and soul
And I worship you.

When the music swelled on the last line, something rose from deep inside her and squeezed her throat. She closed her eyes. This wasn't like any song she'd ever heard at Christ Community. It was more . . . personal. This wasn't singing about God, this was singing to him, and it was far more intimate than anything Joan had ever done. Like opening up her heart and letting God see what was inside, in the place that no one, not even Joan, dared look.

And it was scary.

Tears prickled behind her eyes, and she squeezed her lids tight. Her fingers clutched the back of the chair in front of her. Whatever this was, she didn't like it one bit. She would not lose control and cry in front of all these people!

Thankfully, the song ended quickly. If the praise team started another one, she would leave. She half turned, ready to pick up her purse and head for the exit, when the pastor stepped to the podium. The people all around her sat down, and with a sigh of relief, Joan took her seat as well.

The pastor introduced Robert and Mary Alice. They both stood as the congregation applauded to welcome them. Mr. Sachs lifted a hand to wave as Mrs. Sachs mounted the stairs and went to stand behind the podium. Odd that he left the speaking to his wife. She had spoken of their work together in Afghanistan. Why didn't he tell his side of the story?

As Joan expected, Mrs. Sachs's message was the same as

the one she gave at Christ Community Church. But instead of being bored, Joan sat fascinated along with the rest of the congregation as she heard again how God miraculously provided the thousands of dollars necessary to build an orphanage in the midst of a war-ravaged village. The skin on her arms erupted with chills when Mrs. Sachs told them of a small pot of soup that somehow managed to fill the bowls of almost fifty starving children.

Then came the part that had hovered on the edge of Joan's thoughts for the past week and a half. She told how God answered the seemingly insignificant prayer of one orphaned boy.

Mrs. Sachs told the spellbound congregation, "We teach the children that our God is a personal God, that he cares for each of them more tenderly than any earthly father, and that he delights in giving them the desires of their hearts. Eight-year-old Rahim took us at our word. He came to Robert one day and said, 'My brother is a soldier. He told me ice cream is the most delicious food in the world. Do you think God would give me some ice cream?'" Mrs. Sachs paused. "Now this is hard for us in America to understand, because we can walk down to the corner store and buy an ice-cream bar anytime we want. But in that village, treats like that simply don't exist. They often don't have the food they need to survive, much less the ingredients to make ice cream. They don't have ice. They don't have electricity."

She directed a tender grin toward her husband. "But my husband has the faith of a giant. And he's a man of few words. His response to Rahim was, 'What flavor?'"

Joan laughed along with the rest of the congregation.

"I scolded him later for getting Rahim's hopes up, because I couldn't see any possible way to get chocolate ice cream for that boy. But we serve a God who loves to accomplish the impossible. Two days later, a helicopter was scheduled to deliver some much-needed medical supplies from the headquarters of a relief organization. The pilot told us their refrigeration unit malfunctioned right before he left camp. It wouldn't be fixed for days, and the director sent some of the frozen food along with him to donate to the orphanage."

Mrs. Sachs paused, and even though Joan knew what she was going to say, she held her breath.

"I nearly fell over in a dead faint when that man handed Robert a five-gallon container of chocolate ice cream."

The congregation burst into spontaneous applause, and Joan joined in, chills coursing down her spine.

Mrs. Sachs leaned forward on the podium. "You see, our God doesn't supply only what we need to scrape by. The almighty God is our Father. He loves us. He delights in delighting us. He wants to give us treats and enjoys hearing our joyful laughter in return."

That was it. That was the part Joan drove to Lexington tonight to hear. She leaned against the cushioned back of her chair, her mind whirling as she tried to grasp the point Mrs. Sachs had just illustrated. Was it merely an incredible coincidence, or did God really arrange for that little boy to have chocolate ice cream delivered via helicopter to his front door? The God Joan knew didn't act like that. Of course there was only one God, so why did he take such an active part in the life of an orphaned boy on the other side of the world, while he ignored her? That boy didn't have a father, but neither did Joan.

She didn't hear another word of Mrs. Sachs's message. An ache in her heart became a physical throb as her thoughts circled around a question. What was wrong with her? Something must be, because both of her fathers, earthly and heavenly, had deserted her.

When Mrs. Sachs sat down, the congregation responded with thunderous applause. The pastor announced that a love offering would be taken to help finance another orphanage the Sachs hoped to build, this one in Africa. He also said they would be in the coffee shop if anyone had any questions or wanted to chat. The service ended with another song led by the praise team, but Joan didn't even pretend to sing along. Instead, she scribbled out a check and tore it from her checkbook while the music blared from the speakers all around her.

When the congregation filed out of the auditorium, Joan followed along. She dropped her check into a bucket held by an usher at the door and smiled distractedly at the man's thanks. She paused only a moment before turning to the left and following the crowd past a bookstore and into a large café that looked like a Starbucks, only more crowded.

Clusters of smiling people stood scattered around the room, the sound of their chatter nearly drowning out the hiss of an espresso machine operated by two young women behind the counter. The smell of rich coffee, tinted with hazelnut, teased Joan's nostrils. Moments later Mr. and

189

Mrs. Sachs arrived, escorted by the pastor. A lively group of people immediately surrounded Mrs. Sachs. Joan backed up against a far wall, watching. She'd love an opportunity to talk to Mary Alice Sachs, to find out if her passion was as evident up close as it was when she spoke in front of a group. If only there weren't so many people milling around.

Maybe she could get a latte and wait for the crowd to thin. But the line at the counter was huge, and with only those two teenagers working, it would probably take forever.

She glanced at her watch. Nearly nine o'clock. She should probably just leave. She turned, her hand fumbling inside her purse for her car keys, and nearly ran into someone standing beside her.

"A little intimidating, isn't it?"

Joan looked up into the dark liquid eyes of Robert Sachs. His rich baritone held the hint of a chuckle. "The crowd, I mean. A lot different from your church over in Danville."

He recognized her? Inside her purse, keys jingled as her fingers made contact. "Yes, it is."

Large white teeth gleamed in his brown face as he smiled down at her. It was an infectious smile, and Joan's nervousness began to fade as she returned it. "I'm surprised you recognized me. We didn't meet when you were at my church."

"I never forget a pretty lady. You sat in the front on the right side of the sanctuary, beside an older woman."

"My grandmother." Joan's cheeks warmed at the

compliment. What an amazing memory! "I'm sorry we didn't stay to speak with you after the service. We had relatives coming for dinner."

"No apology necessary." He stuck out a hand. Joan switched the keys to her left and allowed him to engulf hers in a warm grasp. "Robert Sachs."

"Joan Sanderson."

He pumped her hand once before releasing it. "Nice to meet you, Miss Sanderson. I'm curious. Why did you come all the way up here to hear Mary Alice say the same thing all over again?"

Joan avoided his eyes, instead watching his wife who was the center of an animated conversation on the other side of the room. After a moment she shrugged a shoulder. "She's a very good speaker."

"That's why she does all the talking. I'm great with a hammer, but put me in front of a crowd and I freeze solid."

Joan smiled at his candid reply. "I'm sure I'd be the same."

She didn't look at him but watched Mrs. Sachs as she gestured with her hands to illustrate a point. After a moment, her gaze swept the room and came to rest on her husband. She beckoned him over with a quick wave.

Mr. Sachs smiled down at her. "I think I'm being summoned. It was nice to meet you, Miss Sanderson."

"You too." He stepped away, and Joan saw her chance for answers to her questions slipping away with him. She raised her voice and spoke to his back. "Uh, Mr. Sachs?"

He turned, his brows arched politely. Her breath caught

in her throat. She couldn't pour out her questions to this man, this stranger. But she had to say something to let him know the torment she was going through.

"I just wondered why God hasn't ever delivered chocolate ice cream to me."

What an idiotic question. She felt like a complete imbecile and wanted to slink into a corner and hide her face.

But Mr. Sachs didn't act as though it was a foolish question at all. One eyebrow rose as laughter twinkled in his eyes. "Have you ever asked him?"

"Uh . . . well, no."

A wide grin split his face. "Maybe you should."

He left Joan standing against the wall. She stared after him as he joined the group of people gathered around his wife.

Just ask? Cold fear clutched at Joan with an icy grip. She couldn't do that, couldn't ask God for anything. What if he said no? What if instead of ice cream, the helicopter that came to her house delivered something disgusting, like five pounds of frozen spinach?

More likely, nothing would happen at all. She'd be left wondering if that was God's way of saying no, or if he was just ignoring her. As usual.

~ *14* ~

"Hop in, boy." Ken held the door open, but Trigger extended his neck to stare suspiciously into the car and didn't budge.

"We're not going to the vet. Come on, get in."

Trigger looked up at him, obviously understanding Ken's request and considering whether or not to obey. His head drooped, and he turned to slink back to the safety of the house.

Ken held the leash in a firm grip when the dog reached the end of it. "You're not a dog. You're a gigantic chicken." He bent over and scooped the timid pup into his arms, and then deposited him without ceremony into the passenger seat. Trigger, apparently realizing that he had no choice in the matter, managed to reduce his size to half by curling into a tight ball while Ken slid behind the wheel and fastened his seat belt.

"Don't worry, we're not going far," he told the miserable animal.

Hot afternoon air blew into the car as Ken drove to the apartment complex where Mike lived. His bag in the backseat contained the equipment he needed to remove the boy's stitches, in case his mother hadn't already done so. He just hoped the kid remembered their agreement to meet today.

He pulled into the parking lot between the last two brick buildings. No sight of the group he saw last week, but there was one skinny boy sitting on the big rock that bordered the playground. When the Probe glided to a stop in a nearby parking space, the boy jumped down and walked toward the car, favoring his left foot. Ken did a double take. It was Mike, but his shaggy hair had been shorn, leaving a uniformed quarter-inch of fuzz all over his head.

"Hey, Mike," he called through the open window. "I didn't recognize you."

The kid ran a hand over his head. "Yeah, my granny said I couldn't start school looking like a beatnik, whatever that means."

Ken turned the key, and when the engine stopped, Trigger uncurled and hopped into Ken's lap to press a wet nose into his neck.

Mike's eyes grew round as he caught sight of him. "Hey! You got a dog."

Ken opened the car door. "Yeah, he's my roommate. His name's Trigger."

Trigger leaped out of the car and immediately jumped up to plant his paws on Mike's chest. Ken gave a stern "Down!" command, but the boy, with a delighted laugh, was already raking his hands roughly through the dog's neck and back fur, so Trigger ignored him. Shaking his head, Ken got out of the car. Karen's visit seemed to have put their obedience training back a few steps.

He retrieved his bag from the backseat. "How are those stitches doing?"

Mike shrugged. "Okay. They don't itch anymore."

"That's a good sign. You been keeping them clean?"

He nodded as Trigger jumped down and began investigating the grass in front of the car, his leash trailing behind him.

"Is it okay for him to check out the place, or should I put him in the car?"

"He's alright. Nobody here cares."

Looking around at the trash-covered ground and the broken-down playground equipment, Ken could believe it.

"So are we going to go to your place to take the stitches out?"

The boy's expression grew troubled, and he avoided Ken's eyes. "Uh, my mom's asleep, and she won't like it if we wake her up."

Figured. Though he wanted to get a look inside their apartment, he doubted if the kid's mother would welcome his visit, especially after the way she yelled at him in the emergency room. Did Mike even tell her that he was coming today? He didn't want to ask.

"No problem. We can do it out here. Hop up on the hood and take your shoe off."

While Mike did as directed, Ken opened his bag and pulled out an alcohol swab. Trigger, interested in the procedure, stood on his hind legs with his front paws on the bumper and watched as Ken gently wiped the wound. Not as clean as he would have liked, but a close inspection showed no sign of infection and the incision appeared to be healing nicely.

He tore open the disposable suture removal kit he'd grabbed from the hospital supply closet before leaving work, and took out the small scissors and a pair of sterile tweezers. "You're going to feel me tugging. It might be uncomfortable, but it won't hurt."

The boy nodded and leaned slightly away, his eyelids narrowing as he braced himself. Ken snipped all the stitches first, then pulled them out one at a time. Mike drew a hissing breath twice, but made no other sound.

"Okay," Ken said a minute later, "that's the last of them."

He sat up straight. "That wasn't so bad."

"I told you it wouldn't be." Ken wiped the incision with another alcohol swab and covered it with a bandage. He pressed a handful of extra bandages into the boy's hand. "Keep it clean and covered for another week or so, and be careful about running or jumping. But it should be fine."

"'Kay." He slid down off the car, landing with extreme care on his uninjured foot, shoved the bandages into a pocket, and then gave Trigger's head a brisk rub.

Ken watched Mike from the corner of his eye as he replaced the instruments in his bag. "Want to make a dog very happy?"

Mike looked up, interest brightening his features. "Sure."

Ken leaned through the open window to toss his medical bag into the backseat and pull out a tennis ball. The moment Trigger saw it, he started bouncing in circles on the pavement and managed to get his leash wrapped around a hind leg. Mike laughed at his antics.

"Come here, mutt, before you hurt yourself."

Ken unclipped the leash, then showed Trigger the ball before throwing it into the grassy field between the buildings. Trigger raced after it and managed to catch it on the second bounce.

"Hey, he caught it." Mike laughed, and shouted, "Way to go, Trigger."

When the proud dog bounded back to them, the ball in his mouth, Ken pointed toward the boy. "Give it to Mike."

Trigger hesitated a moment, looking from one to the other, then dropped the ball on the ground between them. Laughing, Mike picked it up and threw it.

"Wow," Ken said, watching the ball sail through the air toward the playground. "Do you play baseball?"

Mike scuffed a toe. "Nah."

"You should. You've got a good arm."

The kid's shoulders straightened, and his chin rose. Trigger raced back, but hovered uncertainly between the two of them and wouldn't release the ball. Mike had to pry it out of his mouth.

"We're still working on that." Ken shook his head as the kid sent the ball flying again. "He seems to understand that he has to bring it back so we'll throw it some more, but once he gets here he doesn't want to let go."

The third time, the dog took the ball straight to Mike. Obviously pleased, the boy ruffled the fur on his back before tossing it again. He rubbed his hand on his pants, a look of distaste coloring his features. "It's slimy."

"Yeah. I hate that part." Ken watched as Trigger interrupted his return trip to sniff at a patch of grass. "So your grandmother cut your hair, huh?"

A dirty hand unconsciously rubbed across the fuzz again. "Yeah. My mom didn't like it, either. She said she was gonna do it, but Granny beat her to it."

"Does your granny live in Danville?"

He nodded, but didn't elaborate.

"So school starts soon?"

"Next week." He scowled as though delivering bad news.

"Don't you like school?"

He shrugged, his eyes fixed on Trigger. Ken leaned against the Probe. Kids hated it when adults asked them about school.

"So where are your buddies today?"

Another shrug. "They're around."

Okay, so the kid decided to clam up all of a sudden. Obviously he didn't like being interrogated.

No other topics came to mind. Ken remained silent, watching the boy and the dog. No more questions. Sometimes all that was necessary was for someone to show an interest. He'd done that just by being here. Maybe that was enough for now.

Joan picked up a platter with two leftover chunks of meat from the center of the table and passed it to Gram across the kitchen counter.

Gram frowned at it. "It was too dry."

Behind Joan, Mom swept the empty mashed potato bowl off the table and took it to the sink. "Nonsense, Mother. Everything was delicious."

"It was better yesterday."

Joan ignored the flash of guilt she felt at the resentful glance Gram gave her. Allie had made plans for supper with friends, so Gram spent the evening alone with a Dutch oven full of Salisbury steak.

"It must have been terrific then," Joan said, "because it was great tonight. Put one of those in a container for me and I'll take it to work for lunch tomorrow. Rosa will be so jealous."

"Well." Gram sniffed. "You can take both pieces and share."

Joan grinned at her as she stacked their plates beside the sink. "She'll love it."

Mom turned on the faucet and plunged a finger under the flow, waiting for the water to warm. "Where did you go last night, anyway?"

Joan turned back toward the table and began gathering silverware. So far she had managed to avoid being questioned about her whereabouts. She really didn't want to discuss it, but she couldn't very well lie about going to church, could she?

Drawing a breath, she said, "I went to hear Mary Alice Sachs at the Open Bible Church."

Hands full of silverware, she turned to find both Mom and Gram staring at her with open mouths. Was it so unusual for her to want to go to church in the middle of the week? Apparently so. She deposited the silverware on top of the plates, avoiding either of their eyes.

Gram recovered herself first. "You said you had an errand to run."

"No, I just said I was going to Lexington."

"But I thought you were going for work." Gram shook her head. "You didn't tell me you were going to church."

"Would it have mattered?"

She gave another injured sniff as she smoothed plastic wrap over the leftover container. "I might have liked to go along if I'd known."

Guilt assaulted Joan. She never even considered that Gram might want to hear the missionary's talk again. How selfish of her. She opened her mouth to apologize but Mom cut her off.

"Honestly, Mother, Joan doesn't have to take you everywhere she goes."

Gram ducked her head at the stinging reprimand. Anger flared up in Joan. Didn't Mom realize how harsh her voice sounded?

She reached across the counter and covered Gram's hand with her own. "I'm sorry. I should have asked."

Mom turned toward the sink, presenting a rigid back. Eyes round, Gram gave Joan a wide-eyed glance and remained silent. Swallowing back a sigh, Joan went to the table to gather the napkins and place mats. Okay, maybe Mom didn't mean to be rude. Maybe she thought she was sticking up for her daughter in some weird way. But did she have to hurt Gram's feelings?

The atmosphere in the cozy kitchen grew awkward as a chilled silence stretched to an uncomfortable length. This never happened when Mom was at work, when it was just Joan and Gram alone in the house. Joan fought a rising resentment as she stepped around the counter and picked up a towel, ready to dry the dishes as Mom rinsed them.

"Actually," she said to Gram, more to break the silence than anything, "you probably wouldn't have liked it. The music was loud. They had drums and guitars."

Mom looked sideways to give her a thin smile. "So did she say anything new?"

Her voice was carefully polite, at which Joan heaved a relieved sigh. Conflict avoided. "No, it was the same talk she gave at our church. But she's a really good speaker." Joan dried the glass Mom handed her and placed it in the cupboard. "I . . . enjoyed it."

Mom rinsed a second glass and handed it to her. Taking it, Joan turned away to avoid her inquisitive blue eyes.

Gram placed the container in the refrigerator. "Alice Shropshire called today. She has a new great-grandbaby, a boy."

She told them all the details of Mrs. Shropshire's great-grandson as they finished up the dishes. Then Mom went downstairs to find her book while Joan and Gram settled on the living room couch in front of the television.

As soon as Mom disappeared down the stairs, Joan said in a low voice, "I'm sorry I didn't ask you to go with me last night. I should have."

Gram patted her arm. "Nonsense. Carla's right. You need to do things on your own. You don't need an old woman tagging along all the time."

Joan squeezed her hand. "I love having you tag along." She fell silent a moment, then asked the question that had burned in her mind since she left the Open Bible Church last night. "Gram, do you think God really does things like Mrs. Sachs described?"

Gram stared at the television set as she punched the remote button. "Oh, I expect he does. Just not here."

"But why not?"

"Because we don't need him to." Gram turned her head to smile at Joan. "We live quiet lives here, so we don't have any need for dramatic miracles. He knows that. For us, it would be disruptive."

Joan looked away. Maybe Gram was right. She certainly spent more time reading the Bible than Joan.

Having found a program she liked, Gram put the remote control down on the coffee table. "Some people aren't like us, though. People like Ken, next door. They like life to have more flare, more drama. That's why there are all sorts of churches, so everyone can find one where they're comfortable. It doesn't mean theirs is wrong, just different."

Joan tilted her head, considering. There was probably some truth in that. Not everybody would be comfortable having a helicopter land on their front lawn to deliver the ice cream.

But surely God knew that. If he wanted to, couldn't he use a quiet, nondisruptive delivery method?

On the other hand, wouldn't it be cool to see something

exciting, something so out of the ordinary that it changed people's lives? Joan understood better than anyone Gram's need for order, for a routine. She felt the same about a lot of things. But maybe a little disruption every now and then wasn't a bad idea.

Mom came back upstairs, her book in hand. "I'm going to make a cup of tea. Does anyone else want one?"

"No, thank you," Gram said, her attention fixed on the screen.

Joan shook her head. Mom disappeared into the kitchen, and Joan heard water running. She pictured Mom filling the teakettle, setting it on the stove, turning the burner on, taking a mug down from the cabinet, going for—

"Mother!"

Beside her, Gram started at the sharp tone in Mom's voice. She looked up as Mom stomped through the doorway, Gram's pillbox clutched in her hand.

"You haven't taken your blood pressure medicine all week."

Gram's expression clouded with confusion. "I haven't?"

Mom tossed her head upward and gave an exasperated grunt. "No, you haven't." She spoke in an exaggerated voice. "What is the point of having this pillbox if you can't even remember to open it every day?"

She shook the pillbox in Gram's direction to emphasize her words. Gram's shoulders drooped as though she were a guilty child being scolded. At the sight of her bowed white head, searing anger shot through Joan. Before she could stop herself, she jumped to her feet and crossed the room in three steps to jerk the pillbox out of her mother's hand.

"What is the matter with you?" she shouted. "Why do you treat her like a child?"

Mom's mouth dropped open, her eyes round behind her glasses. Joan stormed past, fury pounding in her ears. In the kitchen her face felt hot, her heartbeat uncomfortably fast in her chest, but she ignored those things and focused instead on opening the pillbox and filling a glass with water. Then she stomped back to the living room, ignoring Mom as she slapped the pills and water down onto the coffee table in front of Gram.

"Don't worry," she told her wide-eyed grandmother. "I'll remember to check the pillbox every day for you."

With that she left the room and ran down the stairs. She closed her bedroom door behind her, and then paced back and forth between the closet and her nightstand. Her pulse raced, while a sick feeling settled deep in her stomach, turning her dinner into an uncomfortable lump. What had she just done? She never shouted, not since she was a kid. As teenagers Allie and Tori threw fits all the time, and Mom raised her voice whenever she was angry, but Joan was the calm one, the one who never lost control.

In some distant section of her brain, a part that was calmly observing this un-Joan-like behavior, she realized the irony of shouting at her own mother because she shouted at hers.

A knock sounded on the door. Mom, of course. Joan considered telling her to go away. She wasn't ready to talk yet, not while her breath was still coming in angry gulps and blood still roared in her ears.

But Joan was accustomed to obeying and habit stepped in. She took a deep breath. "Come in."

Mom opened the door wide enough to slip her thin frame through, and closed it behind her. Her lips were pressed so tightly together that deep lines creased her skin at the edges of her mouth. Her eyes blazed as she captured Joan's gaze and held it.

"You want to tell me what that was all about?" Her lips clamped shut the minute she forced the words out.

Joan dropped into the chair beside her bed. "I just don't see why you have to be so disrespectful to her."

Mom's eyebrows disappeared beneath her bangs. "Disrespectful? I'm trying to keep her healthy."

The words shot out of Joan's mouth before she could stop them. "Sounds to me like you're trying to get rid of her."

Mom's jaw dropped. "What are you talking about?"

"Oh come on, you're always talking about how forgetful she is, and the other day you took her to that nursing home." Her mother sucked in a breath, but Joan corrected herself. "Excuse me, *assisted living center*."

Mom's eyelids narrowed at the sarcasm in Joan's tone. "So that's what this is about. You think I'm trying to come up with a reason to send her away."

Joan clenched the arms of the chair. "Aren't you?"

"No." She gave her head a firm shake. "But I do admit I think Waterford would be good for her."

Her words washed over Joan like a bucket of icy water. Her anger fled in an instant, leaving a sick feeling in her stomach and her hands clammy. She rubbed them on her pants.

Mom crossed to the bed and perched on the edge of it. "I have a couple of reasons for thinking that. First of all, she isn't as alert as she used to be." Joan drew breath to protest, but Mom held up a hand to stop her. "I'm not saying she's senile, far from it. But she used to be so active and have so many friends. Now instead of getting out and doing things, she stays home and alphabetizes the laundry. She's lonely, honey. There are lots of people her age at Waterford, and several of her old friends. Socializing with them would keep her alert."

"But if you take her out of her home, away from everything she's ever known, she'll go downhill." Her voice trembled, and she swallowed hard. "She'll die."

Mom shook her head. "Joan, you don't know what you're talking about. That place isn't a cold, impersonal institution. It's more like a country club."

Tears stung behind Joan's eyes, and she drew a shuddering breath as she fought to keep them back. "But this is her home. She deserves to grow old gracefully in it if that's what she wants."

"I absolutely agree."

Startled, Joan searched Mom's face. "You do?"

"Of course I do." Her shoulders drooped as she heaved a sigh. "I know I'm sometimes too harsh with her, but I love her, and blood pressure medicine is nothing to mess with. I'll start laying her medicine out when I get home so she remembers to take it. I should have done that before, instead of buying that pillbox."

"I don't mind doing it."

"I know you don't, and that's the second reason I think Waterford would be a good move. Because of you."

Joan sat up straight in the chair. "Me?"

"Yes, you. You've taken too much responsibility for her care." She smiled. "That's commendable, honey, but you're twenty-five years old. You've got your own life to live."

"I am living my own life. Maybe this is what I want." Joan's chin rose. "She's my grandmother."

"Yes, and she's my mother." Mom's mouth stretched into a tight smile. "If she's anybody's responsibility, she's mine."

The words shot into Joan like a bullet. That was the problem. If it ever came down to a decision, Gram would bow to Mom's wishes. Mom, not Joan, was in control. Mom had the power to send Gram away, just like she'd sent Daddy away.

Unshed tears prickled painfully. Someone she loved dearly, someone who loved her, could be taken away from her and she wouldn't be able to do a thing about it.

Mom's voice cut softly into Joan's fierce struggle to contain the sob that threatened to choke her. "Joan, when did I become the enemy?"

When you drove my daddy away. But Joan couldn't say that, couldn't say anything. Her throat felt caught in a vise.

Mom stood and crossed the room to stand in front of her chair. She leaned over, took Joan's shoulders in her warm hands, and pressed a kiss on the top of her head. "I love you, honey. You know that, don't you?"

Joan closed her eyes. Mom's favorite lilac-scented lotion

filled her nostrils as the padlock on her emotions clicked open. A hot tear slipped first down one cheek and then the other. That was the problem, of course. She knew Mom loved her. But Mom never understood her, not like Daddy did. Daddy was quiet, introspective, peaceful to be around. As a little girl, Joan would crawl into his lap at the end of the day and they would sit in silence, just enjoying one another's presence without having to say a word. Mom was talkative and boisterous, like Allie and Tori. She didn't have a clue what it meant for Joan to lose the only person in the family who was like her.

And Joan didn't have the words to explain it to her.

She put her hands over her mother's and squeezed. "I love you too, Mom."

It was true, but it didn't make anything better.

~ 15 ~

"You are coming, and that's all there is to it."

Joan leaned against the sales counter and swallowed a sigh so Tori couldn't hear it through the phone. "I've had a really busy week, and I was looking forward to just sitting at home tonight."

"Joan, listen to yourself! This is Saturday night. You can sit at home every other night of the week, but not on Saturday. And besides, if we don't do this soon, we may not have the chance for a long time. Allie's going to have the baby next month, you know."

Tori had a point. When Allie married Eric, the dynamics of the sisters' relationship had been altered. Another personality was inserted into their trio, his presence felt even when he wasn't there. The arrival of a baby would mean even more drastic changes.

Actually, Joan had another reason for not wanting to go to Lexington tonight for a Sanderson Sister Sleepover, but she felt hesitant to mention it. She wasn't sure how Tori and Allie would react when she told them she wanted to be home in time for Sunday school in the morning.

"Maybe we could do it next Saturday, and that way we can make some plans."

Tori's voice held a faint touch of criticism. "You can't plan your entire life. Be impulsive! Be reckless! Let something spur-of-the-moment disrupt your schedule every now and then."

Joan's legs went wobbly, and she dropped into a chair. Did Tori just use the word *disrupt*, the very word Gram used two nights ago to describe the miracles Mrs. Sachs talked about? Surely that word choice was a coincidence. God wouldn't arrange something as trivial and unreligious as a Sanderson Sister Sleepover just to introduce a little disruption into Joan's life.

Would he?

Why did she feel suddenly like God was watching, waiting to see what she would do? Clutching the receiver, she steadfastly refused to look toward the ceiling, which, of course, was stupid. God wasn't up there peeking through a peephole in the roof. That was beyond stupid, just like the notion of God putting the idea of a sleepover into Tori's brain. To think her materialistic little sister could be a messenger from heaven was laughable. Tori never even talked about God, and she refused to go out with Ken because he did.

Joan's head swam. Maybe a night with her sisters wasn't a bad idea after all. Heart pounding, and still avoiding the ceiling, she schooled her voice to remain calm. "You're right. I'll be there."

"Terrific!" Tori's giggle sounded in her ear. "Allie's expecting you to pick her up at 7:30. She's bringing a bunch of DVDs, and I'll go to the store and stock up on Doritos and Dr Pepper."

"Sounds good. I'll see you tonight."

Joan replaced the receiver and sat listening to her pulse pound in her ears. What a totally ludicrous thought that God would want her to choose a sleepover with her sisters over Sunday school. An evening of Doritos and Dr Pepper? Nothing even remotely religious about that. She risked an upward glance. Nothing up there but the ceiling, and the feeling of being watched was gone. A ridiculous notion, anyway. She was letting her imagination get the best of her.

∞

"I love this place." Allie waltzed through Tori's front door and executed a 360 as she admired the spacious living room. "You're so lucky, Tori."

Joan followed, an overnight bag slung on each shoulder. While Tori closed the door behind them, she looked at the entertainment center that dominated an entire wall, and ran a hand across the top of a big flat-screen television set. "This is new, isn't it?"

"I've had it about a month." Tori caught her in a hug, her grin so wide double dimples punctuated her cheeks. "I'm so glad you guys are here."

Allie pulled a stack of DVDs out of the plastic sack she carried and held them up with a flourish. "We're going to have a Hugh-fest tonight."

"Hugh-fest?" Joan asked.

"Hugh Jackman and Hugh Grant."

211

Tori grabbed *Kate & Leopold* and clutched it to her chest. "I love this movie! Let's watch it first."

She whirled and dropped to her knees to put the disc into a DVD player.

"I'm starved." Allie turned toward the kitchen. "What's there to eat?"

"I ordered pizza about ten minutes ago. It'll be here soon."

"Where are we sleeping?" Joan patted hers and Allie's overnight bags. "I'll put these away."

Tori jumped to her feet and grabbed the bags from her. "I don't have any furniture in the second bedroom yet, so I'll put them in my room. But it won't matter," she said over her shoulder as she disappeared down the hallway. "Nobody's sleeping tonight anyway."

"Maybe not," Allie said, coming out of the kitchen with a handful of Doritos, "but I'm going to get comfortable in my PJs and slippers."

Joan snatched a chip from Allie's hand, chuckling. Nobody ever slept at a sleepover. They'd eat and laugh and watch movies all night long. They'd be tired and cranky in the morning, and they'd probably be in bed by six o'clock tomorrow night.

Tori came back into the room carrying the open Doritos bag and a can of bean dip, which she put on the coffee table. She dropped into a chair while Allie positioned herself on the sofa within easy reach of the dip. Joan sat on the other side.

"So what's up with the religious nut?" A chip poised before her mouth, Tori pierced Joan with a blue stare.

Joan gave a bewildered shrug. "I haven't seen any sign of him in a week."

Actually, she hadn't even thought about Ken much for the past couple of days. Instead, her thoughts had revolved around Mrs. Sachs and her ice cream story, and Thursday night's conversation with Mom.

"I'm totally shocked," Tori said. "The way he was checking you out last Sunday, I was sure he would call you."

"Me too," chimed in Allie. "Especially after his sister told Joan he was interested in her."

"What?" Tori's eyelids narrowed. "You met his sister? What did she say?"

Joan searched her little sister's face but saw no sign of jealousy there. One thing about Tori, when she decided to move on, she didn't hold any grudges. There wasn't a resentful bone in her dainty little body.

But there was something else there, something that made Joan uneasy. Disdain, maybe? Ken's outspokenness about his faith had apparently left a bad taste in Tori's mouth. That worried Joan who suddenly realized she would feel weird dating a guy her sister disliked.

But for that to happen, Ken would have to actually be interested enough in her to ask her out on a date. And so far Karen appeared to be wrong.

She shrugged again. "She said she thought he liked me, but if he does, he has a funny way of showing it."

"Men are weird." Allie scooped bean dip on a chip. "Take Eric, for instance. Do you know what he wants to name our baby?" She paused for effect, looking first Joan and then Tori in the eye. "Wilhelmina."

Tori threw back her head and laughed, while Joan raised an eyebrow. "Wilhelmina? Is it, like, a family name or something?"

Allie shook her head. "No, he just heard it somewhere. And that's not all. He wants to call her Willie."

She bit into the chip as Tori exclaimed, "Willie? What is he trying to do, destroy the poor child's life? The kids at school will terrorize her."

"Don't worry." Allie chomped a few times and swallowed. "I won't let that happen. I've gone through life as Alana Grace, remember? No weird names for my kid."

Joan turned a surprised stare on her older sister. "What's wrong with Alana Grace? I've always thought your name was beautiful."

Sheer disbelief stole over Allie's features. "You've got to be kidding. Whoever heard of Alana? It sounds like something out of Greek mythology. I swear Mom and Daddy were high on something when they came up with that one."

"But it's unique, it's special."

"It's weird." Allie grimaced, and then patted her belly protectively. "My daughter's going to have a normal name."

Tori leaned forward and fished a chip out of the bag. "And no nicknames, please. Don't do that to a poor innocent baby."

"Don't worry, I wouldn't."

Joan's head swiveled from her younger to her older sister, even more stunned. "What's wrong with nicknames?"

"They're embarrassing, that's what," Tori said.

Allie nodded. "For the first week of every school year,

before the teacher learns your nickname, they call you by your real name in front of everyone. I was mortified. I hated starting school because of that."

"C'mon, I'm sure that happened to a lot of kids. Nobody noticed."

Tori tilted her head, thinking. "Nope. I'm sure I was the only one in my class who suffered that public humiliation. And yes, the other kids did notice." She shuddered. "I'll never forget Rodney Black's voice when he teased me. 'Vic-TOOOO-ree-uh.' And do you know how many Queen Victoria jabs I put up with?"

"At least Victoria is a name somebody heard of," Allie complained. "In fourth grade Mrs. Vaughan didn't pronounce mine right. The kids used to call me Alana Banana on the playground."

Joan couldn't believe what she was hearing. She had no idea her sisters felt this way. She'd always considered their names beautiful, unlike her own. "But nicknames are cool," she insisted. "They're a term of endearment. Not like my name."

Tori cocked her head. "What are you talking about? Joan is a great name."

"Oh puh-lease!" Joan scoffed to hide a rising resentment. "It's so . . . plain. You guys got the good names, the ones with personality. Who was I named after? Some old dead aunt."

"She died of breast cancer when Mom was pregnant with you." Tori's voice held a hint of reprimand. "She was Gram's only sister, and everyone said she was a really neat lady."

"Maybe she was," Joan admitted, grudgingly. "But she had a boring name. Did you ever notice that nobody called me by a nickname? I was always just plain old Joan."

"You just don't remember," Allie told her. "Daddy had a nickname for you."

Joan swiveled toward her older sister. "He did?"

"Sure. When you were little he called you Buggie."

Joan stared at Allie as forgotten memories resurfaced and washed over her. Her throat threatened to close up. She could see Daddy catching her up in his arms, swinging her high in the air and saying, "How's my little Buggie today?"

"I remember that," Tori said, smiling. "I always wondered where it came from."

Allie smirked. "When she was about three, she ate a June bug."

"Eeewwww, disgusting!" Tori made gagging noises.

"Daddy told her she couldn't eat bugs or she would turn into one. He teased her by calling her his little Joan Bug, and then it got shortened to Buggie."

Joan managed a smile. "You're right. I had forgotten."

The doorbell sounded, and Tori jumped up. "There's the pizza."

"Thank goodness." Allie settled back into the cushion. "I'm starving."

Joan went into the kitchen and filled three glasses with ice and Dr Pepper while Tori settled up with the pizza guy. They watched *Kate & Leopold* while they ate. Tori's big television screen made Joan feel almost like they were at the movies. They sighed over Hugh Jackman's sexy good looks and poked fun at Meg Ryan's ragged haircut in loud voices that would surely have gotten them evicted from a theater.

When the movie ended, Tori replaced it in the machine with *Notting Hill*.

"Ah." Allie gazed dreamily at the DVD cover. "I just love Hugh Grant."

Tori giggled. "Bad boys are the most fun, aren't they?"

Joan thought of Ken. Definitely not a bad boy. Was he fun? She didn't know. And the way things were going, she probably wouldn't have an opportunity to find out.

"Not for marrying," Allie said. "You girls need to find a decent man to marry, like I did."

Tori returned to her chair and picked up the remote control. "I don't think I'm going to get married."

Joan looked at her. "Why not?"

"I don't want to take a chance." She picked up an un-eaten pizza crust and used it to emphasize her words. "The divorce rate is too high these days."

"It's scary," agreed Allie. "But some things are worth the risk. You know what they say, ''Tis better to have loved and lost than never to have loved at all.'"

Tori turned a sharp look her way. "Do you think Mom feels that way?"

A blast of disgust burst from Joan's lips, drawing surprised stares from both her sisters. "I highly doubt it."

"Why do you say that?" Tori nibbled at the crust.

"Well . . ." Joan looked from her to Allie. "Obviously she's not pining over lost love. She's the one who chose divorce. She kicked Daddy out."

Allie's eyebrows drew together. "Are you serious?"

Why did she have such a look of disbelief on her face? Joan swept her gaze to include both sisters. "Well, that's what happened."

"So you would have let him stay? You would put up with a pot-smoking husband who slept with every woman he knew, including your best friend?"

Joan's jaw dropped. No! That wasn't true. Not Daddy. He didn't sleep around. He couldn't have. Surely she would have known something like that. And yes, she remembered that he smoked, but pot?

"Daddy fooled around on Mom?" Tori's eyes were wide as saucers.

"Constantly." Allie peeled a piece of pepperoni off a slice of lukewarm pizza and popped it into her mouth. "Once when I was about thirteen, I came around the corner of the house and caught him kissing Jessie Nelson's mother."

"I remember her," Tori said. "She lived down the street at our old house."

Joan remembered her too. And she remembered that although Mom was always kind to Jessie when she came over to play, she didn't like Mrs. Nelson and wouldn't speak to her. Joan gulped. She also remembered coming home from school one day to find Mom standing in the front yard with her best friend, Patti Keller. Mrs. Keller stood beside her car, crying, and Mom's face had been full of anguish. They wouldn't look at each other when she ran up to give Mom a hug. Something terrible had happened, but when she asked what was wrong, Mom told her to go inside the house. She never saw Mrs. Keller again.

"Cigarettes," she managed to choke out. "Daddy smoked cigarettes, not pot."

"Don't be so naïve, Joan." Allie gave her a disgusted look. "He got stoned every night. I found his stash out in the garage and took it to Mom."

"Daddy?" Tori's voice shook. "Our father was a pot-head?"

Allie turned a look of compassion on her. "Maybe I'm exaggerating. He probably didn't get stoned every night. But he definitely got high."

"Why haven't you talked about this before?" Joan demanded. "If you knew this all along, why didn't you tell us?"

"Hey, don't get hyper with me. You know very well the subject of Daddy has been taboo since he left. That's the way Mom wanted it, and I respected her wishes."

Tori nodded slowly. "Mom's always been really close-mouthed about Daddy. I've never had the nerve to talk to her about him. I didn't want to hurt her."

Joan was aware that Allie was watching her closely, but she had trouble meeting her sister's eye. Tori was right. They'd all seen how Mom clammed up whenever they mentioned Daddy. He was one subject the sisters had learned to avoid almost instinctively. Even among themselves.

"I can't believe you didn't know this, Joan," Allie said. "You were twelve when they divorced. That's old enough to notice things."

Joan stared at the floor, numb. "I guess maybe I didn't want to notice."

Allie scooted over on the couch and laid a hand on

her arm. "I'm sorry. I shouldn't have been so harsh. But I think silence is unhealthy. It's time we talked about this."

Tori got out of the chair and came to sit beside them on the cushion Allie had just vacated. She leaned over to put a hand on top of Allie's, and laid her head on Allie's shoulder. "I always wondered why Daddy left. I . . . figured it was my fault."

Joan's eyes flew to Tori's face. "Your fault? How could it be your fault? You were only nine."

She lifted a shoulder. "They say kids always blame themselves."

"I know I did." Allie's forehead creased. "I knew about his affairs, but I figured if I hadn't told Mom about the marijuana, if I'd kept his secret, maybe she wouldn't have felt the need to kick him out. She'd put up with his affairs for so long, but it was like that pot was the last straw. I always wondered if she was trying to protect us from being around drugs."

A vise squeezed around Joan's chest, and each breath came hard. All these years she'd interpreted Mom's silence as an admission of guilt. Joan blamed Mom for driving her father away, when it turned out Mom was only protecting her girls.

"But she didn't even let him visit," she said, her voice choked with unshed tears. "Why didn't she let him come see us, or even call us?"

Allie's hand squeezed her arm. "You think she kept him from us? No, Joan. She wouldn't have done that. The minute the divorce papers were signed, he took off and she never heard from him again. He never paid a cent of child support, the jerk. That's why we had to move in with Gram and Grandpa."

Joan squeezed her eyes shut, shaking her head. No, that wasn't right. She didn't want to think that about Daddy. He wasn't a jerk. He was just weak. He'd never been strong enough to stand up to Mom in anything. He was gentler, quieter, more like her. That's why it was easy to forgive him, to find someone else to blame.

But what kind of father would desert his own daughters?

She swallowed back the tears that threatened to slip down her cheeks. "I . . . guess I knew that. But for some reason I placed the biggest part of the blame on Mom."

"Transference," Allie said. "It's a normal reaction."

Giggling, Tori sat up. "I love having our own personal psychologist."

"This is serious." Allie poked her arm with a fist, then turned back toward Joan. "Daddy hurt you, but you couldn't express your anger toward him. So you turned your anger on someone else. And Mom was a safe target, because you knew she would continue to love you even if you were mad at her. You knew she would never leave you."

"This is exactly why I'm not getting married." Tori stood. "Look what their divorce did to us. And the statistics say children of divorced parents are a lot more likely to divorce themselves. I don't want to go through another one. It's not worth the risk."

Allie's hand curled around her tummy. "But don't you want to have children yourself someday?"

Tori shrugged. "If I do, I'll visit a sperm bank. That way nobody gets hurt."

Joan laughed at the outrageous idea of Tori calmly sifting through a stack of forms to select a donor for her child. "Not me. I want my children to have a father, a good one." She smiled toward Allie. "One like Eric."

Only Christian.

Startled, Joan brushed at a crumb on her jeans. Not often your own thoughts surprise you, but that one came out of nowhere. Probably her conversation with Karen the other day was still rolling around in her mind.

Tori bent over and placed both hands on Allie's belly. "Yes, but Eric is one of a kind." She straightened. "I'll be right back, and then we can start the next movie."

She left the room, and Allie grinned at Joan. "She'll change her mind when she meets Mr. Right." She heaved herself off the couch. "I'm going to use her other bathroom."

Alone in the living room, Joan wondered if Allie was right. Was there a Mr. Right out there for Tori? And one for Joan, maybe even a Dr. Right? A grin stole across her lips at the thought, but then it faded. What if her judgment was somehow damaged when it came to men? She thought she knew Roger, but he hurt her, left her for another woman. She sucked in a breath. Just like Daddy!

These revelations about Daddy's affairs and his pot smoking had come as surprises, but she knew deep inside that they were true. Which meant she had known as a girl, but chose to ignore the signs. The father she thought she knew wasn't real. He had deserted her. She always thought he was out there somewhere, thinking of her, loving her from far away. But now she realized she never really knew Daddy at all. And what good was love from a distance, anyway?

Mary Alice Sachs's voice sounded in Joan's mind, as if in silent answer to her unspoken question. *The almighty God is our Father. He loves us. He delights in delighting us.*

A heavy stillness stole over the room, an almost electric feeling that prickled the skin along Joan's arms. A clock on the wall ticked, echoing her heartbeat. The answer to her questions was all around her, as though a curtain had been suddenly opened to flood the room with bright sunlight only her soul could see.

She did have a father, and he was almighty God.

She squeezed her eyes shut against a wave of tears. But if he loved her, why was he so remote? He wasn't distant from Mr. and Mrs. Sachs, or from Ken, or even from that orphan boy, Rahim. But for Joan, God was just like her own father, out there somewhere, loving her from far away when what she really needed was someone right here. No dramatic miracles, no helicopters. Just a little reminder every now and then that he cared.

She heard the bathroom door open, and Tori's footsteps go into the kitchen. A drawer opened, silverware rattled. Joan gulped a deep breath and managed to get her emotions under control as her little sister came around the corner.

"Okay, I'm ready." Tori's hands were full, and she turned to share her burden with Allie, who followed her into the room.

"Oh, yummy," said Allie. "Moose Tracks, my favorite."

Joan's jaw dropped as Tori thrust something toward her.

She stared at it without moving, her hands lying like lead in her lap.

"I knew that's what you liked." Tori grimaced in Allie's direction. "But I think it's disgusting. So I got each of us a pint of our own. This is your favorite, isn't it, Joan?"

Joan could only nod as she took the spoon and a pint of chocolate ice cream from her sister's hand.

~ 16 ~

Joan awoke to a pain in her right shoulder. She rolled onto her back, reached up with her left hand, and grabbed the hard object. A peek through groggy eyes confirmed that she'd been lying on the remote control to Tori's television.

She struggled to sit up, her back stiff from sleeping on the hard floor. Beside her, Tori was curled into a ball, hugging a pillow. A backward glance told her Allie had moved to the couch sometime during the night.

Correction. Sometime during the morning. At 4:00 a.m., bellies bloated with pizza and ice cream, they spread Tori's comforter out on the floor in front of the entertainment center and propped themselves on pillows to watch *X-Men*. The screen showed the disc menu now, though she must have lain on the Mute button. The only sounds in the room were the ticking of the wall clock and a gentle snore coming from the direction of the couch.

She glanced at her watch. 8:24. If she hurried, she could get back to Danville in time to shower and still make it to Sunday school.

Her jeans were in Tori's bedroom, and she tiptoed down the hall so she wouldn't disturb her sisters. She didn't know why it seemed so important to go to Sunday school this morning. But if God was interested in having an up-close relationship with her, and apparently he was, she needed some answers. Church seemed like the logical place to get them.

Dressed and clutching her overnight bag, she hesitated in the living room. Should she wake Tori and Allie, let them know that she was leaving? No. They'd want an explanation, and Joan wasn't sure she could explain herself. Or that they would understand.

She left a note telling them she'd see them at home for Sunday dinner and slipped out the door.

Ken swiped the last of the shaving cream from his chin with his razor, watching his reflection in a cleared section of the steamy mirror. He yawned hugely. It had been a long, boring night at the hospital, and what he really wanted to do was fall into bed for a few hours. But it was Sunday morning, and if he wanted to find a church in town, he had to stay awake long enough to attend one. From the clock radio in his bedroom, the Newsboys admonished him to *Shine!* as he splashed warm water on his face.

Someone pounded on the front door. Trigger leaped up from his position in the center of the doorway and ran, barking excitedly, through the house. Ken dried his face and glanced at the clock. 9:15. Odd time for a visitor.

He slipped on a handy pair of scrubs and followed Trigger into the living room.

"Calm down," he told the excited dog, who was twirling in circles in front of the door.

He grabbed Trigger's collar and hauled him backward, holding on so the pup didn't assault whoever waited on the front porch. When he swung the door open, his eyes widened in surprise.

"Joan."

She looked tired. Her hair was pulled sharply back from her high forehead, and her eyelids drooped over her eyes. The skin beneath them was puffy, like she'd had a hard night.

"Is everything alright?"

"Uh," she stammered, "fine. Everything's fine."

Her gaze dropped to his chest, and then she turned her head to look away, her cheeks red. An answering heat crept up his neck. Why hadn't he taken a minute to put on a shirt?

"Hey, Trigger." A smile lit her face as she ruffled the dog's ears. Trigger's tail looked like he might take flight. "How've you been, boy?" She raised her smile to Ken for a second. "He's growing."

"He's eating me out of house and home. But he's learned a few things. Watch this." He bent over to look Trigger in the eye, and when he had the dog's attention, released his collar. "Trigger, sit."

The dog's hindquarters dropped to the ground.

"Hey, that's great!"

At Joan's exclamation, Trigger leaped up, this time to plant his paws on her chest, his tail going crazy.

"No, down!" Ken grabbed him by the collar and hauled him into the house. "You just stay in there for a minute." He ignored the reproachful canine expression and closed the door. Then he turned back to Joan with a sheepish grin. "We're working on not jumping on people, but he forgets."

"You're doing a good job with him." She plucked at a string on the pocket of her jeans. "I was wondering if you'd like to go to church with us again this morning."

That was a surprise. He'd thought of her several times during the week, but something always stopped him from calling her. His hesitation was only partly due to a busy schedule.

"Well, uh, actually I was thinking of trying another church today."

"Oh." She nodded. "Okay. No big deal."

She flashed a brief smile his way, and then turned to leave. Something about the droop of her shoulders made Ken want to keep her here, to keep her talking. "Uh, Joan?"

She stopped, looking back at him.

"Are you alright?"

A tired smile lit her face. "I'm fine. Allie and I spent the night at Tori's, and I didn't get much sleep, that's all."

As if to prove her point, she covered a yawn with her hand. Why were yawns contagious? Ken hid his own, which made her laugh.

"I guess I'm not the only one who didn't get any sleep last night."

"Long night at the hospital."

She nodded, and backed down the first step. Then she

stopped again. "I don't know how far you want to drive to go to church, but there's one in Lexington you might like. It's called the Open Bible Church. I visited there Wednesday night."

"You did?" That was a surprise. He'd figured her for a Sunday-morning-only gal.

"They have a good praise band, and though I didn't hear their pastor speak, he seemed really . . . ," her gaze shifted away as she tried to come up with a word, ". . . genuine."

She continued to surprise him today. Where was the flirty girl of last week? He folded his arms across his chest. If only there was a dirty sweatshirt within reach.

"Thanks. I'll keep that in mind."

She raised a hand in farewell before she went down the rest of the steps. He watched her walk across the grass, seized by indecision. He really didn't want to go to her church again, but suddenly he wanted to spend the morning with her.

"Uh, Joan?"

She turned, her eyes round with questions.

"Maybe I'll go with you after all. I really should give it a second try, don't you think?"

The grin that lit her face made his head go light.

Joan walked through the doorway to the Sunday school room, nervously aware of Ken on her heels. She wanted to kick herself for caving in to the impulse to stop and invite him to come with her this morning. What was she thinking? She had no idea, just as she had no idea what she was doing here when she could be sleeping in at Tori's.

Brittany Daniels, seated at the far end of the long table that dominated the classroom, simpered when she caught sight of Ken. Beside her, Eve Tankersly straightened in her chair, her eyes going round. Ryan Adams searched the empty doorway eagerly, but his face fell when he realized Tori wasn't with them. A few others sat around the table, each with a Styrofoam cup of coffee or a bottle of water in front of them.

"Good morning." Ken's smile swept the room.

"Good morning," the girls breathed in unison.

Instead of rolling her eyes, as she wanted to do, Joan nodded a greeting and stepped up to one of the empty seats nearest the door. She started to pull it out, but Ken was quicker. He grinned down at her as he slid the chair out and waited for her to be seated.

"Thank you." Her pulse did a tap dance as she slid onto the hard plastic seat. She avoided looking his way as he sat in the chair next to hers. No sense reading anything into a polite gesture. Ken was nothing if not a gentleman. On the other hand, the fact that he'd agreed to join her this morning when he obviously wasn't impressed by the church last week gave her hope that maybe Karen was right. Maybe he really was interested in her.

Across the table, Brittany heaved a disappointed sigh. Joan hid a smile. Well, maybe holding her chair was a *little* more than a polite gesture.

Mr. Carmichael arrived a moment later, pacing through

the door with his funny little shuffle, a stack of papers in his hands. He glanced around the table, his eyes going wide when he caught sight of Ken. "Dr. Fletcher, we're happy to have you back." His tone, and the alarmed expression on his face, said the opposite.

Beside her, Ken's smile broadened. "Thank you."

Mr. Carmichael cleared his throat as he fumbled to arrange his Bible, Sunday school book, and papers in neat piles in front of him. He opened his teacher's guide to a place marked with a paper clip, set a page of handwritten notes inside it, and then handed the stack of student papers to Ryan to be passed around the table. With another nervous glance in Ken's direction, he cleared his throat again and began.

"This week's lesson is taken from the tenth chapter of Deuteronomy and is entitled 'Walking in His Ways.'" He removed his glasses and began cleaning them with his tie. "Now an interesting fact of which you may not be aware concerns the name of the book. Deuteronomy means 'repetition of the law,' and it arose from a mistranslation in the Septuagint and the Latin Vulgate of a phrase—"

"Uh, excuse me, please." Joan raised a hand.

Every head in the room swiveled toward her. Mr. Carmichael, in the process of replacing his glasses on his face, gave her a wide-eyed stare of disbelief. "Yes?"

Suddenly self-conscious, Joan tapped a finger on the edge of the table. She'd been thinking about the Open Bible Church, trying to pinpoint the differences between the service she attended and the services at Christ Community. Besides the obvious difference in the music, there was another one she'd noticed.

Joan gulped air and coughed politely. "I'm sorry to interrupt, but I have a question."

He shook his head. "But I haven't even started the lesson yet."

"It's not about the lesson." Joan let her gaze sweep the faces around the table. "I was wondering if anybody is interested in doing something together as a class."

Ryan cocked his head. "Huh?"

"I mean . . ." Joan hooked her index fingers on the edge of the table, flustered. She didn't really know what she meant, but she remembered that bulletin at the Open Bible Church, with the long list of activities. "Don't most churches have young adult groups that get together and do things?"

Brittany leaned forward. "You mean, like, go bowling or something?"

Her expression said she didn't think much of that idea. Joan agreed with her. Bowling was something Mom did, and she had not the slightest interest in. "Not that, necessarily, but something besides Sunday school."

Beside her, Ken was staring at her with an intensity that made her skin tingle. She kept her gaze fixed on the others in the room, but out of the corner of her eye, she saw him studying her.

"I think I know what Joan means," Gordy said. "We're supposed to socialize with each other, make sure we have other single Christians to hang around with during the week. There sure isn't anybody my age at my work to go out with." His grin swept the table. "Maybe you guys could keep me from becoming a couch potato."

"That's exactly what I mean." She nodded in his direction. "We could meet for coffee or go to a movie or to dinner. And we could . . . pray together. Or something." Joan glanced toward Mr. Carmichael, who sat watching with his hands clasped and a long-suffering expression on his face.

Eve raised a tentative hand. "Well, I go to a singles Bible study every Wednesday night in Lexington."

Joan looked at her in surprise. "You do?"

She nodded. "It's at St. Matthew's over on Richmond Road." She looked around the room. "Any of you are welcome to come with me any time you want. They're a great group of people, and I'm learning a lot."

Brittany twisted in her chair to look at Eve. "If you like St. Matthews so much, why don't you go there on Sunday morning?"

Eve shrugged. "I was raised here. My parents go to this church, and my brother and his wife. I like it here." She turned an apologetic smile toward Mr. Carmichael. "I like St. Matthews too."

Ryan leaned forward to look at Eve around Brittany. "I wouldn't mind going with you sometime."

Eve smiled. "That'd be great."

Joan sat back in her chair. She had no idea Eve went to a Bible study somewhere else, nor that Ryan Adams would have the slightest interest in attending one. She looked around the room. She'd been in this church with these people most of her life, and she didn't really know any of them.

"Maybe we should try to do something like that here," Gordy suggested.

"Yes, but who would teach it?" Brittany asked.

They all tried not to look at Mr. Carmichael, who became engrossed in his notes. Joan felt a flicker of sympathy. Apparently the poor man wasn't any more interested in teaching a Bible study than they were in having him teach.

Eve shook her head. "No offense, but my Wednesday night Bible study is pretty intense. I don't think I can commit to another one. I mean, I'd love to get together with you guys, but can't we do something else?"

Ken, who had been listening quietly up until now, laid an arm on the table and turned his body so he could see everyone as he spoke. "Since you've never really done much together outside of Sunday morning, maybe you need to have some sort of kickoff. An event of some kind to launch yourselves as a group."

"An event." Excitement prickled Joan, and she sat up straighter. "I like that. We could do a project."

"You mean build a house like Habitat for Humanity?" Brittany's brow creased with alarm. "Y'all, I'm totally useless with a hammer."

"Well," Ken said, "maybe you should start out smaller. Is there a job your church needs to have done? It doesn't have to be a building project. Maybe there's something in the community."

They sat in silence a moment, exchanging glances. At the front of the room, Mr. Carmichael cleared his throat and glanced at his watch. Guilt washed over Joan. She had sidetracked his class.

"Maybe we should talk about this later," she said. "Are

you guys free any night this week? Not Wednesday, of course." She sent a quick smile toward Eve.

Ken spoke up. "I could do Thursday."

She turned a wide-eyed look his way. Ken wanted to get involved? Heart pounding, she swallowed against a dry mouth. "Thursday's good for me." Nods up and down the table indicated that Thursday worked for everyone. "Okay, then. Say around 7:30 at my house?"

The date and time confirmed, she sat back in her chair and turned her attention to Mr. Carmichael. Her apology, delivered by way of a shy smile, was met with a long-suffering sigh.

"Well then, let's continue. As I was saying, the word Deuteronomy . . ."

Ken put an arm across the back of her chair and leaned close. His warm breath tickled her ear and set her stomach fluttering. "Good job."

Joan didn't hear a word of the lesson.

"I can't believe you ditched us!"

Hands on her hips, Allie stood inside the front door as Joan stepped into the house. Gram and Mom followed right behind her.

"She came home to go to church with us." Gram kissed Allie on the cheek before climbing the stairs to disappear into the kitchen.

Mom enveloped her oldest daughter in a hug. "Good to see you, honey. How are you feeling?"

"Tired and cranky." Allie sniffed. "My sisters kept me up all night long and fed me junk food."

"Puh-lease!" Joan laughed at Allie's injured expression. "Nobody forced all that pizza down your throat. And who kept throwing chocolate-covered peanuts at me every time I tried to go to sleep?"

"You were missing the best parts of *Four Weddings and a Funeral*."

"Like we haven't seen it seven hundred times already."

In the living room, Tori bounced off the sofa and came to hug Mom. "I'm thinking Joan didn't just come home to go to church." She arched an eyebrow in Joan's direction. "I saw *him* out the window."

Allie's eyes widened. "Dr. Gorgeous went with you again? Well, why didn't you say so? There are very few acceptable reasons for ditching your sisters in the middle of a slumber party, but a hot date is definitely one of them."

Joan shook her head, laughing. "I'd hardly call Sunday school and church a hot date. Especially since he wouldn't even stay for dinner."

An unladylike snort came from Tori. "For a religious nut, that's about as hot as you're going to get."

Joan avoided her little sister's probing stare. If she thought Ken was a religious fanatic, what would Tori say if she knew her own sister thought God used her and a pint of chocolate ice cream to deliver a message? It did sound nuts. Heck, maybe it *was* nuts.

"I think Dr. Fletcher is a nice young man," Mom told them. "And he would have accepted our invitation to Sunday dinner, but he worked all night and he has to be back at the hospital at 6:00. He went home to get some sleep."

Allie yawned. "I know the feeling."

Mom went downstairs toward her bedroom, probably to change out of her Sunday clothes, and Joan headed toward the kitchen. Tori put a hand on her arm, halting her.

"Nice or not, he's too serious when it comes to religion." Her eyes captured Joan's. "Be careful with that guy, okay?"

An uneasy feeling cast a shadow over Joan's happy mood. No doubt about it. Her sister had taken a dislike to Ken. That would make for some awkward family dinners if Joan actually managed to develop a relationship with the guy. Or maybe it was religion in general Tori disliked? Odd, she'd never picked up on that before.

She laughed, making light of her growing discomfort. "Are you afraid he's going to convince me to dress like a Pilgrim and shave my head? Maybe drink poisoned Kool-Aid?"

"Don't laugh," Tori insisted. "Some of those fanatics are scary people."

"I don't think Ken is scary-religious." Allie slipped past them and into the kitchen. "He's just been so heads-down on his medical career that he's not well-rounded. He hasn't developed a social life. Joan can help with that."

Heat crept up Joan's neck as she returned Tori's stare. Deep inside she felt certain there was way more to Ken's faith than merely the lack of a social life. And she was on the verge of figuring out what it was. She tore her gaze away from Tori's and followed Allie into the kitchen. "Yeah,

I'm such an expert in social situations. I haven't been on a date since Roger. And Ken sure hasn't been beating down my door."

Of course, he had volunteered to come to her house on Thursday night to help organize the group's project. But given Tori's hostility, Joan didn't want to mention that.

With relief, she realized she had managed to mention Roger the Rat without wanting to spit. Maybe she was starting to get over her anger.

"Well," Tori trailed her, stopping to lean against the doorjamb, "I just think Joan could do better, that's all."

Allie whooped with laughter. "Better than a doctor?"

"Absolutely." Tori raised her chin. "She could get a brain surgeon, easy."

A rush of gratitude washed over Joan, and she whirled to hug her baby sister. "I don't know about that, but I'm glad you think so."

"Could someone help me with this?" Gram held two pot holders toward Joan and inclined her head in the direction of the open oven door.

Joan took the pot holders and lifted out the roasting pan, inhaling the savory odor of onions and roasted meat. The juices sizzled as they sloshed against the hot sides of the pan. It wasn't heavy, but if Gram's joints were bothering her today, Joan was glad she asked for help. Better not to risk another lasagna incident, this time with witnesses.

Allie was at her elbow in an instant with two big slotted spoons. She lifted the steaming roast from the pan and deposited it onto a waiting platter, inhaling. "Mmmm, it smells wonderful, Gram."

"I hope it's not overdone." Gram hovered over the roast, poking it with a fork and fretting. Apparently satisfied, she turned a grin on Joan. "At least it's not fried."

As Joan fished carrots and potatoes out of the pot, Gram went to the refrigerator for a jar of homemade pickles. Mom came into the room as Gram set them on the counter and put a hand on the lid, her jaw set.

"Mother, let me do that. You might want to get the table ready."

Relief lightened Gram's features as she yielded the jar. Mom easily twisted the lid off and dumped the pickles into a dish while Gram picked up a stack of napkins and went into the dining room.

Joan scooped the last carrot out of the crock pot, struck by the tender expression on Mom's face as she watched Gram place a napkin and silverware beside each plate. With last night's revelations fresh in her mind, she might have been seeing her mother with different eyes today. Maybe her actions were a little rough at times, her voice a little too harsh, but she loved Gram. She was doing what she thought necessary to take care of her, to protect her. Like she had protected her daughters.

Anxiety twisted a knife in Joan's gut. If only Mom didn't think a nursing home was the best way to provide that protection.

~ 17 ~

Ken parked in the physician's lot at ten past six. He slammed the car door and jogged toward the hospital entrance, trying to shake the lethargy that added weight to his limbs. He hated being late. He'd have to remember to turn the volume up on the clock radio. But after only four hours' sleep, he doubted if he would have heard the alarm even if it had blared through a bullhorn beside his ear. Thank goodness he'd forgotten to put Trigger outside before he fell asleep. If the dog hadn't decided to bark in tempo with the radio's music, he'd still be sleeping.

Of course, now he had a huge mess to clean up when he got home. The stack of medical journals he hadn't managed to read yet had become enough confetti to fuel the Macy's Thanksgiving Day Parade.

"Sorry I'm late," he said as he burst through the ER doors.

Dr. Boling, seated at the nurses' station, rose at his entrance. Apparently it hadn't been a busy day, because the older doctor seemed relaxed and unstressed as he shook his head in Ken's direction.

"No problem. The wife's visiting her mother for a week, so I've got an empty house waiting for me at home." He tilted his head to peer through the bottom half of his glasses. "You look tired."

"I'm not awake yet." Ken ran a hand through his hair. "I'll be alright, as long as there's coffee."

"Always. It's a key ingredient in a doctor's blood. Our veins would collapse without it." He rounded the desk and headed toward the back office to give report. Ken fell into place beside him.

The nurse lifted her head from her computer monitor. "Dr. Fletcher, there's someone out in the waiting room to see you. She's been here about twenty minutes."

"Me?"

She nodded. "She's not a patient. Says she wants to talk to you about a personal matter."

He looked toward Dr. Boling, who waved good-naturedly. "Go. I'm in no hurry."

Curious, Ken walked through the double doors leading to the ER waiting room. The room was empty. Odd. Maybe the woman got tired of hanging around and left. As he turned to go back to the treatment area, he caught a glimpse of movement through the revolving door. A tall woman stood outside, smoke curling above her head from the cigarette she held to her lips. He sauntered across the room and stepped into the warm August evening.

She turned when he came through the door. Deep creases framed her mouth, caused by decades of sucking on cigarettes. "You Dr. Fletcher?"

"Yes. I understand you wanted to see me?"

She crushed her cigarette in the receptacle before thrusting her hand toward him. "I'm Beverly Lassiter."

Lassiter. "You're Mike's grandmother." He shook her hand, searching her face for any sign of trouble. "Is he okay?"

"That boy?" Her thin chest huffed a single proud laugh. "Never better. Startin' school tomorrow, though. By the end of the week, I 'spect he'll come up with some sickness or other that'll keep him home."

Ken laughed with her. He'd played his share of hooky at Mike's age. Her love for her grandson couldn't have been more obvious if she'd whipped out a stack of photos to show him. Something heavy inside Ken shifted a fraction. At least Mike had a grandmother who loved him.

Mrs. Lassiter drew her shoulders up. "I come to thank you for what you done."

"What I . . . oh, you mean removing his stitches?" Ken shook his head. "That was nothing."

"Twern't '*nothing*.'" Both hands clutched at the strap of the handbag hanging from her shoulder. "Not many folks woulda checked on the boy. He said you came twice. I'm beholdin' to you."

She raised her chin to look him in the eye as she delivered her thanks. Not an educated woman, certainly, and judging by the worn state of her clothing, not a wealthy one. But she carried herself with quiet dignity and knew the social graces, knew that a good deed required an acknowledgment.

He dipped his head. "You're welcome. I was glad to do it."

242

She hesitated, her grip on the shoulder strap tightening as her gaze slid away. "Holly ain't a bad girl, not really. She was just so young when Michael came along. And she's always been mule-headed, wanting to do for her own self instead of letting me help." She looked away. "Not that I can do much, but she and the boy'd be better off living at home with me rather than in that dump."

Ken suspected a girl like Holly wouldn't relish the thought of living under her mother's observant eye. Mrs. Lassiter didn't seem the type who would keep her mouth shut if her daughter was doing something she didn't approve of.

"I got a glimpse of some of Mike's friends the other day." He watched the traffic beyond the entrance to the parking lot. "I hope when school starts up again he'll find some different kids to hang out with."

Mrs. Lassiter shook her head. "Not if he's like his mama. If there's a bad one around, she'll hook up with him, and next thing you know they're in trouble together." She peered into his face. "But my grandson likes you. Maybe you could talk some sense into the boy."

A smile twitched at the edges of Ken's lips. "You know, when I was a boy, I wasn't much different from Mike. I got into my fair share of trouble."

She squinted, her gaze dropping to the stethoscope hanging around his neck. "You done alright with yourself."

A look of understanding passed between them. He was being given tacit permission to do what he'd wanted to do since the night he met Mike Lassiter—provide a positive influence. It was a huge responsibility, and not something to agree to lightly. But Ken, of all people, knew what a difference a positive influence could make in a child's life. Maybe now was the time to give back a little of what he'd been given. From the first night he met Mike, he knew in his heart God wanted him to do something for that boy.

Grinning, he said, "Maybe Mike would like to go out and get a pizza with me one night. Or take in a ball game."

Her clutch on the shoulder strap relaxed, and she reached into the bag to withdraw a set of keys. "I reckon he would."

"Would you like to come inside?" Ken asked as she turned to leave. "It isn't a busy night, and I might be able to find us a cup of coffee while we talk."

She shook her head. "I need to get on home. I just wanted to thank you for taking care of them stitches." Her heel scraped on the asphalt as she headed for a rusty four-door sedan.

"Maybe I'll see you again sometime," Ken called after her.

She turned. One side of her mouth rose in a crooked smile. "I 'spect so."

Joan slipped out the front door at 6:40 Monday morning and closed it quietly behind her so she didn't wake Gram or Mom. She paused on the porch to inhale the fresh air. In the east, the rising sun dominated a clear blue sky. Her skin felt sticky even in the relative cool of the early hour. Though they'd enjoyed a few low-humidity days unusual for August in Kentucky, summer refused to let go. Today promised to be a hot one.

She stepped onto the sidewalk and stretched her muscles for a moment before taking off at a slow jog. Today's exercise would probably hurt. Her body was sure to punish her for the overindulgence with junk food over the weekend.

The Hendersons' cat watched from its perch in the front window as she ran past. When she got to the Faulkners' flowers, she heard her name called from behind.

"Joan, wait up."

A quiet groan sounded in her throat when she turned to see Ken and Trigger running to catch up with her. Why did he have to pick now to show up, when she hadn't taken the time to do more than splash water on her face and throw on some workout clothes? A hand went to her hair. She'd barely even pulled a brush through it before putting it in a ponytail.

She hid her embarrassment by bending down to rub Trigger's ears. "Hey, fella. What are you doing up so early?"

"Early?" Ken laughed. "What are you talking about? It's late. Almost my bedtime, in fact. But the book I've been reading says the reason this guy's digging holes in the backyard is because he's not getting enough exercise. So we thought we'd run with you."

She glanced over his green hospital scrubs and white sneakers. "Are you a runner?"

"Not really, but I think I can keep up. Is that okay?"

Joan looked away to hide a grin. "Sure." She started again, and Ken fell into step beside her while Trigger led the way, straining at the leash.

"So, have you come up with any ideas to talk about Thursday night?"

She shook her head. "I really haven't thought about it yet. How 'bout you?"

"Maybe." He gave her a sideways smile. "There are a couple of things I want to check on."

They ran past a few houses in silence.

"I was surprised when you said you wanted to come. I mean, our church didn't seem to impress you much."

"It didn't," he admitted. "But you do."

Exercise had nothing to do with the way her heart pounded in her chest. "Me?"

She faced forward, aware that he turned his head to look at her. "Yes, you. You were different yesterday, and I've been trying to figure out what prompted the change."

"I . . ." She stopped. The whole ice cream thing sounded too weird to put into words. The last thing she wanted was for Ken to think she was strange. "Remember that Open Bible Church I told you about?" He nodded. "I went there to hear a missionary talk about building orphanages in Afghanistan, and the church is so different from mine. Karen told me a little about your church in Indianapolis, and I realized it must be like that one."

"And you want to try to make your church more like that?" He sounded skeptical.

Joan shook her head. "Not really. I mean, I don't think the praise band and the audio system and all that would go over too well at Christ Community. But . . ." She ran on a few paces. Talking about her reasons didn't come easily, especially when she hadn't really figured them out herself. "I saw a bulletin that listed all the activities Open Bible has going on during the week, and I realized we don't do anything like that. We call ourselves a community, but we're not, not really." She gave him a quick look. "I guess I'm beginning to think there ought to be more to church than sitting in a pew and listening to a sermon."

Ken's breath was starting to come hard with the exertion, but he smiled in her direction. "I think you're right."

A thrill shot through Joan at his words.

They rounded the corner and started down the next block. Ken trudged valiantly beside her, huffing heavily. By this point Joan was usually completely warmed up and at her peak speed, but she set a pace slower than normal. Even Trigger was starting to pant.

"But I don't think . . . ," huff, ". . . Mr. Carmichael was too thrilled."

Joan laughed. "Did you see the terror on his face when we brought up the Bible study?"

"Nice guy . . . but . . ." Huff, huff.

"But he's not a great teacher," Joan finished for him.

Ken nodded.

"I know. He's been teaching that class since he retired a few years ago. I'm sure he spends a lot of time on the lessons. He's always telling us about the root meaning of this word, or the other uses of that one. He's really into the historical and intellectual aspects of the Bible."

Again, Ken nodded but didn't speak. His face looked like he'd been sitting in a sauna for a couple of hours. Trigger no longer surged out ahead of them. Instead, he trailed along behind, panting heavily. A newspaper headline flashed into Joan's mind.

DANVILLE DOCTOR'S DYING WORDS:
"I THOUGHT I COULD KEEP UP!"

Hiding a smile, Joan slowed to a brisk walk. "You know, they say walking is the best aerobic exercise you can do. It gets your blood pumping but doesn't jar your joints."

Casting her a look of gratitude, Ken slowed. "Guess I . . . wasn't in as good . . . shape as I thought."

At that moment, Trigger apparently decided enough was enough. He came to a dead stop and flopped into the grass, wheezing.

Joan laughed out loud. "Neither is your dog."

~ 18 ~

"I'm home!" Joan let herself in the house and inhaled deeply. The scent of warm chocolate lingered in the air. "Mmm, what smells so good?"

When she came through the kitchen doorway, her heart skipped a beat. Gram stood tiptoe on a dining room chair, reaching up to the top shelf of the pantry.

"Gram!" She dropped her purse on the floor and rushed forward. "What in the world are you doing up there?"

"Getting these." She extracted a package of paper napkins.

Pulse pounding, Joan held out a hand to help her down. She heaved a relieved breath when Gram leaned heavily on it to step to the floor. "Do me a favor? Next time, wait for me. I'd rather you not climb up on a chair."

A frown added creases to her forehead, and she spoke irritably. "I can manage."

"Gram, please." Joan held her breath until her grandmother gave a slight nod. Relieved, she turned her attention to a tray of fudgy goodies on the counter as her pulse slowed to normal speed. "You didn't have to make brownies."

She resisted the urge to pinch a corner off one of them. No sense indulging in the extra calories. With Ken and Trigger now accompanying her on her morning *walks*, she wasn't getting nearly the workout she was accustomed to.

"I can't have guests in my house and not offer them something." Gram looked askance at the suggestion of such blatant inhospitality.

Joan laughed at her. "Well, thank you. I just hate for you to go to any trouble, especially since we're interrupting your Thursday night schedule."

"Nonsense. I'll watch *CSI* downstairs on your television." She opened the package she'd retrieved and stacked some napkins beside the brownies. "And besides, what else do I have to do all day?"

"You can't fool me. You do plenty just taking care of me and Mom." Joan hugged her. "Now I'd better go change clothes before they arrive."

Gram followed her down the stairs and into her bedroom. "Are you sure you won't have something for supper?" Her voice cracked with worry. "Maybe a sandwich and a bowl of soup?"

"I had a late lunch," Joan told her. "And besides, there's no time. They'll be here any minute. I don't want to eat in front of them."

She brightened. "I can fix them a sandwich too."

Joan clasped her grandmother's shoulders. "That's not necessary. They're just coming for a meeting." She leaned forward and kissed a wrinkled cheek, reveling in the powdery smell she always associated with Gram. "Thank you for taking care of me, but I'm not going to wither away from lack of food."

The doorbell rang. Joan glanced at her watch. The first person was five minutes early.

"Would you get that, please? Tell whoever it is I'll be right up."

Gram's brow cleared as she scooted out of the room, intent on her mission. Joan grinned as she donned jeans and a blue shirt. By the time Joan got upstairs, she'd be stuffing brownies into whoever had just arrived, regaling them with the history of her recipe and the story of the first time she made them for Grandpa.

As she mounted the stairs, the doorbell rang again.

"I'll get it," she shouted.

Eve and a familiar-looking brunette stood on the stoop.

"You remember Marissa?" Eve nodded toward her friend. "She's been to church with me a couple of times."

"Sure." Joan stepped back so they could enter. "Hi, Marissa. Glad you could come."

"Thanks." Marissa returned Joan's smile with a shy one.

Behind her, Gram said, "Come on in, girls, and tell me what you'd like to drink. I have lemonade, sweet tea, milk, and 7UP. Or I could make coffee."

Joan turned in time to see her step into the living room with a tray of cheese and crackers. Apparently the brownies weren't her only project. She had prepared a full buffet of snack food. Joan chuckled as she swung the door closed. Leave it to Gram.

An arm shot through the doorway. She pulled the door back open and looked up into Ken's smiling face.

Would her stomach ever stop fluttering at the sight of those breathtaking green eyes?

"I'm not late, am I?"

"You're right on time." She stepped back to let him inside. "I'm glad I finally get to hear your secret idea."

All week long during their morning walks, he'd been hinting that he had a great idea for the group but wouldn't tell her what the project might be. He slipped inside and stood looking down at her, his face barely six inches from hers. Definitely inside her hula hoop, but Joan had no desire to step back.

"I hope you're not disappointed after all the buildup."

Disappointed in anything to do with Ken? Not likely.

By 7:40 everyone had arrived, and they had to bring extra chairs from the dining room. Joan did a quick count. Eight, counting herself. Not bad. All the Sunday morning regulars had showed up, and Brittany called Crystal, who attended sporadically. Joan realized there were a couple of others she should have thought to call and made a mental note to do that before their next meeting.

Gram's brownies were a hit, and she was obviously enjoying herself, flitting in and out of the room refilling everyone's glasses if they got more than three sips low. Joan realized she would have to get things going. She felt like they should begin with a prayer.

She had never prayed in public! Blessings before family

meals didn't count. Praying wasn't something that came naturally to her, not prayers like the one she heard from that preacher at the Open Bible Church. Or Ken, even. When he had said the blessing at dinner, he made it sound so easy. Not professional, like Rev. Jacobson's, but more like a normal conversation. Maybe he would do it, if she asked.

No, this was her idea. It was up to her. She cleared her throat. "We ought to get started, you guys. I, uh, guess I'll open with prayer."

The chatter fell silent and everyone bowed their heads. Joan gulped a breath. Just talk to him. "Dear God, thank you for the great turnout tonight. We're here because we're hoping to come up with ways to support each other, and also to do some good in our church and maybe in our town. We hope you'll give us some ideas and that, uh . . . ," her eyes squeezed tighter, "that your Holy Spirit will lead our discussion. In Jesus' name, Amen."

A huge wave of relief washed over her. That wasn't so bad. In fact, it felt sort of good, especially the part about the Holy Spirit leading them. Ken must have thought so too, because he smiled at her.

"Okay," she said, looking around the room. "Has anyone come up with any brainstorms?"

On the sofa, Brittany raised a hand. "I thought we might paint the Sunday school classrooms. It's been years since the last time anybody did it."

"I wondered about planting fall flowers around the churchyard." Eve glanced around the room. "And in another month we could rake leaves for some of the elderly people in our congregation."

Beside her on the love seat, Ryan laughed. "There are plenty of those, that's for sure." He ducked his head as Gram made another pass through the room with the tea pitcher.

"What a shame it's not closer to Christmas," Brittany said. "We could do the Angel Tree."

"What about volunteering at the food pantry?" Crystal absently swirled her soda, ice tinkling against the glass. "They need help all year-round."

Gordy's head swiveled toward her. "Does Danville even have a food pantry?"

She shrugged. "If they don't, Lexington does. Or maybe we could start one here."

Joan tapped a finger against the arm of her chair, listening to the ideas being thrown out. These were some good projects, but she was holding out to hear what Ken had come up with.

"I like the idea of doing something for the community," Ryan said. "The church I went to in St. Louis when I was a teenager used to print labels with John 3:16 and put them on cold bottles of water. Then we'd go out as a group and pass them out to homeless people."

Eve sat up in her seat, her face brightening. "What a terrific idea."

"Except I don't know of any homeless people in Danville." Gordy reached for a handful of peanuts from a dish on the coffee table. "We could maybe go to Lexington or Louisville, though."

Joan's gaze slid to Ken, her eyebrows arched. Was he ever going to speak?

He caught her looking at him, and grinned. "What do you know about Shadow Ridge?"

"The housing project?" Gordy scowled. "It's a place for low-income families, most of them on welfare. And it's a dump."

"Yeah, some scary people live out there." Brittany shuddered. "There's a high crime rate. I hear a lot of drugs are sold in Shadow Ridge."

Ken nodded slowly. "I figured that. A couple of weeks ago I met a boy who lives there. He's not a bad kid, but if the only role models he has are the people selling drugs in his apartment complex, where's he likely to end up?"

Silence fell on them as everyone considered the question. Joan looked at Ken. "What did you have in mind?"

"I've been out there a couple of times. You're right." He nodded at Gordy. "It's a dump. Trash everywhere, beer bottles all over the place, even on the playground. And the equipment is broken down and dangerous." He leaned forward, his forearms resting on his thighs as he looked around the room. "I thought maybe we could clean it up, make it safe for the kids who live there."

Ryan shook his head. "It's not a bad idea, but I don't see how cleaning up their playground will help keep those kids off drugs."

"Maybe it won't, but doing it says somebody cares about them."

"You know," Crystal said thoughtfully, "I'll bet some of those kids have never had an adult take the time to do anything just for them."

Ken stared at the floor in front of him. "If we demonstrate

Christ's love in a real, practical way, it will make a difference. I know it will."

Joan watched him, saw a muscle in his jaw flex. She felt certain he was speaking from personal experience. Had someone done something for him as a kid, something to influence his life? Maybe after his parents died?

A smile brightened Eve's face. "I like the idea."

Joan caught his eye and grinned. "I do too."

She saw nods around the room.

"But are we allowed to go in there and do a cleanup project?" Ryan's eyebrows drew together as he looked at Ken. "I mean, are there permits we have to get or permission or anything?"

"None. I spoke with the complex manager a few days ago." Ken held up a hand to forestall any argument. "I didn't commit us to anything, not before we decided as a group, but I asked him what we'd need to do to get permission. He seemed thrilled." His lips twisted as he caught Joan's gaze. "But he wanted to make absolutely sure we understood the complex couldn't pay for anything."

"I work for a hardware supplier." Ryan cocked his head sideways. "Maybe I can get the owners to donate at least some of the material we'll need."

"Hey!" Brittany clapped her hands together. "I can call some other businesses in town and see if they'll help too. I'm good at that."

"You know what we might do?" Marissa blushed as everyone looked at her. She ducked her head and swallowed, but continued. "We could put up a notice in advance. Maybe some of the parents would want to help us if they knew what we were doing. That way we'd have an opportunity to work alongside them, to get to know them."

"That's a great idea," Eve said. "There are bound to be caring parents in that complex, people who are just down on their luck. Maybe this will help them too."

Excitement vibrated throughout the room as each of them voiced enthusiasm for their first project. Joan couldn't help grinning at Ken.

"I don't want to forget about the other ideas we've discussed," she told everyone. "We'll keep a list and do some of those things later. But it sounds like we're all in agreement that our first project will be the Shadow Ridge playground?"

They all agreed.

"Good. Let's start ironing out the details."

Joan went to the kitchen for a calendar and a notepad. Time to make a list. She might be lousy at calling people for donations, and she didn't know what good she'd be repairing broken playground equipment. But details were her forte. She could organize anything.

She didn't bother to hide an excited grin. Allie said she needed a goal. Looked like she was right.

~ *19* ~

Bark, bark, bark, howl.

Ken reluctantly let go of his dream and struggled to consciousness. His eyes felt weighted down. He labored to open them and peer at the clock. 10:36 Saturday morning. He groaned. Last night at the hospital had been a killer. Seemed like they ran nonstop, and he'd even had to bring in the on-call doc to help. When he finally got home after a fourteen-hour shift, he'd barely been able to make it to the bedroom before he collapsed. He didn't even get to take his morning walk with Joan, which was fast becoming a highlight of his and Trigger's day.

What was wrong with that obnoxious dog, waking him up after only two hours' sleep?

Bark, bark, bark, howl.

With a groan, Ken launched himself out of bed, stumbling against the doorjamb as he headed toward the back door. Drat Trigger. Drat Karen for making him get Trigger. Drat the whole world for not letting him sleep!

He opened the door to the back porch, bracing himself for Trigger's enthusiastic greeting.

"What is the matter with . . ."

Odd. Instead of leaping on him in uncontrolled joy, as he normally did, the dog ran out the doggie door. Ken watched through the window as he raced across the yard, barking like crazy. Probably going for his ball, the irritating mutt. Ken felt sorry for the poor thing, alone all night long and ignored for much of the day, but he had to get some sleep, didn't he?

Trigger ran back to the porch and stood just outside, barking and watching Ken through the window.

"I know, fella, and I'm sorry. We'll take a long walk later, I promise."

Trigger ran to the doggie door, stuck his front half through and barked frantically. Extremely odd. If he didn't know better, Ken would think Trigger was acting like Lassie, trying to get his master to follow him.

Ridiculous thought. Trigger was a mutt, not a rescue dog.

Still, when he backed out of the doggie door and zoomed across the yard to stand barking at the side fence, Ken knew something had gotten the pup's attention. Probably a cat. The quicker he checked it out, the quicker he could get back to bed. Giving in to a huge yawn, he followed through the back door into the yard. The pitch of Trigger's bark rose. The dog leaped up on the fence, his front paws resting against the chain link, barking toward the house next door.

Joan's house.

A fist of alarm squeezed Ken's gut. Joan and Carla weren't there. He'd noticed their cars gone when he came home from the hospital. That meant Grace was alone.

Ken's feet went into motion. He ran to the gate and unlatched it, Trigger racing through ahead of him. Sure enough, the dog ran straight around to the back of Joan's house and up onto the deck. Ken dashed up the stairs after him. In a barking frenzy, Trigger stood on his hind legs, front paws on the glass French door.

Ken hauled the dog back. He knocked on the glass.

"Grace? Are you in there?"

He couldn't hear a thing over Trigger's barking. The blinds were closed so he couldn't see in. He twisted the handle. Locked. And he knew they kept the front door locked as well. The tiniest gap at the side of the blinds gave him a crack to peek through.

His stomach clenched into a knot. He saw a movement inside, down low. A white head. Grace! Lying on the floor!

"Grace! Grace, are you alright?" He jerked the doorknob frantically, his gaze sweeping the back patio. He'd have to break in. But with what? There, lining the back flowerbed, dozens of big landscaping rocks the size of his head. He ran down the stairs, grabbed the biggest one he could find, and raced back up on the deck.

"Grace, I'm coming in."

He raised the rock high above his head.

Joan sat in the back office, going over next week's labor schedule. Since school started again, the two high school students she'd hired at the beginning of the summer could only work weekends. Rosa agreed to pick up some extra hours next week, but she still hadn't decided whether or not she was moving to Las Vegas with Luis.

A twinge of loneliness struck Joan at the thought. If Rosa did go, where would Joan find someone to take her place? And not just at work. Her gaze fell on the colorful picture of Cinderella taped to the wall above the desk, the left edge ragged where Tiffany had torn it from the book. Rosa was more than an employee. She and Tiffany had become her extended family.

She tightened her lips and typed Rosa's name into the Tuesday–Thursday evening schedule next week. Better not to think about that until she had to.

Actually, what she really wanted to think about had nothing to do with work. She'd much rather plan the Shadow Ridge playground project. Her finger tapped the notebook containing her lists. Brittany called last night, ecstatic with her success in securing a truckload of playground mulch. The lumberyard that agreed to the donation wanted to know if there would be any free publicity involved. Brittany wondered if they should contact the *Advocate-Messenger*, letting them know about the project and the generosity of local vendors. They might even send a reporter to cover the event. Joan had to smile at that. She might actually be the subject of a newspaper headline!

She gave in to the silly grin that kept twitching her lips. Things were really starting to look up. True, Ken hadn't asked her on a date yet, but she was getting to know him, and so far she really liked what she saw. No matter what Tori thought, he was a great guy, and completely normal. His faith only enhanced his appeal, in Joan's opinion. And he seemed to be enjoying her company as well. This morning was the first time he'd missed walking with her in almost a week.

And this church project was fun, exciting even. It gave her something in common with Ken. But more than that, she felt like she'd finally stumbled onto something she could get enthusiastic about.

Brrring, brrring.

Joan clicked the Save button on the computer before she picked up the phone. "Good morning, Abernathy's."

"Joan?"

Her heart stuttered at the sob in Allie's voice. "What's wrong?"

"Eric just called. It's Gram."

Gram? Joan's ears stopped working. Blood roared in her head, and for a moment her senses shut down. The office, the computer monitor, everything dimmed as a gray shroud descended over her vision. Something wrong with Gram? Was it a stroke? Joan closed her eyes, guilt threatening to drown her. She hadn't been checking the blood pressure medicine. Mom said she would do it, so Joan didn't. But she should have!

Allie's voice came back into focus. ". . . ambulance, and Ken will meet us at the hospital."

Joan's grip on the receiver tightened. "Ken's at the hospital?"

"Aren't you listening?" Hysteria tinged Allie's voice. "Ken found her. He called 9-1-1 and got Eric."

"Mom?" Joan's voice came out in a croak. "Has someone called Mom?"

"Ken did. He called the hospital and had them get her from the fourth floor. She'll be waiting in the emergency room when the ambulance arrives. I'm leaving right now."

"Me too." Joan jumped up from the chair and threw the receiver in the general direction of the desk. She slid the drawer open and grabbed her purse, fumbling for her car keys as she ran through the loading dock area and into the showroom. Customers dotted the store, all of them turning to stare when she shouted at Pat, "I'm going to the hospital. It's my grandmother."

She shot through the front door in a flash, aware but not caring that Pat was shouting questions after her. No time for that right now. She had to get to Gram.

Her car zoomed to the hospital with a mind of its own. A good thing too. Joan's brain refused to concentrate on anything. She was dimly aware that she stopped at a stoplight. Her heart threatened to pound through her chest while her hand thumped a frenzied pattern on the steering wheel. What if Gram . . . Joan choked back a sob. If anything happened to Gram, she couldn't handle it. She'd lost so many people in her life. Daddy. Grandpa. Roger. She couldn't handle losing Gram too.

God, why is this happening? Don't you care?

The light changed. Tears blurred her vision. She scrubbed them out of her eyes with an impatient gesture. *Don't think about that. Think about driving. Turn into the emergency room parking lot. Turn off the car. Pocket the keys.*

She leaped out of the car and dashed toward the revolving door.

Inside the hospital, she rushed to the registration window. "My grandmother, Grace Hancock. Is she here?"

The woman at the desk peered over a pair of reading glasses. Joan's throat convulsed as a look of compassion crossed her face. Why did she feel sorry for her? Was Gram . . . was she dead?

"She's here," the woman acknowledged. "Are you Carla's daughter?"

Struggling to hold back her tears, Joan nodded.

"Just a minute. I'll tell them you're here."

She stood up and disappeared through a doorway behind her at the same moment Allie shot through the revolving door. Seeing Joan, she made a beeline across the room and threw her arms around her. "Is she okay?"

Joan pressed her head next to Allie's and hugged her shuddering shoulders. In the face of Allie's tears, Joan knew she had to remain calm. Allie was hysterical enough for the both of them. That couldn't be good for the baby. She swallowed back a sob. "I don't know. They just went to get Mom."

The double doors leading into the treatment area swung open. Joan turned and saw Ken stride through them. As one, she and Allie ran toward him.

"Is she alright?" Allie's eyes, puffy and red, begged for information. Joan's breath caught in her throat, waiting for his answer.

Ken put a hand on each of their shoulders, his face an oasis of calm. "She's doing as well as can be expected. Her vitals are good, except her blood pressure's high, but that's not unusual after a trauma like this. Ortho is on their way to do some X-rays, and we've just called in a surgeon."

"Surgeon?" Joan searched his face. "X-rays? Didn't she have a stroke?"

He shook his head. "No, we think she broke her hip."

Her hip? Not a stroke. "She's not going to . . . die?"

The most welcome sound Joan could have hoped for was Ken's gentle laughter. He squeezed her shoulder. "No, she's not going to die."

Joan's knees threatened to buckle from a sudden wave of relief. Allie's sobs grew louder, and in a single gesture, Ken pulled them both to him. His strong arm lent Joan strength as she buried her face in his shoulder. She stood there, one arm around Ken and the other around Allie, and let the news sink in. Gram broke a hip. She wasn't going to die.

Ken continued. "I don't want to make light of her condition, though. An injury like this for someone her age is serious. We'll have to check those X-rays and let the orthopedic surgeon give us a prognosis. No matter what he says, I think it's safe to assume we're going to keep her here for a while."

Joan drew in a shuddering breath, and felt a measure of control return. She lifted her head, pressing Allie's back with her arm. "What happened?"

Before Ken could answer, someone came through the revolving door. Allie gave a cry and flew to her husband's side. A fresh wave of weeping overtook her as Eric comforted her. She looked so pitiful, leaning over her big belly to reach Eric.

With something like a shock, Joan realized Ken's arm still lingered at her waist. She stepped away, casting an awkward half smile up at him, just as Allie recovered herself and pulled Eric toward them.

"Ken was just about to tell us what happened," she told him.

Ken grinned down at Joan. "It was Trigger. He must have heard her cry or something. He barked and howled like a madman until he woke me up from a dead sleep, and then wouldn't be ignored. He led me to your house, and I found her on the dining room floor." His grin turned sheepish. "I'm afraid I did quite a bit of damage to your back door getting inside. I'll get someone out there to fix it this afternoon."

Eric thrust a hand toward Ken. "Hey, man, don't worry about that. I'll take care of it. We're grateful to you."

As soon as Ken released Eric's hand, Allie threw her arms around his neck. "Thank you so much, Ken. If you hadn't found her, she could have laid there all day. Then she really might have had a stroke."

"But how did it happen?" Joan shook her head. "Surely her hip didn't just snap for no reason."

"She fell off a chair." Ken frowned disapproval. "I talked to her for a few minutes while we waited for the ambulance, and I told her she had no business climbing up on a chair to begin with. She said she was trying to rearrange the baskets on top of the china hutch. Something about putting them in size order?"

Allie groaned, while guilt stabbed at Joan. This was her fault. Why hadn't she done more the last time she caught Gram standing on a chair? She should have been firmer, should have extracted a promise. She gulped. She should have told Mom. Gram would have listened if Mom told her not to go climbing on chairs. But Joan didn't want to tell Mom, because she was afraid. The threat of the nursing home loomed like a dark shadow.

"Listen," Ken said, "it's against the rules to have too many family members in there at once, but since your mom is a nurse here, I'm sure nobody will mind if you want to go back and say hello."

Allie rubbed at her tearstained cheeks. "We do."

Unable to speak, Joan nodded. She allowed Ken to guide her through the double doors and down a long hallway, past several empty hospital beds with curtain partitions. Two were closed, presumably with people inside. Ken led them to the last bed and pulled back the curtain. Inside, Mom sat in a hard plastic chair beside the bed. She rose when she caught sight of them, and Allie rushed into her open arms. Joan stood, frozen, staring at the bed.

Gram looked small and vulnerable lying there. An IV needle was inserted in the back of her hand, attaching her by way of a clear tube to a plastic bagful of liquid. The bag hung from a pole fixed to the head of the bed. Her blue eyes seemed abnormally big, her face pale. She was strapped to a yellow plastic stretcher that lay on the hospital bed, her right leg immobilized. She still wore her own clothes, though the way her long-sleeved blouse had twisted around her waist looked uncomfortable. Why didn't someone straighten it? When Gram's eyes closed against a sudden pain, Joan realized they probably didn't want to move her any more than they had to.

She shook off her shock and stepped to the opposite side

of the bed from Mom's chair. A faint smile lifted the corners of Gram's lips as she raised her hand for Joan to take.

"Are you okay?" Joan kept her voice at a whisper. Whispers hid emotion, helped her maintain control.

"I'm fine." Her voice shook with something . . . fatigue? Pain? "But you know what? They say they're going to have to cut my slacks off. These are my favorite slacks. I've had them for more than twenty years."

Allie stepped up to the opposite side of the bed, teasing laughter in her puffy eyes. "Then it's high time you got some new ones."

"You're both here." Gram's head turned as she smiled at Allie. She sounded woozy. They had probably given her something for pain. "Is Tori coming too?"

"She'll be here as soon as she can." Allie smoothed the hair from Gram's forehead. "She has to drive from Lexington, you know."

Gram sighed. "The whole family here, and I don't have a thing to serve you."

Even Joan joined in the laughter. How like Gram.

A man in scrubs wheeled a big machine into view. A flash of surprise crossed his face when he caught sight of all the people stuffed inside the curtained area.

Ken stepped up to the bed. "They're here to do the X-rays. I'm afraid you'll have to wait outside."

Joan squeezed Gram's hand and laid it gently down on the sheet. "We'll be right outside if you need us."

When they moved away from the bed, the man wheeled the machine in and closed the curtain behind him. Allie and Eric headed toward the waiting room, but Mom hesitated.

Ken touched her on the arm. "You can stay. She might feel more comfortable with you there."

Before she could disappear through the curtain, Joan stepped in front of Mom. She looked up into her face, her jaw quivering. "This is all my fault." Her voice cracked with a sob. "I should have stopped her."

Mom's arms went around Joan. The gesture seemed to break down a barrier, and Joan felt tears gush into her eyes. She returned the hug, wetting Mom's shirt, aware that Ken stepped discreetly away.

"That's silly, honey," Mom whispered. "You weren't even there. She fell, that's all. There was nothing you could do to prevent it."

Joan shook her head. "You don't understand. I caught her on a chair the other day. I told her not to do it again, but I didn't make her promise." She buried her face in Mom's shoulder. "I should have told you. I was being selfish, afraid you'd send her away if you knew she was doing something dangerous. And now look what's happened. I'm so sorry, Mom."

Her breath came in shuddering heaves while Mom patted her back. After a few moments, Mom took her shoulders and pushed her gently to arm's length. "Listen to me, Joan. Mother is not your responsibility. This is not your fault. It's no one's fault. It was an accident, that's all." She ducked her head, forcing Joan to look her in the eye. "Do you understand?"

Still miserable, Joan nodded.

Mom pulled her close for another hug. "She's going to be fine. Don't worry about her." She chuckled. "And I can pretty much guarantee she won't be climbing on any more chairs."

Joan couldn't help laughing. She backed up to give Mom a trembling smile. "You'd better get in there before that man tries to cut her clothes off. He might need someone to defend him."

Mom's gaze softened. "I love you, honey."

New tears sprang to Joan's eyes. How many times had Mom said those words? At least a million. But never before had they fallen like absolution on Joan's aching heart.

"I love you too, Mom."

The pounding of Eric's hammer rang through the house. Joan watched as he placed another board across the broken door and nailed it into place. Outside the window, deep darkness covered the backyard.

"There." He stepped back to eye his work. "Nobody's coming through that. You'll be safe and secure until the new door is installed next week."

"Thank you, Eric." Mom stood behind him, a mug of tea in her hand. "I'm so glad we have you to help us with things like this."

"Me too." Tori, curled up on the love seat, called from the other room. Exhaustion made her voice faint.

She arrived at the hospital in time to hear the news from the orthopedic surgeon. Gram had fractured her right femur just below the hip joint. It was a bad break, not easy to repair. She was scheduled for surgery at 6:00 in the morning to have a rod and pins inserted to secure the bone while it healed. Given Gram's age, the surgeon said the hardware would probably never be removed. A hip replacement would have been far easier to recover from. At this point he wasn't sure Gram would ever walk without a walker.

Even while she recognized the serious nature of Gram's injury, Joan felt nothing but relief. She was alive. She would recover. That's all that mattered.

Allie heaved herself out of the recliner. "Can we go home now? I'm so tired I can hardly move."

She looked it. Her eyelids, no longer puffy from crying, now drooped as she gave an open-mouthed yawn. Her feet had swollen from hours pacing the hard hospital floors, and she'd slipped her shoes off. Joan decided they looked slightly less bloated after elevating them in the recliner the past hour, but not enough to get her shoes back on.

"Come on, girls." Eric threw an arm around the small of her back for support as he helped her toward the door. He placed a hand over her belly like he was palming a basketball. "Daddy will take you home and put you to bed."

Mom set down her mug and followed them to the door. "You don't need to come to the hospital in the morning. I'll call you when she comes out of surgery."

Allie raised her chin. "Just try and keep me away."

Eric gave her a stern look. "If you can't get your shoes on, you're staying home." He forestalled her argument with a kiss on her bangs. "I watch out for my girls even when they're too stubborn for their own good."

Allie must have been tired. She didn't even argue as he guided her out of the house.

Mom shut and locked the door behind them, and then returned to the living room. She picked up her tea and sat beside Joan on the sofa, heaving a sigh. "What a day."

"I'll say." Tori's eyes didn't open. "And tomorrow's going to be another long one."

"Why don't you go to bed, honey? I'll wake you in the morning."

"Good idea." She sat up, swung her feet to the floor, and stood, wobbling slightly. "G'night, Mom. G'night, Joan." She stumbled down the hallway toward the spare bedroom.

Mom watched her go, then turned to look at Joan. "You're quiet tonight."

Joan mustered the energy to smile. "I'm always quiet."

"True, but you're extra quiet tonight. Are you alright?"

Joan stared at her feet, which were propped up on the coffee table. Gram would have a fit if she were here. "Yeah, I think so. I was really scared, though."

"You know what?" Mom held the mug with both hands and stared down into it. "I was too. For a few minutes, before I knew what was wrong, I thought, *I can't handle this. I've lost too many already.*"

Joan felt her eyes going wide. "I felt the same way."

Mom placed a hand over hers. "She's eighty-three. I know it's going to happen some day. But I'm sure glad it wasn't today."

Joan closed her eyes, enjoying the comfort of her mother's touch. For the first time, talking to Mom felt easy. She wasn't struggling to come up with words that wouldn't give away what she really felt. Maybe because, for the first time, Joan felt no hint of the hidden resentment she'd held for so many years.

"Mom, can I tell you something?"

"Of course."

Joan looked down at the warm hand on top of hers. "I blamed you for Daddy. All these years, I blamed you for making him leave. I think that's why I've been so angry over Gram. I felt like you were trying to take somebody else away from me."

Mom's hand curled around hers. Joan looked up to see her sad smile. "I know, honey. It's okay."

"No, it isn't. I never realized what you went through. I want you to know I think . . ." She swallowed and turned her hand over to squeeze Mom's. "I think you were right. To send him away, I mean. I just don't understand why you didn't tell us, make sure we knew your reasons."

"You and Allie have been talking?"

Joan nodded.

Mom released Joan's hand and blew out a deep breath. "I know how important it is for a girl to have the love of her father. A lot of her developing self-esteem is based on that relationship. I figured if you blamed me, you wouldn't feel like he deserted you."

Tenderness for this woman, who had given so much for her, welled up and threatened to clog Joan's throat. She scooted across the cushion that separated them to lean her head on her mother's shoulder. "Moms are important too."

Mom's hand came up to caress her cheek. "You've always had the love of your mother."

Joan closed her eyes. "I know."

At 9:30 Joan took her cell phone to a quiet corner of the hallway outside Gram's hospital room and dialed Brittany's phone number.

"Hello?"

"Hey, it's Joan."

"Hey! I'm just getting ready to leave for church."

"I hoped I'd catch you." Joan shoved the slip of paper with the phone number on it into her jeans pocket. "I wanted to let you know I won't be there this morning."

She brought Brittany up-to-date on Gram's accident.

"Oh, the poor thing! Is she going to be okay? Do y'all need anything?"

"She'll be fine." A real smile lightened Joan's tone. "She's still in recovery, but the doctor said her surgery went better than he could have hoped. She should be back to her room any minute."

"You know what I'm going to do?" Brittany giggled. "I'm going to make brownies for when she comes home."

Joan laughed. "She'll love that. Listen, at Sunday school could you ask if we can meet at someone else's house this Thursday? I don't know if she'll be released by then, but if she is, she'll need to stay quiet. And I know Gram. She won't be able to do that if there are people in her house."

"Do you want to postpone the playground project? You're going to have so much on your mind this week."

"No way." Joan leaned against a window, watching a man in a hospital gown shuffle down the hallway, pulling his IV pole beside him. "If we wait too much longer, the weather will turn cold and the kids won't have enough

275

time to enjoy their new playground. No, this Saturday is the perfect day."

"Okay, if you're sure."

The elevator door at the other end of the hallway opened, and an orderly wheeled a hospital bed out.

"I'm sure. You guys just pick another place to meet this week."

"What about Cracker Barrel? We could have dinner together while we work out all the plans."

Joan grinned. This singles class was fast becoming a real social group. Maybe she wasn't the only one who needed something to get involved in. "Sounds great."

The hospital bed rolled slowly down the hallway, stopping in front of Gram's room. That was no orderly. Joan pushed off the wall to stand up straight. "Ken just brought Gram back from recovery, Brittany. I need to go."

"Okay. We're going to pray for your granny this morning. And you call me if there's anything we can do, you hear?"

Touched, Joan smiled. "Thank you. Tell everyone I'll see them Thursday."

She pressed the End button and joined her family in the hallway as they filed out of the small private room to make way for Ken to roll the bed in. Gram's eyes were closed. A surgical cap still covered her head, and a white blanket had been tucked up around her neck. Only her left hand, the one with the IV tube, lay outside the cover.

A nurse came out from behind the nurses' station and followed them into the room. Ken handed her a chart

276

and then leaned over the bed. "Grace, you're back in your room. And you have some visitors."

Her eyelids fluttered open. Joan joined Allie, Tori, and Mom in rushing forward to her side as the nurse transferred the IV bag to a machine with a digital display. Ken stepped back to stand beside Eric in the doorway.

"Hi, Gram," Tori said, her tone low and soft.

"We're all here, Mother," Mom said.

Joan placed her hand over the one with the IV. It was cold. Gently she slipped her other hand beneath Gram's palm to warm it. "How are you feeling?"

Her eyes unfocused, Gram's head turned to look at each of them. Her lips barely parted as she spoke. "I've been better."

Allie laughed softly. "How does it compare to childbirth, Gram?"

"Much worse," she whispered. "No reward when it's over."

"Don't say that to Dr. Winterton," Ken warned. "He's just spent several hours putting Humpty Dumpty back together again, and making sure your leg will heal correctly. That's a pretty big reward."

The last two words came out in almost a slur. Joan peered at Ken. He looked exhausted, dark circles beneath his red-rimmed eyes. He did get a few hours' sleep yesterday afternoon, but then he'd had to report back to the emergency room for work at 6:00 last night. He hadn't been home since. With a glance at Allie, she yielded her place. Allie's hands slipped around Gram's as Eric stepped forward to stand beside his wife.

Joan went to Ken in the doorway. "You've been here all night. You need to go home and get some sleep."

He brought a hand to his face and rubbed at his eyes. "I'm going now. I just wanted to be here when she got out of surgery."

Joan laid a hand on his arm. "You've been so kind to us."

Mom left Gram's bedside and came to stand beside them. "Yes, you have. We can't thank you enough."

From her place by the IV pole, Allie nodded. Tori's eyes caught Joan's for a second. Her lips tightened. Joan bit back a sigh. She had some work to do on her little sister.

Ken said, "Grace, I'll be back tonight to see how you're doing."

Gram's head dipped once in acknowledgment before her eyelids closed again.

Joan smiled up at him. "I'll walk you to the elevator and bring you up-to-date on the playground project."

They all said goodbye and Joan fell into step beside Ken. She told him about Brittany's success in securing playground mulch and about a message from Eve saying she bought a bunch of fall flowers to plant around the grounds. When they reached the elevator door, she told him about their next meeting at Cracker Barrel as he pressed the button.

He grinned down at her. "So I guess that means you and I are having dinner together Thursday night."

Her pulse fluttered, driving coherent thought out of her mind. "I . . . I guess so."

He frowned. "But you could also say you're having dinner with Gordy."

Joan recovered enough to raise an eyebrow. "And you could say you're having dinner with Brittany."

Ken leaned toward her. Her eyes captured by his, she found herself unable to look away. Heart pounding in her chest, his warm breath caressed her cheek as he said, "I don't want to have dinner with Brittany."

He was going to kiss her! Her breath caught in her throat as she leaned ever so slightly forward . . .

The elevator doors slid open. A wave of disappointment swept over her when Ken stepped back to let two women out. He took their place in the elevator, his eyes holding hers as he punched a button.

"Will I see you later?" His lopsided grin made her mouth go dry.

Oh, you can count on it!

She managed a self-possessed nod as the metal doors slid closed.

~ *21* ~

Joan stood on the front porch Tuesday morning, stretching and trying not to look toward Ken's house. His car sat in the driveway, which meant he wasn't working late. Yesterday she didn't see him at all, and though he probably just got caught up at the hospital, she couldn't help wondering if he was sorry for their almost-kiss. He wasn't avoiding her, was he?

His front door opened when she stepped onto the sidewalk. A foolish smile took possession of her lips. What was the matter with her, grinning like an idiot? If he wasn't sorry already, he certainly would be if she simpered all over him like a teenager. She schooled her expression as an ecstatic Trigger pulled him down the driveway.

She hid her face by stooping to give Trigger an enthusiastic ear rub. "There's my hero. What a good dog you are. You saved Gram, Trigger! I'm going to buy you a big, juicy steak, that's what I'm going to do."

"Hey, what about me?" Ken gazed at her mournfully. "I helped too."

Joan straightened, laughing to hide her nerves. "You want me to rub your ears?"

"No, but that steak sounds pretty good."

They started walking. Joan set an aggressive pace. If she couldn't run, at least she was going to get her blood pumping, and theirs too. Trigger knew the way by now and ran in front, straining at the leash.

"Do you think he'll ever learn how to walk on a lead?" Ken shook his head.

"Your book should tell you how to train him. Aren't you supposed to shorten the leash so he has to walk right at your side?"

Ken nodded, then turned his head to grin at her. "But if I did that, where would you walk?"

She raised her chin. "I'd run ahead, and you boys could try to keep up."

He laughed. "No thanks. I learned my lesson that first morning." They walked a few steps. "I stopped by to see Grace this morning. She looked good."

"She had a lot of pain last night." Joan spent Monday evening in Gram's room after work. "The physical therapist is supposed to come today to teach her some techniques for transferring from bed to a chair. I don't know, though. It's really fast, don't you think?"

Ken shook his head. "You'll be surprised how quickly they'll have her up and around."

"Well, as long as they don't push her too hard."

They turned the corner. Trigger had settled into their rhythm, and no longer jerked Ken's arm forward with every step.

"You have a very special relationship with her."

Joan nodded. "She and my grandfather helped Mom raise us after . . ." She kept her eyes focused ahead of her. She hated talking about this. "After my father left."

Ken's voice softened. "Were you close to your father?"

Close? She always thought she was closer to him than to anyone else. Now, she didn't know how to answer that. "Not as close as I thought we were."

Ken watched his feet for a few steps. "I was close to my father. When he and Mom died, I felt like something inside me died with them. I didn't have anybody like Grace. Only Karen, and she was just a teenager." A sad smile hovered around his mouth. "My great-aunt raised us, but we weren't close. I don't think she knew what to do with an angry teenage boy."

"Angry?"

"Oh yeah." He switched the leash from one hand to the other. "I was angry at the world, had a great big chip on my shoulder. I felt like everyone was against me, and of course I was always looking for anything I thought could even the score. Alcohol. Drugs." His gaze slid sideways to meet with hers. "I was on a path to nowhere."

Joan could hardly believe that this man, this doctor, could have a past like the one he described. "What happened?"

"A man took an interest in me. Mr. Wallace." He smiled. "He went to the church my aunt dragged me to every Sunday. He didn't do much, just paid a little attention to me. One Sunday he plopped down on the back row next to me, asked me how things were going, and sat there through the service. He did that every Sunday morning for weeks—just sat by me, trying to get me to talk. Then one day he invited me to his house after church to have dinner with his family and shoot a few hoops." Ken laughed. "He had three little girls who had no interest in basketball, and he loved it. He taught me to love it too. I played in high school, and he came to most of my games."

The playground project was starting to make sense. "So a man showed an interest in you and it changed your life."

Ken tilted his head, considering. "Yes, and no. He showed an interest in me, and became my friend when I desperately needed one. But what changed my life was when he introduced me to Jesus Christ."

Changed his life. Joan, too, became a Christian when she was a young teenager, but did it change her life? If she was honest with herself, she'd have to say no. As a Christian she believed she'd been changed on the inside, but did that change carry over to the outside?

Of course, she'd never been a rebel, never been on a path like Ken described.

"Maybe that's the difference, then." She didn't intend to speak, but the question in Ken's eyes urged her to explain. She shrugged a shoulder. "I was never in trouble, never a rebel. So when I became a Christian, the change in me was less noticeable." Something about the expression that stole over his face made Joan uncomfortable, and a little defensive. "What's that look for?"

"Do you really want to know?"

She nodded.

"I was thinking that God's life-changing power is the same no matter how good or how bad the person is who accepts him."

"But doesn't the Bible teach that God meets each of us where we are?" Joan didn't want to look at him.

"Yes, and he has also given us the ability to make our own choices. He'll change us as much as we allow him to."

She jerked her head sideways to look at him through narrowed eyelids. "Are you saying I didn't allow God to change me, and you did?"

A muscle in his jaw twitched. He was silent as they ducked beneath the low-hanging branches of a sugar maple. Inside, Joan felt as though a tornado was ripping through her emotions. This conversation had taken an uncomfortable turn, and she wanted to end it now. Why did tears feel so close to the surface all of a sudden? She struggled to regain control, focused on her footsteps, the sidewalk, the rising sun's rays filtering through the trees.

"Do you want to know what really made the difference in me?" Ken came to a sudden stop, forcing Trigger and Joan to stop with him.

Though fearful of his answer, Joan nodded.

"It was when Mr. Wallace told me about a promise God made. God said, 'I will never leave you, nor forsake you.'"

Joan's breath caught in her chest. God said that? God, who wanted to be her father, who sent chocolate ice cream when she asked for a sign? He promised not to leave her?

Ken went on, his voice soft. "See, my father left me.

True, he died, but to a twelve-year-old kid the result is the same. When I heard that verse, I realized that God wanted to be a real father to me. I'd always thought of him as some ghostlike spirit sitting on a throne of judgment somewhere, watching from a distance. But suddenly I knew he was right here"—Ken held his hands out, gesturing around them—"right with me every moment. And he promised never to leave. No other father in the world can keep that promise."

But fathers were unreliable. They lied, they cheated, and they left.

She shook her head. No, that was Daddy. She couldn't accuse God of having the same faults as her father. A little girl might do that, but not a grown woman.

"I'm—" She stopped when she realized her voice came out choked. Ken's face was blurred through tears. No! The last thing she wanted to do was cry in front of Ken.

She whirled, and before she could think about her actions, she ran.

❧

Trigger leaped from a sitting position, pulling Ken's arm nearly out of its socket in his effort to follow Joan. Ken knew how the dog felt. The pain in her eyes touched his very soul, and he wanted to go after her, to hold her and tell her it would be okay, that he'd take care of her. He allowed Trigger to drag him forward three steps.

No.

He stopped. The Lord didn't often speak so firmly in

the negative, but there was no doubt in Ken's mind from where that direction came.

"But she's hurting," he whispered. "I want to help her."

In his heart, Ken knew he couldn't relieve Joan's pain. Only God could do that, and he wanted to. But she had to let him.

He stood still, watching her retreating back while Trigger strained at the leash and barked his frustration.

"Lord, reach out to her. She needs you. I can't stand to see her in pain because . . ." He paused, wonder stealing over him as he realized the truth in the words he was about to speak. "Because I love her."

❈

Her Nikes pounded the sidewalk, each step taking her farther from Ken and Trigger, who barked after her. She didn't look back, just ran blindly, tears jarred from her eyes at each step.

God was not like Daddy. Of course he wasn't! But maybe she'd been so hurt by her father's desertion she refused to allow her heavenly Father a place in her life. Blinking to clear her vision, she knew she had discovered the truth. When she heard Mrs. Sachs speak about God's power, didn't Joan feel God nudging her? When Ken talked about how his faith affected his life every day, didn't she feel a tug deep inside? When Karen asked, "What do you believe?" didn't Joan feel the weight of God pressing her, waiting for her answer?

She slowed to a walk, her breath coming in gasps. An

oscillating sprinkler watered the yard beside her. Heavy drops splashed onto the pavement with a loud *tap, tap, tap* in the stillness of the early morning, a wet accompaniment to her thoughts. She had turned another corner and could no longer see Ken and Trigger.

But she did respond to those feelings. She took charge at Sunday school, organized their group, got them focused on a project that could really do some good. Didn't that count for something? Surely God was happy about that.

A slight breeze blew cooling moisture into her sweaty face. Maybe God was pleased with her actions, but what was her motivation? Did she really come up with this project idea because she wanted a closer relationship with a heavenly Father? Or with Ken? Or was she just bored?

She stopped. The sun, rising above the houses behind her, cast long shadows on the road. She drew in a deep breath. The truth was, God had been trying to get her attention and she had ignored him because she was afraid. Afraid of being called a fanatic. Afraid of giving up control. But most of all, afraid of being hurt again.

I will never leave you, nor forsake you.

Was it true?

Oh, how desperately she wanted to believe it! Suddenly she realized she didn't care if Tori and Allie called her a fanatic. If only she could believe that she had a real Father, one who loved her and would never leave her. If she could believe that, she would give her whole heart to him.

"God, I want to believe in you." She closed her eyes, her head tilted back to the sky. Sweat dampened the skin on the back of her neck. Anyone driving by would think she was a lunatic, but she didn't care. "I want you to be real in my life the way you're real in Ken's. I want you to be my . . . my Father. And I promise to be whatever you want me to be."

The whirling tornado of emotions slowed, and a peaceful calm stole over Joan's heart. With an assurance that left her lightheaded, she knew what God wanted of her. He wanted her to be his daughter. His beautiful, cherished, much-loved child. Her limbs felt light, and before she knew what she was doing, she started running again. Like a little girl running into her Father's outstretched arms.

Joan unlocked Abernathy's front doors a few minutes before 9:00 with her heart still light. She stepped outside to breathe the fresh air. Big, puffy clouds were rolling in, painting patterns with sunlight on the parking lot. Before today they were just clouds. Now they were tools in the hands of an Artist who wanted to color the world just for her.

Rosa's car, with two people in the front seat, pulled into a parking space. Ah, it looked like she would finally get to meet the infamous Luis.

She lifted a hand in greeting as Rosa stood from the passenger side, her happy mood dimming when Rosa did not return her smile. Instead, she looked sad, hesitant, as their eyes locked across the top of the car. Joan lowered her arm. So. The decision had been made.

Luis stood, and Joan studied him in surprise. He was shorter than his wife, with the same jet-black hair and sun-kissed skin tone. He walked beside Rosa, staring at Joan through eyes so dark they might have been all pupil. His gaze shifted away from her face. Why, he looked timid, almost fearful. This was the man who evoked such passionate emotion in the willful, determined Rosa?

Gathering the comfort of all her professionalism around her, Joan held her hand toward him. "You must be Luis."

His grip was firm. He pumped her hand and then shoved his into his pocket without a word.

"Luis want to meet you." Rosa was having trouble looking Joan in the face too. She stared at the concrete between them. "He want to explain to you our reasons to move to Las Vegas."

"You don't owe me an explanation." Joan was proud that her voice betrayed none of the hurt and disappointment she felt. She was losing her friend.

"Miss Joan." His voice a high tenor, Luis made her name sound even more exotic than Rosa did, the J coming out as a Y. "We come to *Los Estados Unidos* to make money we not can make in Mexico. Here we make *mucho* to send back to our family in Juarez. But we . . . ," his hands waved as he searched for a word, "we lonely to be together. What good is money if we not have each other?" He put an arm around his wife and pulled her close to his side. "Rosa is my family. Tiffany is my family. If I do not have my family, money is no good for me."

The love shining from his eyes as he gazed at his wife, and in Rosa's as she looked at him, pierced through a barrier in Joan. She felt the beginning of tears prickle the back of her eyes, an all-too-familiar feeling lately. What would she give to have someone love her that much?

Wonder stole over her as she realized she did. Her Father

had told her just this morning how much he loved her, and that he would never leave her. For some reason, that made Rosa's departure not as devastating as it would have seemed before. Joan would miss her, but she knew this was the right thing for her friend.

And for Tiffany too. That little girl deserved to have both her parents with her. She especially deserved a father who loved her, as Luis obviously did. She was young. She'd adjust to her new home, make new friends, and be happier because she was part of a real family. An American family, just like Rosa wanted for her.

Joan reached for them both, pulled them into a hug. "I hope you'll be happy in the home you build together."

Joan stepped through the hospital's main entrance. Her watch read 7:15. Gram would have finished supper an hour ago, and was probably watching her evening game show.

As she hurried toward the elevator, her eyes fell on the person leaning against the reception desk. Shock coursed through her body, bringing her to a standstill.

Ken.

Stomach in her throat, her face heated in a flash as their gazes locked. She knew he'd be here, knew she would run into him tonight. But she didn't think he'd be waiting to waylay her inside the front door. He must think her a total infant after the way she behaved this morning.

He crossed the room in three steps, his eyes never leaving hers. "I knew you'd be here soon."

She tore her gaze away, staring instead at the stethoscope hanging around his shoulders, the collar of his white jacket, anywhere but at his face. "I wanted to see Gram."

She swallowed. Of course she did. He knew that. Why was she stating the obvious?

"I know. I won't keep you. I just wanted to make sure you were alright. And that you weren't"—his head dipped, trying to catch her eye—"mad at me."

She gave an embarrassed laugh. "Of course not. I'm just feeling a little foolish for running off like I did this morning."

His warm finger touched her chin, tilting it gently upward. She couldn't breathe, the breath snatched from her lungs by the green depths of his eyes.

"I don't think you're foolish, Joan."

The way he said her name, drew it out like he wanted to savor the taste on his tongue, washed over her like a caress. Who needed a nickname? When Ken said it, her name flowed into her ears like heavenly music. All awkwardness fled as his finger rose to brush her cheek. If she leaned forward and tilted her head, their lips would touch.

If only the woman behind the reception desk wasn't staring at them with such obvious interest. Ken noticed and his hand dropped to his side. Mouth twitching, he took a step backward. "I'll let you get up there."

Blushing to the hair roots, Joan nodded. He fell in step beside her as she walked to the bank of elevators. When she punched the Up button, the door swooshed open immediately. Just her luck.

He leaned against the side panel to keep the door from

closing. "Dr. Boling is going to be late tomorrow, so I'll be stuck here in the morning. I'll miss our walk."

Disappointment washed over her, but she nodded. "Do you want me to take Trigger? I've got an old leash at the house I can use."

"He'd love that."

"It won't be the same, though." She gave him a shy smile. "I was sort of hoping we could continue our conversation. I promise not to cry or run away."

The elevator door tried to close, and he shoved it back with his shoulder. "Any time. Maybe we could go to dinner one evening."

A lopsided grin turned her stomach into a fluttering mess.

"Just the two of us."

A date! He was asking her for a date! Breath shallow, unable to tear her gaze away from his eyes, she managed to respond in a composed voice. "I'd like that."

Triumph shone in his face. "Me too."

He stepped back, and the doors swished closed.

Joan melted against the elevator's back wall. They hadn't set a time or place, but she had definitely been asked for a date. Two almost-kisses and an almost-date! Tori might not approve, but Allie would be thrilled with her progress.

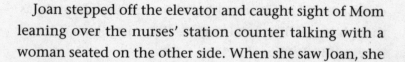

Joan stepped off the elevator and caught sight of Mom leaning over the nurses' station counter talking with a woman seated on the other side. When she saw Joan, she straightened. Her face took on a guarded expression, which sent a shock of fear coursing through Joan. Was something wrong? Surely Ken would have mentioned it. Unless he didn't know.

Joan approached, bracing herself for bad news. "What's wrong? Has she taken a turn for the worse?"

Mom's brow cleared. "No, not at all. She's doing really well, in fact. It's just . . ." She glanced at the seated nurse, grabbed Joan's arm, and propelled her down the hallway. They stopped in the deserted waiting room at the end. "She's being released tomorrow."

"But that's good news."

"It is." She nodded. "But she's not being released to come home. She needs some extra help and some PT that Dr. Winterton feels she won't get at home."

Cold fear tickled in the back of Joan's mind. "I'll take off work. I've got some time off coming—"

"Joan." Mom stopped her with a hand on her arm. "You're not a nurse or a physical therapist. Mother will be better off at a facility where they have skilled people who can help speed her recovery."

"A facility like Waterford?" The word rolled off her tongue with a bitterness that was more habit than a true expression of her feelings.

Mom winced. "They have an excellent nursing program. I promise you, it's only temporary. In a couple of weeks when she's recovered enough to take care of herself, she'll come home." Mom rested her chin on clasped hands, as though beseeching her to agree. "I'm sorry, Joan. I know how you feel about this."

Joan stared at the pleading in her mother's face. With a growing amazement, she realized Mom didn't know how she felt—because Joan didn't feel the same as the last time they talked about the assisted living center. True, she wasn't happy about this development and could get angry or upset if she allowed herself. But there really wasn't any reason to feel that way. Gram wasn't being taken from her. She knew that now.

I will never leave you, nor forsake you.

From somewhere deep inside, a sense of calm welled up to drive away the fear that she would lose someone else she loved. No matter what happened, Joan would never be alone.

She took both of Mom's hands in hers. "It's okay. I understand."

At 10:40 the next morning Joan pulled her car into a parking place in front of Waterford Manor. She'd driven by the facility many times since it opened, but this was the closest she'd ever come. Peering over the steering wheel at the covered entry, the ornate front door, the well-tended flower garden lining the trim brick building, she had to admit the place didn't look like a depressing nursing home from the outside.

Allie's car pulled to a stop beside her. Mom must have also called her about Gram's pending arrival at Waterford. She heaved herself out of the car with some effort, and then leaned against the door to rest. As she waddled around the car, Joan realized with a shock that her belly was noticeably lower than just two days ago.

"You've dropped."

Allie rolled her eyes. "Tell me something I don't know." She winced, her hands carrying her round abdomen as she walked. "She's pressing on something in there, and it feels awful. If I stand up too quickly, you'd better be ready to catch her when she falls out."

"But you've got three more weeks."

She glared. "Don't remind me."

They made for the shade of the canopy and stopped to scan the parking lot.

"I don't see Mom's car," Allie said.

"We probably beat them here. Mom said they had to get some paperwork signed before they'd be able to leave."

"Let's go in and see what it's like."

Steeling herself with a deep breath, Joan opened the door for her sister. When they stepped inside, Allie gasped and Joan's eyes went wide.

They stood in a foyer with high, vaulted ceilings and marble tiled floor. Richly upholstered wingback chairs sat on each side of a gleaming mahogany table, a marble statuette posed elegantly on its surface. The subtle scent of lemons hung in the air, reminding Joan of the furniture polish Gram used at home.

"Ohmigosh," breathed Allie. "Mom said it was nice, but I had no idea."

The sound of a chair scooting across the floor drew their attention to a neat reception desk. A gray-haired woman rose from behind it. "May I help you?"

Her pleasant smile made a homey contrast to the elegant surroundings. Joan returned it, hoping hers wasn't stiff with surprise. "Our grandmother is going to be here for a couple of weeks while she recovers from surgery. She should arrive any minute."

"Oh yes." She ran a finger down a pad of paper on the desk. "Mrs. Hancock. We're expecting her."

Allie pointed toward the two chairs. "Is it okay if we wait over there?"

The woman nodded. "Of course. But if you'd like to take a look around before she arrives, I'll be happy to give you a little tour."

"That would be nice, thank you."

She came out from behind the desk. "I'm Edna Carter."

"Allie Harrod, and this is my sister Joan Sanderson."

Her hand, slender and lined with veins, felt cool in Joan's. They fell in beside her as she led them beneath a wide archway. Allie pointed upward toward the stained glass in a dome-shaped ceiling. Eyes wide, Joan nodded as she stepped through a doorway on the other side. She'd never seen stained glass that size outside of a church.

"This is the dining room." Mrs. Carter's gesture swept the room. "Breakfast and lunch are available, of course, though some residents prefer to have those meals in their apartments. But no one misses dinner in the dining room. We have a grand time every evening."

Round tables covered with white tablecloths filled the carpeted room, eight high-backed chairs surrounding each one. Large chandeliers cast a warm light over the furnishings. A statue stood sentry beside the door—a life-size maître d' holding a burgundy menu for display.

Allie stooped to read it. "Tonight they're having chicken cordon bleu or poached salmon with hollandaise sauce, potatoes au gratin, and green bean casserole. And peach cobbler or carrot cake for dessert." She ran a tongue across her lips. "Can I come for supper?"

The older woman laughed. "Of course you can, dear. We love guests. I'll put in an order for an extra meal if you like."

They proceeded through the dining room, across a hallway, and through a set of doors beyond.

"This is the library." Mrs. Carter's announcement was unnecessary. A large stone fireplace dominated one side of the long room, but two walls were composed of floor-to-ceiling shelves of polished dark wood, stuffed full with books. A candle burned on the mantle, filling the room with the scent of vanilla. Two women seated at a computer broke off an animated conversation at their approach. Joan caught sight of an eBay list on the monitor. They smiled and nodded a greeting before continuing their discussion about how much their maximum bid should be.

Mrs. Carter gave a sniff as she pointed toward a closed door in the wall opposite the fireplace. "The study is through there. This entire building is nonsmoking, but a few gentlemen *insist* on stepping out on the patio to smoke their cigars. We keep the door closed because of the smell."

Joan smiled at Mrs. Carter's obvious disapproval of such behavior. They returned to the hallway. Paintings decorated the walls, along with the occasional plant stand or uphol-stered chair placed in cozy nooks beside an end table with an assortment of magazines. The doors on the rooms they passed each had a plaque with the name and a picture of the resident. Through open doors, several people called a greeting as they passed.

Joan turned to Mrs. Carter. "This is a beautiful place. But I don't see any sick people. I thought this was a nurs-ing facility."

"It is that too. We offer several levels of care here, what-ever the resident needs. Your grandmother will be on Re-spite Care, I noticed, which means she'll receive full care but only temporarily, while she's here." Her face bright-ened. "Would you like to see one of the apartments?"

"We'd love to." Allie smiled her gratitude.

"Come this way."

Joan followed Allie and Mrs. Carter, peering at the various wreaths and hangings on many of the doors. They crossed the dining room again and into another hallway, passing a laundry room, a chapel, and even an exercise room.

"You have a gym?" Allie's eyebrows arched high.

Mrs. Carter waved a hand dismissively. "That's nothing but a few machines. All residents have full membership at the wellness center next door. They have exercise classes and a swimming pool there."

Allie turned an open-mouthed look Joan's way. "I want to live here!"

Joan agreed. The place was like a country club. She felt more than a little foolish for making such a big deal out of Mom bringing Gram here to visit her friend.

Mrs. Carter stopped in front of a door, her hand on the doorknob. She turned a worried face toward them. "Now I wasn't expecting guests, so don't look too closely at the dishes in the sink."

Joan's jaw went slack. "This is your apartment?" The older woman nodded. "I thought you worked here."

"Oh no, dear. Janet had to step away to take care of a resident. I was just covering the desk for a minute."

Joan took a second look at their guide. Mrs. Carter wasn't anywhere near as old as Gram. Come to think of it, many of the residents she'd seen looked younger than Gram. She shook her head. She couldn't have been more wrong about this place.

Mrs. Carter's apartment was homey, comfortable, and stuffed full of furniture. A sliding glass door off the main room opened on to a private patio with a pretty little flower garden. The kitchen area boasted a half-sized refrigerator, a microwave, and a sink with a small cabinet. They stepped through a doorway into a separate bedroom with a full-sized bath.

Allie walked through, Joan right behind her, then turned a smile on Mrs. Carter. "It's lovely."

The older woman's gaze swept the room. "It's small, but plenty big for me. And now we'd better get back up front and see if your grandmother has arrived."

She had. Mom's empty car sat beneath the canopy out front. Mrs. Carter led them down another hallway to a room whose door stood open. Inside, Joan found Mom and a young, pleasant-faced nurse's aide on either side of Gram's bed.

This apartment was smaller than Mrs. Carter's, an efficiency, probably intended for temporary use only. It was more comfortable than a hospital room, with a vinyl recliner beside a nice little table and lamp, but the bed was standard hospital issue. It had the same kitchenette as Mrs. Carter's, and a private bathroom.

"There you girls are." Mom set Gram's suitcase on the floor and shrugged her purse off her shoulder. "I saw your cars out front."

Allie eased into the recliner. "We were getting the grand tour. Wow, Gram, this is quite a place you've landed in."

Joan went to the bedside to take Gram's hand. The IV had been removed, and a piece of gauze beneath plastic tape covered the place where the needle had punctured her skin. Her eyelids looked heavy as she tried to focus on Joan. "Do you think Myrtle will come visit with me?"

"Mrs. Mattingly?" The young aide patted her other arm. "I'm sure she will later. But right now you need to get some rest." She placed a call button on the bed next to Gram's right hand. "I'll be in to check on you every so often, but ring this when you wake up."

Gram nodded and, with a soft sigh, closed her eyes.

Mom spoke in a low voice. "The trip over took a lot out of her. We've given her something for pain, so she'll sleep for hours."

"Are you saying I have to go back to work now?" Allie blew her bangs off her forehead. "I told them I'd be gone most of the afternoon."

"Go home and take a nap," Mom advised. "You look tired, honey."

Joan held a hand out to help her sister out of the chair. "Well, I'm going back to work, but I'll come again later. Will I see you this evening?"

"Oh yeah." Allie smiled. "I'm coming for dinner. Mrs. Carter ordered me some of that chicken cordon bleu."

They filed quietly out of the room. Joan paused in the doorway to look back at the bed. Gram's breath came slow and steady, her face peaceful in sleep. A matching peace descended over Joan. Gram might have a painful and slow recovery ahead of her, but she was going to be fine.

~ *23* ~

Cracker Barrel's dining room bustled with activity. Joan had to raise her voice to be heard by Eve, who sat at the far end of the long table. Their number had grown tonight, since Gordy and Crystal both brought friends. Joan was ecstatic at the popularity their little group was enjoying. Of course, it might just be the food that drew people. Who didn't love Cracker Barrel?

She tried not to bump Ken's arm with her elbow every time she took a bite. It wasn't easy since the ten of them were crowded around a table meant for eight. The way his eyes kept fixing on hers, though, she didn't think he minded.

When the server cleared their plates, she set her notebook on the table in front of her. "So, we've got two gallons of kid-safe paint, four vinyl-coated swing chains, and four sling seats, compliments of Ryan's boss." She smiled across the table at him. "Anything else in the way of equipment?"

Gordy spoke up. "Nick and I ran by there on the way over here tonight. The slide's in pretty good shape, but there are some rusted bolts we'll need to replace, and some rough spots that I think we can smooth out. We'll bring what we need for that."

Crystal waved her hand above her head, bouncing in her seat. "Guess what I got?" She didn't wait for anyone's guess. "I got a new backboard and basketball hoop donated from Gart Sports in Lexington."

"Hey, that's fantastic," Ken said, and several people clapped. "I've been looking at that court. Unfortunately I don't think we can do much with the cracked asphalt, but I'll bring some weed killer so we can clean it up enough to dribble a basketball."

Joan recorded the basketball equipment in her notebook. "We have a truckload of mulch coming at one o'clock." She glanced at Brittany for confirmation. "And Eve's got flowers to plant."

"A bunch," Eve said. "So everybody bring a shovel."

Joan made a note to herself. "What else do we need?"

"Garbage bags," Nick said. "And thick gloves for picking up broken glass. We saw a lot of that."

"I'll get the bags," Joan said, making another note. "What about the notice we said we were going to post?"

On the other side of Ken, Marissa leaned forward to look at Joan. "I made one and put up copies over there yesterday." She reddened. "I hope that was okay. I thought we needed to get it up a few days in advance."

Joan smiled. "That's perfect. I'm so glad you thought of it." She glanced around the table. "I think we've got everything covered."

Brittany clapped her hands, a wide smile on her face. "This is going to be fun, y'all!"

Scanning her list, Joan noted a satisfying check mark beside every item. The only thing left to do was the work. Grinning at Brittany, she couldn't agree more.

❧

Joan hefted a bulging garbage bag. Where was the trash dumpster?

Behind her, Ryan called, "Hey, Joan, just toss that in the back of my pickup. It'll be easier than carrying them all over one at a time."

Just toss it, huh? She half-carried, half-dragged the bag toward Ryan's truck. Loaded down with not only trash from the apartment complex grounds but also weeds from the overgrown flower bed Eve had laboriously uncovered, she'd filled the bag heavier than she anticipated. A parade of little girls followed, giggling.

"Here ya go, ma'am," a deep voice said. "Lemme git that for ya."

Joan smiled with relief into the stubble-covered face that grinned down at her. "I appreciate that."

As the man heaved the bag into the back of the truck, Joan turned to survey the work. The residents of Shadow Ridge had surprised them, outnumbering Joan's group two to one. True, most of them preferred the role of spectator, and a few even brought chairs out of their apartments to sit on their porches and watch. But some pitched in and worked right alongside Joan's friends. Kneeling, Eve and Marissa worked the ground with hand shovels alongside four women. Pots of white and yellow mums stood nearby ready to be planted. Other women spread out all around the grounds filling green garbage bags with trash. Even a couple of men, like her helper, worked alongside Ken, Ryan, Gordy, and Nick as they replaced bolts and attached the new swings. The new backboard leaned against the existing metal pole, ready to be mounted.

But what sent a thrill through Joan were the children. There were dozens, many hanging back shyly to watch the working adults. But most joined in with the garbage and flower details, while a group of boys eagerly handed tools up to the men fixing the swing set. A few were even helping Joan.

She turned a smile on three girls who stood nearby. "Come on, girls. Let's grab another bag."

Just then a car pulled into the parking lot and two women got out. One had a fancy-looking camera slung around her neck. Joan smoothed a hand over her ponytail. Looked like the newspaper had decided to cover the event. Good. The businesses that donated material deserved a little free publicity.

"Hello." The driver came toward Joan with an outstretched hand. "Pam Baker, from the *Advocate-Messenger*."

"Joan Sanderson." Joan removed her work glove to shake the woman's hand. "I'm glad you came by."

"Sanderson. You're the one who called." Her gaze swept over the working people as she flipped open a notebook. "You've got quite a little project going on here. What made you decide to do this?"

Her pen hovered over her pad, waiting to record Joan's words. What should she say? That she was bored and needed something to fill her time? That she thought church should be more than a Sunday morning lesson? That she wanted to spread God's love around her community? Tori would surely think she'd become a fanatic, that Ken had rubbed off on her.

Joan looked down at the girls. Stains covered their clothing, and their hair didn't look all that clean. But one of them gave her a tentative smile and slipped a hand shyly into hers.

Who cared what Tori thought?

Facing the reporter, she raised her chin. "We're Christians. We want to make a difference in people's lives. What better place to start than on a playground?"

Ken tightened a nut, trying to ignore the photographer's camera. It unnerved him, having that thing pointed his way, clicking over and over while he worked. The kids loved it, though, and wore huge grins whenever the lens swung toward them.

If only Mike had showed up. Ken dropped by Thursday afternoon to tell him about the cleanup project, and he said he'd be here. But so far he hadn't made an appearance.

Ken glanced across the playground at Joan. She stood beside the reporter while Brittany explained something. A little girl clutched her hand. Standing there with a stray strand of hair blowing in the slight breeze, smiling down at the child, Joan must be the most beautiful woman in the world.

"Dude, you done up there?" Ryan, holding the ladder on which Ken stood, broke into his thoughts.

"Yeah, that's the last one. I think we're ready for the paint."

The faces of their young helpers lit with excitement.

"I want to paint!"

"Me too! Can I paint too?"

Gordy held up a hand. "I've got four brushes, so you'll have to take turns. And nobody on the ladder except me, you hear?"

While they worked out which four got to paint first, Ken climbed down. As he jumped from the second rung to the ground, he noticed a few older kids coming around the side of the building. They must be the same ones he'd seen a few weeks ago, with the baggy jeans and T-shirts with gang designs on them. Today there were three boys around thirteen or fourteen years old and . . . and Mike.

Mike caught sight of Ken and a smile split his face for a second. Then he glanced up at the boy beside him and the smile disappeared, replaced by the same bored, insolent expression the older kid wore. The leader of their little gang, he puffed on a cigarette as he crossed the grass toward them.

"Mike," Ken called, ignoring the others. "Glad you made it."

They approached the playground. Beside Ken, Ryan was sizing up the three older ones. The leader noticed and insolently sucked on his cigarette, blowing out a long, slow stream of smoke.

Ryan's eyelids narrowed. "A little young to be smoking, aren't you?"

Looking him straight in the eye, the kid took another puff. "I'm old enough."

"What's your name, kid?"

The boy's glance slid toward one of his buddies and back to Ryan. "Bob."

"Bob, huh?" Ryan cocked his head. "You spell that with one O, or two?"

Ken turned away to hide his laughter. It took Bob a little longer to work out the insult, but when he did, he glared at Ryan and whirled to march away.

"Oh, come on, Bobby, I'm just kidding around. You ever hung a basketball goal?"

The kid stopped, his scowl deepening. "No."

"Neither have I." Ryan stepped forward and clapped Bob on the back. "Why don't you put that thing out and come help me figure it out?"

Bob stared at him. For a moment Ken thought he would leave, but then the scowl slipped a little. He dropped the cigarette on the ground and crushed it with a beat-up tennis shoe. "Can't be that hard."

"That's what I thought, till I got a look at the instructions." Ryan put an arm around Bob's shoulder and steered him toward the basketball court, winking at Ken over his head. "I hope one of you guys can speak a foreign language, because I swear these instructions are not written in English."

The two older boys followed Bob and Ryan, leaving Mike beside Ken.

"Hey," Ken said. "Come here a minute. I want to introduce you to someone."

In Bob's absence, the insolent expression fell away from Mike's face. He looked around expectantly as he walked beside Ken. "You didn't bring Trigger?"

"Are you kidding?" Ken laughed. "Nobody would get any work done with him around. He'd pester us to death trying to get us to throw his ball."

"I'd do it."

Ken rubbed his buzzed head. "I know you would. Tell you what. Maybe your mom will let you come over to my house one day next week to help me build some shelves. Then you can throw the ball for Trigger till your arm falls off."

He grinned. "Alright!"

Joan saw them approaching and excused herself, leaving the reporter in Brittany's capable hands. She met them halfway across the grass.

"Joan, I want you to meet somebody. This is Mike Lassiter, a friend of mine. Mike, this is Joan Sanderson. She lives next door to me."

The boy's chest swelled with pride at the introduction. He stuck his hand out like a perfect gentleman. "Pleased to meet you, ma'am."

Joan's lips twitched as she shook his hand. "Nice to meet you too, Mike."

Mike's gaze slid up to Ken, a shrewd look in his eyes. "Is she your girlfriend?"

Joan's face went red.

Ken put a hand up to hide his mouth from Joan and in

a stage whisper said, "Not yet, but I'm working on it, so behave yourself."

Blushing, Joan shook her head. "You two are trying to embarrass me." She walked away, but not before giving Ken a coy smile.

As he watched her walk away, Ken filled his lungs. Joan was one pretty woman.

"You like her," Mike teased, looking up at him.

"Yeah, I do." He grinned down at the boy and shoved his shoulder playfully. "So don't mess it up for me."

Joan slumped against the chair back, fatigue clawing at her body. She looked down the table and saw tired expressions on the face of every member of the CCCS group. That was the name Brittany dubbed them for the reporter, the Christ Community Church Singles.

A server brought a tray of sizzling fajitas to the next table, and the spicy onion smell revived her a bit. She had suggested Casa del Sol, where Rosa worked part-time, when everyone said they wanted to get something to eat. Rosa could use the extra tip money to tide her over until she found a job in Las Vegas.

"Look at the smiles on those kids' faces." Eve held her digital camera toward Gordy so he could check out the little screen. She looked as tired as Joan felt, but also as happy. "They're going to have so much fun on that playground."

"I didn't want to leave," Brittany complained. "They

looked so sad, especially Shawneda. She wanted me to do her nails like mine." Brittany held up a hand. "'Course, they're a sight right now. I'm almost ashamed to take these things to church tomorrow."

"We ought to do something else for those kids," Crystal said. "We could have a sleepover at the church or something."

Brittany straightened. "Or a tea party!"

"Yeah," Gordy said, "the guys would love that."

Ryan tore the paper off a straw and rolled it into a tight wad between his fingers. "Ken and I are going by there next Thursday afternoon to shoot a few hoops with some of the older boys."

Beside Joan, Ken nodded. His arm rested casually across the back of her chair, mostly because he was on the end and the position let him more easily face the rest of the table. But she hoped he had another reason for invading her hula hoop.

Marissa seemed to be having her own hula hoop invaded by Ryan. And she didn't seem to mind either. She didn't blush when she spoke this time. "What are we going to do next? We came up with some good ideas at our first meeting."

Where was the list? Joan couldn't remember what she did with it. She shook her head, too tired to think. "I have them written down. Somewhere."

Rosa arrived with baskets full of warm tortilla chips and spicy salsa. Her eyes slid toward Ken, and then she wagged her eyebrows at Joan as she set a basket on the table in front of her.

"Whatever we decide," Nick said, "I'd like it to help somebody in need. You know, like collecting winter coats for the homeless, or food for the rescue mission, that kind of thing."

Rosa placed the other basket at the opposite end of the table. "If you want to help hungry people, go to Juarez." She put a hand to her chest. "My family, they are not hungry because my Luis sends money to feed them." She beamed with pride, then her face became sad. "But some are not so lucky there. Many children go hungry."

A spark of interest flared in Joan as Rosa's words sunk in. Hungry children in Mexico, maybe even people Rosa grew up with? How could she stand the thought?

Joan straightened in the chair. "Rosa, what kind of help would those people need? I mean, what could we do?"

From the corner of her eye, she saw Ken studying her. The rest of the CCCS group fell silent, all of them waiting for Rosa's answer. A glance around the table told Joan that several of them had the same idea that was beginning to form in her mind.

"Ai, Joan, they need everything." Rosa waved a hand. "Food. Clothes." Her gaze slipped to Ken. "Medicines. And houses. Many have no place to live in. Others, they sometimes fall down. Their children sleep in . . . *como se dice* . . ." She waved a hand in the air, searching. "Hutch?"

"You mean huts?" Ryan asked. "Or shacks?"

"*Sí*, like that." She shook her head sadly. "Is very poor, my old home."

Joan caught Eve's eye.

313

Excitement lit Eve's face as she leaned toward Joan. "Are you thinking what I'm thinking?"

Nick's eyebrows drew together. "You mean taking up a collection of food and stuff to send down to Mexico?"

Joan and Eve grinned at one another. Joan shook her head, enthusiasm chasing away the last of her fatigue. "I was thinking more along the lines of delivering those things ourselves."

Crystal gasped. "You mean plan a trip to Mexico?"

"That's a terrific idea," Marissa exclaimed.

Eve drew a noisy breath, eyes wide. "We could hold Vacation Bible School for the kids." She looked up at Rosa. "Do they speak English?"

Rosa shrugged. "Some yes, some no. But they all like to learn. Joan maybe can teach them a little English."

"Me?" Joan laughed. "I don't speak Spanish. How can I teach English to Spanish children?"

Rosa put a hand on her hip. "You have been teaching me. *Habla español bien bastante.*"

A couple of seconds ticked by while Joan translated. *You speak Spanish well enough.* She slitted her eyes as she dredged up an appropriate response from her rusty memory. "*Sí, pero solamente un poco.*"

Gordy's eyebrows shot up. "Sounds pretty good to me."

Laughing, Joan shook her head. "I said I only speak a little. And that's only textbook Spanish."

Ken's hand moved from the back of her chair to clutch her shoulder. His eyes mirrored her excitement. "I have always wanted to volunteer in Central or South America."

His grip tightened. "And now I'm a doctor. I can really help people down there."

His face shone with passion, the same passion so evident when Mary Alice Sachs spoke of her work with orphans. Joan realized with a growing amazement she felt that passion beginning to flicker in herself too. Teaching English to people in Mexico would be fun. And she'd be putting her degree to good use.

Brittany clapped her hands. "We're going to have so much fun! While we're down there can we go to Cancún?"

Joan laughed. She might even be able to interest Tori in a mission trip that included a visit to Cancún.

Ken followed Joan's car as it pulled onto Elmtree Drive. He was tired, so tired, but he only had about an hour to get cleaned up and get to the hospital. He really should have skipped the Mexican restaurant, but he didn't want the day, the fellowship, to end. Maybe he'd get lucky and it would be a slow night. He could catch a quick nap on an empty gurney.

This day had been amazing, an affirmation of how God was involved in his life in so many ways. First, his relationship with Mike had taken a giant step forward as they spent several hours together working on the playground. Then one of his deepest desires, to help poor people in other countries, opened up right before his eyes. And all because of Joan.

Her car pulled into her driveway, and he swerved into his own next door. He sat a moment, hands on the steering wheel. There was one more thing he wanted to accomplish today.

"Hey, Joan."

Walking around the front of her car, she looked up when he called, a tired smile on her lips. He crossed the grass to meet her at the bottom of her porch steps. A big strand of hair had fallen out of her ponytail and wisped around her face. He caught himself in the process of reaching up to smooth it behind her ear. No. She was so beautiful this way, tired and disheveled, her expression so open. Like all her defenses had crumbled away.

He shoved his hand into his pocket. "Today was terrific."

"It really was. I liked your friend Mike." Her smile deepened into a playful grin as her eyes twinkled up at him. "Even if he was a little nosy."

"Yeah. Kids." Ken laughed to hide a flash of embarrassment. His gaze slid away from hers, toward the street, as he rocked back on his heels. What was the matter with him? Had he developed a sudden shy streak?

"Uh, listen." He cleared his throat. "I managed to finagle next Wednesday off, and I was wondering if you'd like to have dinner with me."

He couldn't mistake the pleasure in her expression. Something inside Ken lifted as he saw it.

"I'd really like that, Ken."

A silly grin took possession of his mouth. He didn't even try to hide it. "Good." He took a step backward. "So, I'll see you then. Uh, I mean, I'll see you before then. But I'll see you then too. Right?" He clamped his mouth shut.

She laughed. "Good night, Ken."

Her low laughter sent a thrill through him as she let herself into the house. He turned toward his own home, his step light.

"Excellent!"

Joan knocked twice on Gram's door at Waterford late Wednesday afternoon. Hearing no answer, she peeked inside. Empty. She was probably down in the community room, where she'd spent a lot of time lately. Now that she was mobile, the nursing staff had to practically force her to her bedroom to rest.

Sure enough, Joan found her among a group of elderly people clustered around a game table. At their center, four players jealously guarded the cards in their hands. One lady held hers close to her chest.

"Hi, Gram."

Seated in a cushioned chair, Gram's face brightened. "Joan. You're early today. You remember my friend Myrtle."

"Of course." Joan smiled at the woman in the chair next to Gram's. "Hello, Mrs. Mattingly." She bent to whisper in Gram's ear. "I can't stay long, Gram. I have a date tonight."

Gram's head whipped toward her, eyes round. "With Ken?" Joan nodded. Gram's smile widened and she explained to Mrs. Mattingly in an embarrassingly loud voice, "My granddaughter has a date with a *doctor* tonight!"

The announcement drew exclamations of approval from the entire room, while Joan's face warmed. She nodded at several congratulations, and then spoke in a low voice. "I just wondered if you needed anything."

"Yes, in fact, I do." Gram reached for the walker behind her. Joan positioned it for her. "Could you bring my mantle clock next time you come?"

Her mantle clock? Joan bit back a gasp of dismay. Every day Gram asked for a few more personal items from home. Nothing big, just little niceties to make her temporary apartment more comfortable. But her mantle clock? That was . . . that was furniture!

Gram braced her arms on the walker, her face set in a grimace of pain as she began the process of standing. Joan placed a hand under her arm to help, but Gram spoke crossly. "Let me do it myself."

Joan stepped back and watched, wincing in sympathy. Finally on her feet, Gram rested a minute.

"It's getting easier," she said.

Her pace was slow and laborious, but at least she was mobile. Joan walked beside her down the hallway, trying to think of an excuse not to bring the mantle clock.

"About that clock, Gram—"

"I miss the chimes." She winced as her right foot shuffled forward. "I hated the thing when your grandfather first gave it to me. So noisy! But I've grown used to it over the years. Funny, the things we miss."

"But, Gram, if you keep bringing stuff here, we're going

319

to have to hire a moving van when you're released to go home."

Gram watched the floor as her feet took each painful step. "When do you suppose that will be?"

Joan spread her hands. "I don't know, but with the progress you're making, I wouldn't be surprised if it was this week."

Gram's eyes widened. "Oh no, I can't go that soon." She lowered her voice to a conspiratorial whisper. "There's a pinochle tournament week after next. I've been watching these people play. I think I can take them."

"There you are!" Mom's voice interrupted Joan's whirling emotions. She stood in the doorway of Gram's apartment dressed in pink scrubs. She stepped out of the way to let Gram pass into the room, looking at Joan in surprise. "Why did you leave work early?"

In the process of lowering herself into the recliner, Gram lifted her head. "You don't know? Joan has a date with Ken tonight."

Mom's glance slid to Joan. "Well, well, well. That's good news."

When Gram was resting comfortably in her chair, Joan bent down to kiss her cheek. "I've got to go get ready. See you tomorrow, okay?"

Gram nodded. "And don't forget my clock."

Joan speared Mom with an alarmed gaze. "Walk me to my car, would you?"

A puzzled frown creasing her brow, Mom nodded. "I'll be right back, Mother."

Closing the door, Joan whirled to face her mother. "Did

you hear that? She wants her mantle clock. And she told me she couldn't leave before some stupid card tournament the week after next!" Tears stung her eyes. "I don't think she wants to come home."

Mom placed a comforting hand on Joan's arm. "She's been dropping hints about that for a couple of days."

"But she can't stay here!"

"Joan." Mom's expression became serious. "Think about it from her perspective. She's alone all day long, never seeing anyone except us. No wonder she alphabetizes everything she sees. She's bored out of her mind. Then she comes here where she's surrounded by friends and laughter and activities. She's treated like royalty, waited on hand and foot if she wants. Would you want to leave?"

Joan's jaw trembled. "But . . . but I'll miss her."

Mom's face softened. "I know, honey. But she's only a few minutes away. And think how much happier she'll be."

"Did you do this on purpose?" Joan knew her lower lip was protruding and that she must look like a sulky five-year-old, but she didn't care. That's how she felt at the moment.

Mom raised a palm toward her. "I promise I had nothing to do with it. And if she doesn't bring it up, I'm not going to say a word." She lowered her gaze and confessed. "But I did talk to the administrator, just in case, and discovered they have a full apartment available two doors down from Mrs. Mattingly. It's hers if she wants it."

Joan sniffed. "Can she afford it? As fancy as this place is, it must be outrageously expensive."

"She's got some money stashed away from what Grandpa

left her. But I'd hate to see her get into that until she absolutely has to. The only other asset she has is the house."

Joan gasped, her eyes going wide. "You mean we'd have to sell it?"

"Either that, or we'll have to figure out a way to generate income from it." Mom's lips twisted. "We might have to start paying rent."

Momentarily outraged, Joan drew breath to protest. Then the absurdity of her situation stopped her. How many other twenty-five-year-olds had never paid a single penny in rent? Sure, she chipped in on groceries, but other than that, her paycheck had been completely her own since she left college. All her student loans were paid, and her car was free and clear. Maybe it was time to grow up.

Ducking her head, she nodded. "I guess so."

※

The doorbell rang promptly at seven o'clock. Joan spared a moment for one last glance in her mirror. Her hair, freed from its habitual ponytail, gave her a softer look, and she thought she might get used to it. She'd agonized over whether or not to buy a new outfit, but finally decided to put the money toward the mission trip instead. Ken had seen the red Maggy London dress before, but it looked good on her. Hopefully he wouldn't mind.

She dashed up the stairs and stopped to compose herself with a deep breath before swinging the door open.

On the front stoop, Ken's eyes gleamed his appreciation. "You look beautiful."

When he held a bouquet of flowers toward her, Joan couldn't stop a blush from warming her cheeks. "Thank you." She buried her face in the colorful blooms, inhaling deeply. "Would you like to come in while I put these in water?"

He stepped inside but held on to the open front door. "Our reservations are for 7:30, so we need to get going."

"Reservations?" Joan raised an eyebrow in his direction. "There's a restaurant in Danville that takes reservations?"

She entered the kitchen and opened the cabinet where Gram kept odds and ends, looking for a vase.

"Close," he called from the door. "We're going to the Beaumont Inn in Harrodsburg. Have you ever been there?"

Joan almost stumbled in surprise. The Beaumont Inn was a graceful country inn well known for its elegance and southern charm.

"N-no," she managed. "But I've wanted to."

The flowers watered and resting in a place of prominence on the coffee table, Joan allowed herself to be escorted to Ken's car. She grinned up at him when she realized he had driven the car to her driveway. "I could have walked across the yard."

He shook his head, opening the door for her. "Karen told me you might be wearing heels, and girls don't like it when their heels sink into the dirt, or something like that."

While he walked around the front of the car, Joan put a hand over her mouth to hide a smile. He had gotten advice from his sister about their date. He must be nervous. The thought made her relax, and she enjoyed the fifteen-minute drive to Harrodsburg.

Joan had driven by the Beaumont Inn several times but had never gone inside. The beauty of the nineteenth-century former girls' school struck her as she walked between stately white columns into an elegant entry hall furnished with antiques and pictures of Confederate generals. In the parlor to the left, she glimpsed an antique Steinway and old-fashioned upholstered furniture.

The dining room managed to be elegant and homey at the same time. They were seated at a table for two in a secluded corner. Ken examined the menu with obvious delight.

"Fried green tomatoes, Kentucky cured country ham, grits, famous yellow-legged fried chicken. Mmmmm. This place is pure southern!"

Joan nodded. "If you want a taste of Kentucky cuisine, you've come to the right place. Everybody says so. They're famous for their fried chicken and also the corn pudding. And they serve a special orange-lemon cake for dessert. I've heard it's terrific."

"But you've never been here?"

"No, but this is where Eric proposed to Allie. They come here every year on their anniversary."

She didn't tell him Roger tried to bring her here once, but she insisted they go somewhere else instead. From Allie's description, she'd known of the place's romantic atmosphere, and for some unknown reason she didn't think she'd be comfortable here with Roger.

For an equally unknown reason, she felt perfectly comfortable with Ken.

She sipped at her water, nerves fluttering in her stomach. *Slow down, girl. This is only date number one.*

A server in a white apron took their order, and when she left the table, Ken caught her gaze and held it. "Have I mentioned how beautiful you look tonight?"

Smiling, she lowered her gaze to her bread plate. "You have, and thank you. You look very nice too."

He did. She'd seen him in a suit before, at church, but his tailored shirt and casual jacket gave him a dressed-up look that she'd not seen. In fact, the black shirt was so crisp it might be new. Did Karen give him wardrobe advice too?

"So how's Grace progressing?" He cast a look of thanks at the server as she set a glass of sweet tea in front of each of them. "I haven't been out there to check on her this week."

"She's doing well but walking is still painful."

He nodded. "I'm afraid it will be for quite some time. She's lucky to be in pretty good health for someone her age, so I think she will recover eventually. She'll be home before you know it."

"I'm not so sure about that." She told him about this afternoon's visit. "So I'm not sure she'll be coming home at all."

He ducked his head to catch her eye. "You don't seem too happy about that decision."

Heaving a sigh, she said, "I'm being selfish. I'll miss her." She toyed with her spoon. "Actually, I feel like her decision is sort of forcing me to make some of my own. I'm twenty-five years old and I don't know what I'm going to do with the rest of my life." She gave a silent laugh. "I know I don't want to sell furniture forever."

"What do you want to do?"

"I don't know. I've been . . . praying about it." She lifted a shy glance to his face. She still felt awkward talking about her new intimate relationship with her heavenly Father, but Ken of all people would know what she meant. "I'm really excited about this mission trip, but I don't think I want to be a full-time missionary." She tilted her head. "Maybe I'll get my master's degree and teach."

"Spanish?"

They shared a laugh.

"No, I don't think I'll be teaching Spanish anytime soon." She sobered. "Maybe English, though. That's what my undergrad is in."

"You'd be a great teacher." Admiration glowed from his eyes. "One of my favorite Bible verses is in Jeremiah. I memorized it when I was trying to decide about medical school. '"For I know the plans I have for you," declares the Lord, "plans to prosper you and not to harm you, plans to give you hope and a future."'" He reached across the table and placed his hand on top of hers. A thrill shot through her at his warm touch. "I know there's a terrific future in store for you, Joan, whatever you decide to do. And . . ." His throat moved as he swallowed, and his gaze intensified. "And I hope I'll be around to lend a hand."

The dining room around her fell away. Did that mean what she thought it meant? Did Ken just say he wanted to share her future with her?

"Here we go," the server said. "Bleu cheese for the

gentleman, and ranch for the lady. And some warm bread too."

Joan ripped her gaze from Ken's as the noise of the dining room returned. Ken withdrew his hand and smiled his thanks up at the woman.

Her heart threatening to pound out of her chest, her brain buzzing, Joan didn't taste a bite of her salad.

❧

As they were sharing a slice of orange-lemon cake for dessert, Joan's cell phone rang. The shrill ringtone she kept set on high volume pierced through the cozy atmosphere of the restaurant, drawing stares from those at neighboring tables. Embarrassed, she fumbled around in her purse.

"I'm sorry," she said to Ken. "I meant to turn it off."

He lifted a shoulder. "No big deal."

As she silenced the ring, she glanced at the display. Allie's nightly call. She'd call her back later.

They were walking toward the car when it rang again.

Joan was glad the darkness hid her blush as she silenced the phone a second time. "I'm so sorry. Allie must have forgotten I had a date tonight."

They arrived at the car. As Ken unlocked the door, he said, "It's okay if you want to call her back. I don't mind."

"Of course not. She can wait until later." Since he didn't open the door immediately, she leaned against it, her head thrown back, eyes closed as she breathed deeply of the fresh night air. A soft breeze rustled her hair and the leaves of the magnolia trees surrounding the small parking lot.

She felt Ken move beside her, and opened her eyes to find him leaning against the car. His arm on the roof, he gazed down into her face. Talk about a welcome invasion of her hula hoop!

"Thank you for dinner," she breathed. "This place is incredible. So . . . romantic." She gulped. Romantic? She couldn't talk about the delicious food, the graceful furnishings, the beautiful night? She had to mention romance? His nearness was messing with her mind. She couldn't think with him so close, looking into her eyes like that.

"Thank *you* for coming with me. There's not another person in the world I'd rather have shared it with."

Eyes locked, his face moved closer to hers. Oooh, this was it! He was going to kiss her! Her heart stuttered as he neared, her shallow breath mingling with his. She closed her eyes in the fraction of a second before his lips touched hers. His hand softly cupped the back of her neck, pressing her gently into him. A warm thrill shot through her body, making her head spin and her knees weak as she surrendered to Ken's kiss.

And her phone rang again.

Her eyelids flew open and she jerked back as though caught in the act of a crime.

Ken, grinning down at her, pulled away. "She seems pretty determined. Maybe you'd better take the call."

A headline from the front page of tomorrow's paper flashed into Joan's mind:

PREGNANT WOMAN STRANGLED WITH TELEPHONE CORD
SISTER SAYS, "SHE *SO* DESERVED IT!"

"Allie, determined?" She groaned. "You have no idea."

Laughing, he opened her door and walked around the car toward the driver's side.

Vowing to cancel her cell service first thing in the morning, Joan pulled the phone out of her purse. She turned away slightly as she flipped the cover open.

"This had better be important," she whispered into the phone.

"Important?" Allie's voice held a touch of hysteria. "My body feels like an alien has taken control of it, my husband keeps waving a stopwatch in my face, and neither of my sisters are here. I'D SAY IT'S IMPORTANT!"

Standing upright, Joan gripped the phone. "You're in labor?"

"Of course I'm in labor! And they won't give me any pain medicine, either, not for another two centimeters. Even Mom is being mean to me." She sniffed, her voice going pitiful. "I need my sisters."

Joan bounced on her toes. The baby was coming! She was about to become an aunt! She looked across the top of the car at Ken. Smiling, he nodded. "Tell her we're on our way."

Joan almost shouted into the phone, "Hold on, Allie! I'll be right there. Don't do anything without me!"

She heard Allie's outraged voice as she snapped the lid closed. "Like I have a choice!"

~ 25 ~

So tiny. So fragile. So perfect. Perched on the foot of Allie's hospital bed, Joan gazed down into the face of her beautiful little niece, just four hours old. Tori and Mom hovered nearby, each of them itching to take the baby from her, but Joan couldn't make herself hand over this precious armful. Gram rested in the chair next to the bed, having just finished her turn at holding the infant. Ken leaned in the doorway, smiling as he watched Joan admire her niece.

"She is so amazing," Joan whispered. "Look at those tiny eyelashes, those delicate little lips."

"I love her teensy toes," Tori said. "And that soft, soft head."

Allie snorted. "Yeah, well that head didn't feel so soft a few hours ago."

Joan grinned at her big sister. Allie looked tired, exhausted even, but a triumphant smile gave her face a glow that could not be dimmed.

"She's gorgeous, Allie. You did such a good job."

Beside Allie, Eric beamed. "She is gorgeous, isn't she?"

He placed a tender kiss on his wife's head. "Just like her mama."

Allie settled back into her pillows with a happy sigh. "We finally decided on a name. Do you want to hear it?"

"Of course we want to hear it." Mom stepped back and focused her digital camera on Joan and the baby for the five hundredth time. "I want to call my granddaughter by name when I brag about her to all my friends."

Allie and Eric exchanged a secretive smile. "You tell them," Allie said.

Eric's chest puffed with pride. "Her name is Joan Leigh Harrod."

Joan gasped, while Tori, eyes glittering with happy tears, clapped a hand to her mouth.

"You named her after us?" Tori asked.

Allie nodded. "She's named after the two best sisters in the world, who will also be the best aunts, I'm sure."

"Oh, Allie." Joan shook her head. "Don't do that to this innocent little baby. Give her a name as beautiful as she is."

"Her name is Joan." The set of Allie's jaw announced to everyone that she would hear no argument. "And it *is* a beautiful name."

"Then at least switch them around. Or let's just call her by Tori's middle name, Leigh."

Allie's chin rose. "She's Joan, and that's that."

"Well, if you're going to be stubborn about it." Joan blew out a resigned sigh. She leaned close to the baby and whispered, "But I'm going to call you Joanie."

Joan's gaze slid to the doorway, where Ken stood. He

winked, sending a warm thrill through her stomach. She looked back down at the infant. How could she feel such tenderness, such love, for this tiny little person she'd only known a few hours? What must Allie feel when she gazed at her newborn daughter, this brand-new life that she brought into the world?

Joan brushed a soft kiss on the baby's forehead, breathing deeply of her powdery infant smell. Like little Joanie, she too had a brand-new life ahead of her. What was the verse Ken quoted? In all the excitement, she'd forgotten it. She intended to look it up when she got home and memorize it. But even if she couldn't remember the exact words, deep in her heart she clung to the promise of the verse.

Her life was no longer stuck. Her Father had plans for her.

Acknowledgments

The bad thing about thanking people is that I'm bound to leave someone out, and I hate that. But I was raised to say "thank you," so here goes:

My sisters are amazing. They're lively and smart and fun and an absolute wealth of source material just waiting to be written down. I've freely used some of their funnier characteristics to create the Sanderson sisters, which will tell you what a hoot they are. Susie Smith and Beth Marlowe, your support and enthusiasm keep me going. Thank you for loving this story when I needed someone besides me to love it. You guys are truly awesome.

I have other awesome family too, and some of them helped me with *Stuck in the Middle*. Thanks to Maggie Tirey and Sarabeth Marlowe for going with me to tour a beautiful assisted living center in Danville, Kentucky. Amy Barkman (my mom) and Christy Delliskave (my daughter) read my books and feed my ego—but they don't mind telling me when something doesn't work, either. And Corrie Barkman became my sister late in life but is just as precious to me as the ones I was raised with. Thank you all.

I thrive on the feedback of my critique partners because I know they make me a better writer. For this book, I owe a huge "thank you" to the following people: Tracy Ruckman, Julie Scott, Marsha Hornock, Loralee Kudzo, Janelle Mowrey, Jess Ferguson, and Sandra Robbins. Thanks also to the CWFI critique group for faithfully reading various chapters and summaries without ever getting to read the whole book: Richard Leonard, Corrine Eldred, Mary Yerkes, and Lani Zielsdorf. You guys rock.

Elizabeth (Lisa) Ludwig is not only a wonderful critique partner, she's an incredible freelance editor and a great writer. Thank you, Lisa, for polishing my words and for suggesting so many wonderful smells. And for the hula hoop.

The research for this book took me into some areas for which I had no expertise at all. Thanks to the following subject matter experts who freely shared their knowledge with me: Angie Brown, Susan Matherly, Timothy Noel, Crystal Miller, Ronda Wells, MD, and the members of ACFW for sharing their delightfully quirky OCD stories.

My agent, Wendy Lawton, is one of the nicest, sweetest, most encouraging women I know. And she's a savvy businesswoman too. I thank God for her every day.

And where would this book be without the gifted people at Revell? I'll tell you where: still in my computer, where nobody except me and my family could read it. Thank you to Vicki Crumpton (editor extraordinaire), Barb Barnes, Cat Hoort, Cheryl Van Andel, and everyone else at Revell who worked so hard to make this book happen. I may not know all their names, but I am so grateful for their work.

Of course a huge "thank you" goes to my husband, Ted, for loving me and supporting me and believing in me. And for doing the laundry when it piles up and I have my face plastered to the computer screen. And another "thank you" goes to Jonathan Leake, just for being my son. He too is an overflowing fountain of source material, and one day he's going to end up as a character in one of my books. (Consider that a warning, sweetie!)

It's a funny thing. Just when I think I have no more ideas, no stories to tell, the Lord gives me a new one. And his are so much better than anything I could dream up on my own. So he gets the biggest thanks, and all the glory.

Virginia Smith is a writer of humorous novels, speaker, singer, snow skier, motorcycle enthusiast, and avid scuba diver. Someday, she insists, she's going to find a way to do all those things at once without killing herself or her long-suffering husband. She launched her career as a novelist with the release of her debut, *Just As I Am* (Kregel), in March of 2006, and has been cranking out God-honoring fiction ever since. An energetic speaker, she loves to exemplify God's truth by comparing real-life situations to well-known works of fiction, such as her popular talk, "Biblical Truth in Star Trek." She attributes the popularity of that talk primarily to the Star Trek uniform. Visit her website at www. VirginiaSmith.org.

more good books to read?

Be the first to get sneak peak news, reviews,
and previews of the latest books from Revell at:

www.revellbooks.com

Join as many newsletters as you desire and
get only the info you really want!

Sign up today!

ℜ Revell